A Bucket List To Die For

LORRAINE FOUCHET

A Bucket List
To Die For

Translated from the French
by Deniz Gulan

HODDER

First published in the French language as *Entre Ciel et Lou* by Editions Héloïse d'Ormesson in 2016

First published in Great Britain in 2021 by Hodder & Stoughton
An Hachette UK company

2

Copyright © Editions Héloïse d'Ormesson 2016
English translation © Deniz Gulan 2021

The right of Lorraine Fouchet to be identified as the
Author of the Work has been asserted by her in accordance
with the Copyright, Designs and Patents Act 1988.

Deniz Gulan asserts her moral right to be
identified as the Translator of the Work.

A CIP catalogue record for this title is available from the British Library

Paperback ISBN 9781529356779
eBook ISBN 9781529356762

Typeset in Plantin Light by Hewer Text UK Ltd, Edinburgh
Printed and bound in Great Britain by Clays Ltd, Elcograf S.p.A.

Hodder & Stoughton policy is to use papers that are natural, renewable
and recyclable products and made from wood grown in sustainable
forests. The logging and manufacturing processes are expected to
conform to the environmental regulations of the country of origin.

Hodder & Stoughton Ltd
Carmelite House
50 Victoria Embankment
London EC4Y 0DZ

www.hodder.co.uk

For the painter Simone Marini, who,
six months after the death of Isabella Peroni,
gave me a sealed bottle containing her voice.

For the Groix islanders, proud owners
of this small land perched on the ocean.

For those who hail from elsewhere,
yet chose to make Groix their home.

For all those who have been
profoundly affected by Brittany.

Me'zo ganet e kreiz ar mor,
I was born in the midst of the ocean

Yann-Ber Kalloc'h

Whence comes its name?
Is it fairy or witch?
Or from some black inferno,
like the mud of its furrows
They say its joy can be seen
As well as its cross
I speak of the island of Groix.

Gilles Servat, Michelle Le Poder

Behold, an island is outward bound
That has slumbered in our gaze,
since infancy

Jacques Brel

31st October

Joe, Groix Island

My name is Joseph, you always called me Joe. That's me sat in the front row, red-eyed, wearing an oilskin jacket, with a turquoise sweater draped over my shoulders. You used to say the scent of lilies was strong enough to wake the dead. I should have bought you some. You knew the meaning of love, but you had a wicked sense of humour. You spent our married life playing your lousy jokes on me. I still can't believe that a woman as vivacious and lively as you has gone. There must be a catch somewhere. Maybe it's one of your pranks?

Our children arrived by boat. Cyrian drove from Paris with his wife Albane, their daughter Charlotte and puppy Oskar in his black Porsche Cayenne that he left in the car park at Lorient. Sarah took the train, using her walking stick instead of her wheelchair. Cyrian dealt with everything the way he runs his business. He chose your coffin, and took care of the funeral notice and the service booklet which bore a breathtakingly beautiful photo of you. Our son may not be friendly, funny or endearing, but he does do things properly. The church pews are all full—us Groix islanders on one side, mainlanders on the other, your family in the front row. Our friends' children were married here and their parents buried here. We used to sit at the back of the church holding hands. Now here I am, sat in the front row like the teacher's pet, reaching for your hand. The ex-voto boat swinging above my

head is making me giddy. Behind the altar, under the cruci-
fix, there is a big anchor surrounded by two angels. The new
rector, young Father Dominique, conducts the service
himself. In the past, it didn't matter which day of the week
you died because there were priests living on the island. Not
anymore. Good timing, Lou, you left on the right day, so
you'll get the full works. The local La Kleienn choir sings
"Audite Silete" by Michael Praetorius. The music is beautifully intense and charged with emotion. I feel so empty inside;
I long for the sea, our old life, and you. I want you, Lou, you
and our special camembert and caramel pancakes with salted
butter. A cardiologist with a broken heart, ironic isn't it. I'm
badly shaven, I didn't polish my shoes. My daughter-in-law
Albane is shocked that I'm wearing my turquoise sweater.
You gave it to me on our last wedding anniversary, Lou. I
mean I *am* the widower for pity's sake, can't they just leave
me alone! I always wear a sweater on my shoulders, it's my
trademark. Our friends joke that if I die before them, they'll
come to my funeral with a "Joseph" on their shoulders. You
won't be there to see it though . . .

   Life is built up in layers, like an onion. Each layer of your
life is gathered here today in this church. The 7 Gang are
here—our friends from Groix we used to meet for dinner at
Fred's house on the 7th of each month. The SAWIH members
are here too: The Society for Aiding the Wives of Inadequate
Husbands. I started the group with Jean-Pierre back when
we did odd jobs for the wives of friends who were here at
weekends but worked on the mainland during the week. Your
family is in the front row, sitting very upright and looking
impeccable. Your father, the count, died two years ago. You
lost your mother in a car accident when you were just one.
Your elder sisters are all sat together in a row, in height order,
like the famous Dalton Brothers. I haven't seen them since
your father's funeral. They carried on living in the family

château, after I stole you away. They may resemble you physically, but they lack your spark, your bubbly personality, your general craziness and your free spirit. Your old friends from the Catholic private school are here, loyal as ever. You can spot them a mile off in their suits, scarves, moccasins and ballerina pumps; at this time of year, us islanders wear thick warm jackets, trousers and boots. You were involved in the Clara Prize, a short-story competition for teenage writers organized in aid of heart research. Your colleagues and former prize winners have all made the journey from Paris. My old friend, Thierry Serfaty, head of neurology, is here too.

The person who took over my cardio department has also showed up out of courtesy. I couldn't stand the man, right from the outset. I took early retirement just two years ago to finally enjoy the rest of my life with you, Lou, and you stood me up big time!

You left me during the night of Saturday through Sunday, as summertime changed to wintertime. At three o'clock in the morning we all put our clocks back an hour. At that very moment, and as if to say *screw you all*, you drew your last breath, as the nurse was doing her rounds. In Brittany, legend has it that when someone dies, the henchman, Ankou, stops by in his creaking old cart to collect their soul. What did you say to him? *Don't forget to put your watch back an hour or you'll miss it . . .*

We leave the church through the large forecourt door that opens onto the square. The autumn sun lights up the tuna fish weathervane on top of the church spire. Everywhere else in France, the church bell towers tend to be decorated with cockerels, but Groix is an island of seafarers and was France's leading tuna fishing port at the beginning of the twentieth century.

There isn't a single funeral parlour on the island, due to lack of demand. The funeral procession goes around the church then heads for the cemetery on foot. I take this path every day, but this time I don't stop for a coffee at the Triskell and I don't have a newspaper under my arm. My heart is in smithereens. I'm devastated. You believed in your father's god, I believe in the god of the seafarers, but he has abandoned me. I'm shipwrecked on dry land, never having set sail, drowning in my own grief.

The bell tolls. The cars stop. The old folk cross themselves. Fred's beagle, Arthur, cocks his leg up on the hearse wheel. I glance at the dog to say thank you, he is the only one acting normally today. Our grief-stricken children walk one step behind me. I pray that all this is just one of your weird pranks. The procession passes in front of our local restaurant, The 50. Jean-Louis adapts the menu according to what's in season. You would have chosen the tomato *mille-feuille* with brown crab and pepper sorbet, I would have gone for the smoked pollack and seaweed soup. You would have refused a dessert, but I would have cracked and gone for a Poire Belle Hélène and you would have sneakily devoured half of it! Now I'll just have to stuff my face alone. What an awful thought. If I leave you some will you come back for it? We walk past Yannick, Maurie and Perrine's art gallery. I half expect you to leap out of a canvas and give me the fright of my life. Your beauty was such, Lou, that it could have given a blind man his sight back. I didn't see you dead. I refused to, I didn't want this to be my last memory of you, despite my colleagues in psychiatry saying it helps the grieving process. I don't care, I'm on strike, I refuse to mourn.

In the covered market, there appears to be movement, people are wiggling and shaking. Yet I hear nothing. I stop short. Everybody slows down, except for the hearse carrying you. I take a closer look. People are indeed dancing inside. I catch sight of a poster on one of the pillars: *Silent ball organized in protest against the Society of Composers, Authors and*

Music Publishers and its taxation of local business owners who play music. I leave the funeral procession and walk towards the makeshift dance floor in the hall of the former covered market, which nowadays no longer houses any vendors.

"Dad!" whispers Cyrian, in embarrassment.

"Grandpa!" says his wife Albane.

I hate it when she calls me that; they can just piss off. I stretch out my arms, and spin around. Each dancer follows his or her own beat. They all have headphones, headsets, iPods, mobile phones. I move to the rhythm of a Serge Reggiani song in my head. Baffled, the funeral procession stops. Your childhood friends are staring at me, Lou, and your sisters are speechless. Cyrian tries to grab my arm, but I pull away sharply. Then Sarah throws down her stick. The other dancers move back. She takes me in her arms, and we dance together.

"Fellini died on the 31st of October," she whispers in my ear.

We stagger and dance clumsily, each to the beat of the music in his head. Knowing our daughter, she must have chosen Nino Rota.

"I'll be back in a minute!" I snap at Cyrian.

He steps back, disgruntled. His wife purses her thin lips. Their nine-year-old daughter Charlotte doesn't seem bothered. Her half-sister Apple is in floods of tears. Apple is Cyrian's eldest daughter; she is ten years old and lives with us and her mother here on the island. She doesn't know her father very well. Since she was born, he has only made fleeting visits to see her, on her birthday, Christmas, Easter, and Mother's Day, though that was for you, Lou. And he does his best to avoid bumping into his ex, Maëlle, Apple's mother.

I finish the verse. "I love you, you who will never grow old, don't ever leave me please, I love you." I'm speaking to you one last time in my Groix dialect, *me gallon*, sweetheart, *me karet vihan*, my darling. Then I bend down in front of Sarah and pick up her walking stick.

"We need to get back to the others," I say.

"'Cortège' is a poem by Jacques Prévert," Sarah whispers to Apple. "That means 'procession'."

A golden old man with a watch in mourning
A Queen doing manual work with a man of England
And the trawlers of peace with the guardians of the sea.

Apple has her father's eyes: blue with flecks of gold. She is a smart alec and delights in putting Prévert's words back in the right order. We're coming, Lou, but at Sarah's pace. To qualify as a Groix islander, you have to have four name plaques in the cemetery, showing four generations of islanders born and deceased on this piece of rock in the middle of the ocean, three leagues off the coast of Lorient. I was born here and hail from several generations of fishermen. You were born in your father's castle, an heiress worthy of knights and huntsmen. You gave all this up when you married me, though you gained a jewel in return: Groix. And I was your soul mate, your confidant, your *proche*, or *"piroche"*, as Apple used to say when she was little—and the word stuck.

The island protects as much as it isolates. When arriving on Groix, those who are devoted to it get back what they once lost. When leaving Groix, you take its shadow with you, like a hitchhiker, it stays with you, and you live for the day you will return. Groix, a five by two and a half mile bite-sized chunk of reality gets under your skin. It's amazing watching the boat pass between the two lights at the entrance to Port-Tudy and the dock. The magical islands serve as a daymark for the islanders' souls. And anything less than the truth, has no place here.

When Sarah and Cyrian were children, I told them that the Groix islanders' hearts were surrounded by sea water. On the first day of the school holidays, I would take them to swallow a glass of sea water. We would head to the beach, whatever the weather, and drink it looking into each other's eyes. Cyrian, the eldest, was the first to quit this ritual. Sarah held on a little longer just to please me. I still do it with Apple. I tried it with Charlotte the few times she came, but she spat it all out. As for Albane, she shrieked like a hysterical gull, so I gave up.

When I saw you encircled by candles to port and starboard, it reminded me of the death vigils and other morbid jubilations of Lucien Gourong, the globetrotting Groix storyteller. I remember the last time we saw him live, we came back singing at the top of our voices. *She lost her cherry in the Kerlivio valley.* I'm not laughing so much now.

Apple trembles when they lower your coffin into the ground. She tries to take her father's hand, but his arms just dangle. Charlotte stares at her phone. She seems frustrated that there's no signal here. Apple's eyes are misty with tears. Your two granddaughters have nothing in common except their father. Family is important, it's crucial really. But today it's crucifying me.

I'm always amazed in interviews when they ask, *What was the happiest day of your life?* and the reply is invariably, *The day my children were born.* For me, it was the day you smiled at me for the very first time. Our children were a given, a natural consequence of our love. But the true miracle for me was that you loved me, Lou, with that bewitching look of yours and your ravishing beauty. And your dazzling smile, oh yes, I am still blinded by your smile even though you've gone.

When your holier than thou sister said you were happy to be beside the Good Lord, I objected and said no, you were happy with us. God either made a mistake or had gone away for the weekend and his stand-in ticked the wrong name on the list.

I grew up on this island. There were two schools, one blessed by God and one run by the Devil, one Catholic and one secular. I went to both of them. I was then a border at Lorient college before studying medicine in Rennes. I worked my socks off and secured an internship in a Paris hospital. We got married. I refused to go and live in the family château with your father like your obedient sisters' husbands did, something he always held against me. Then our children came along, first Cyrian and then Sarah. I took out a twenty-year mortgage on an apartment in Montparnasse near the station where the trains depart for Brittany. I chose to work in the public health service rather than practise in the private sector where I would have earned ten times more. We always returned to Groix for the school holidays. And then we moved to the island permanently with our cheerful group of young, retiree friends. It was festive and fun. We were care-free again with nothing to weigh us down. Until last spring, that is, when you ruined everything, my love. You were fifty-six years old and I didn't see it coming.

Cyrian and his family live in the Parisian suburb of Le Vésinet, Sarah lives in the Marais area of central Paris. They have both got successful careers in different areas, and have never been any trouble to us at all, even when you insisted on moving into a nursing home at the end of June and I had to agree to it, which just about killed me. I didn't tell anyone why; I was bound by medical secrecy. In any case, it was no one else's business, and you wouldn't have wanted people to know. Our friends didn't understand. Our children were embarrassed at the idea of you being there, but neither of them came to help us. Cyrian buried himself in his work and offered to pay for you to be cared for at home. Sarah took to the bottle and one-night stands. They came back and forth a few times to see you, but you deserved more. Then one day they got here too late ... As for Charlotte, you hadn't seen her in over a year.

I'm one of the lucky ones who always lands on his feet. I usually beat Apple at Monopoly, I always find a parking space in Paris, the tills close after me at the supermarket. I met you, you fell in love with me. I was born under a lucky star, but you took that star with you leaving me in the darkness. You were always late, it was the story of your life. When I think of the number of planes, trains, curtain-raisers, and film screenings we missed because of you. This is the first time that you've ever been early, that you actually beat me to it. That's a good one. When do I laugh?

I don't cry. Whenever we attended funerals together, you would quote Stan Laurel. *If anyone cries at my funeral, I won't speak to him ever again.* I think back to Sarah's poem. I'm a turquoise widower in an inconsolable sweater. A lonely sweater worn by a turquoise *piroche*.

1st November

Apple, Groix Island

Your jacket is still hanging up in the entrance hall, Lou—no one dares take it down. Daddy, his wife and my half-sister Charlotte came down from Paris yesterday with Oskar, their sweet labrador puppy. Before going to the church, Albane took him out in the garden.

"Oskar, number one!" she said.

And I swear to you, the little dog did a wee. Then she said, "Oskar, number two!"

He did what she said and squatted. She took a peg and a little green plastic bag out of her pocket to pick up the dog poop, then told him to stand up. How stupid can you get? Then she said to Charlotte, "Now it's your turn, you should think about going to the little girls' room."

So Charlotte went inside to the bathroom. When she came back, I couldn't stop myself from saying, "One day your mum will slip up and say, 'Charlotte, number two!' and pull out her peg and bag."

She didn't look amused, but I saw Joe's face light up for a moment.

I have Daddy's eyes; Charlotte has his mouth. She has straight red hair like her mother, and I've got dark brown curly hair like Mummy. It's my tenth birthday today. This year I won't be having a cake though because you've just died. Mummy sneakily gave me my present this morning. I hate pink things like Hello Kitty, so my new watch is black, it's a watch in mourning like in Aunt Sarah's poem. I like black things, peeling wallpaper, whistling pipes, an angry sea, jellyfish and mosquitoes. Did you know, Groix Island didn't break away from the mainland. It rose up from the bottom of the sea millions of years ago. I learned that in class. I often have a nightmare that the island is sinking under the water and we all drown. I wake up crying, but never tell anyone about it.

I have about the same number of friends in Primetur and Piwizi. The island was originally divided in two: Primetur to the east and Piwizi to the west. Today, you can get married or make friends on both sides. During the school year, me and Mummy live with my grandparents in the village in a former ship-owner's house. In the summer, we move to Locmaria where we have a small fisherman's cottage that Mummy's parents left her when they died. We do bed and breakfast to help make ends meet. I'm the one who bikes to the village to buy fresh bread for the guests' breakfasts. Mummy does the cleaning, the laundry, the coffee and makes the jams. There's no heating, so we can't have guests in winter.

I've already seen lots of dead things: baby rabbits run over at night by idiots speeding, birds caught by the village cats, and once I saw a drowned man who had been washed up on a beach. I wish I hadn't seen you though, Lou. I prefer to remember you messing up your friend Martine's chocolate cake recipe. My friends' grandmas bake them delicious tarts, desserts and *tchumpôt* cake. But you were such a bad cook that you couldn't even do a nice omelette. But you made them with so much love, that I ate them anyway.

Mummy and Daddy haven't spoken since I was born. Mummy says it has nothing to do with me but she's lying. It was me being born that made everything go wrong. My half-sister Charlotte told me. Daddy wanted Mummy to move to

Paris with him, but she refused to leave Groix saying there was no air in Paris. I don't know if that's true, I've never been further than Lorient. Charlotte says that he wanted her to get rid of me, but she refused. Daddy didn't want me; I was an accident. Every time he comes to the island, Mummy rushes back to Locmaria to avoid him. I have lunch with him in the village. We don't talk much but there is so much I want to tell him, it's hard to keep it all to myself. He kisses me but never hugs me. I call my grandparents by their first names, Lou and Joe. Charlotte calls them Granny and Grampy.

Daddy only ever wears dark suits and ties, never jeans like the other dads here. He is always moaning about the trade union's latest employee demands, the financial crisis and his taxes. His wife Albane is never happy either. She doesn't like Brittany and prefers the south where the sea is warm. Aunt Sarah calls their Charlotte "the obnoxious brat". Aunt Sarah is really pretty, she has loads of boyfriends. She has a rare neuroge de . . . neuro de ge ne . . . something disease with a complicated name, which can't be cured. She walks with a stick and when she has a seizure, she has to sit in a special wheelchair. She has tattoos; she has Federico Fellini on her left arm, wearing a large hat and scarf, and his wife Giulietta Masina on her right arm, complete with the small hat and striped sweater from the film *La Strada*. Aunt Sarah says she has no time to lose, and lives life to the full. She's also a genius; she went to that famous university where all geniuses go. Daddy also wanted to go there but he didn't get in. He took it badly that his little sister is brainier than him. When I'm grown up, I want to be a doctor, like Joe. I'll have to go away to study, but I'll come back and open a surgery here.

I'm sorry that you're dead, Lou, but not as sorry as I was that day in June when that thing happened that I swore I wouldn't tell anyone about. I lied to everyone, even Mummy. I pretended it was Tribord's fault. Tribord is our ginger tom cat.

In the olden days, the sailors from Groix were known as the Greks. When they were out fishing on their tuna boats, the big flat-bottomed *dundees* with all sails set, they used tall, enamelled coffee pots known as *greks*. That morning, we both got scalded by the boiling coffee in our *grek*. I immediately put my face and your hands under cold water. We both ended up with blisters, you on your fingers and me in the corner of my eye. The scar will stay with me forever, and your secret will stay safe with me forever too. After that you moved into the nursing home. At first, I thought it was only for a while, but you never came out again. Death is for life, *for ever and ever, Amen*. In his sermon this morning in church, Father Dominique said we were a united and close-knit family. We're actually just pretending. You were the only one who loved all of us. I don't think Daddy will ever set foot on Groix again. He only ever came to see you. At the cemetery, I took his hand and he stiffened up. I felt ashamed and stepped back. I just wanted to comfort him and not feel so afraid. I know I'm a burden to him. Mummy works at the Librairie principale, one of the island's bookshops, with her colleagues Marie-Christine and Céline. She earns a living and refuses Daddy's money. Charlotte says I weigh heavily on him, which I don't understand because I don't cost him a penny. Plus I'm skinny and she's chubby. She may be my half-sister but she weighs twice as much as me.

During the service, one of your great-nephews, who is a solo soprano singer in a Paris choir, sang such a beautiful hymn that it made a shiver go down my spine. It was called "Pie Jesu". I don't know my cousins very well. When you live on an island, you miss out on family gatherings. Joe, Daddy, Albane and Aunt Sarah will be sailing over to Lorient tomorrow to see the solicitor. I'm going to be alone with Charlotte for the first time.

A few days before *that thing* happened that I can't mention because I promised to not tell a soul, you and Joe taught me how to do cardiac massage. We laughed so much! Joe borrowed a dummy that they use to train first aid workers. I placed my right hand at the bottom of the dummy's chest bone with my left hand in a hooked position and my arms straight and Joe told me to press down regularly doing one hundred presses per minute. I lost count, so you took out your mobile phone and played a song at full volume, telling me to follow the beat of the music. I can't get that song out of my head now. It's a really old song called "Staying Alive" by a band called the Bee something. We were all shrieking along. "And we're stayin' alive, stayin' alive! Ah ha ha ha, stayin' alive, stayin' alive! Ah ha ha ha, stayin' aliiiiive!" I asked Joe if they gave you cardiac massage to this song when your heart stopped beating in the nursing home. He said that you were sleeping peacefully and that staying alive isn't always the best solution.

Lou, on the other side

I'm dead but I remember everything. It's like picking up my emails after a long break. I just had a memory lapse of several months that's all, like a computer glitch.

I had a great send off. "Audite Silete" and "Pie Jesu" were very poignant. Those whom I cared most about were there. My sisters, my school friends, my Clara Prize associates, your old friend Thierry, the colleague you couldn't stand who replaced you, and enough Groix islanders to crew a fishing fleet.

I love you but I can't say it to you anymore and it breaks my heart. I wish I could touch you, dry Apple's tears, and take Charlotte's phone off her. She is just pretending not to care, to hide her distress. I saw you hugging Sarah, my *piroche*; you held on to each other like a boathook gripping a buoy. That turquoise sweater really suits you; I hesitated about the colour, but I made the right choice. I saw Cyrian almost shaking with grief, and Apple trying to take her father's hand. I saw Maëlle hesitating, wondering whether to hug him or not, and Albane looking daggers at Maëlle.

I rewind. I'm back at our wedding. I see our families' glum faces and our lovestruck smiles. I feel your skin against mine, your smell, your taste, I float away with you in frenzied passion. I see your fatherly pride when Cyrian was born. And your joy when Sarah came along. I remember how serious you were as you defended your thesis as a doctor of medicine. And the look of joy on your face when you became head of department. I remember your tears every time death stole a patient from you, and your laughter when you saved one. Your emotion when Thierry put a name to Sarah's illness, and my panic the day Apple got burnt. I can still feel the cool wood of the rifle when you discovered me in your office in the middle of the night. I can still hear the New Year's concert in Vienna, that we listened to again the first evening in the nursing home as we hugged each other tightly. My breathing slows down again as my final moment arrives. I'm not even afraid, Joe. It doesn't even hurt. Like sand running through my fingers. Drops of water don't suffer when they turn into foam, grains of sand don't suffer when they are scattered on the beach.

I smile as I think of the young solicitor from Lorient to whom I gave a tricky task, that you will mistakenly think is a very bad joke. You can do it, Joe, you will succeed. You have never let me down. Well . . . apart from once.

2nd November

Joe, Lorient

You could have picked a local solicitor. But no, you had to take the boat and cross over to the mainland without telling me. You were independent then; you knew what you were doing. And at that time, you still remembered that we loved each other.

I never doubted your love for me and our children. You were so close to them, and I didn't want to intrude, it wasn't my place to. I left them in your charge, entrusted them to you. I did my bit, earning a living to pay for our flat, their schools, their universities, their braces, glasses, music lessons, extra maths lessons, sailing courses, fashionable clothes, computers. I remember admitting to you one day that Sarah was my favourite because I felt guilty about her disability. If looks could kill. You jumped up angrily.

"Sarah is a beautiful, bright, bubbly child! She will grow up healthy and happy."

I tense up when I think of that intern, that stupid bastard who told us that our daughter's illness wasn't hereditary, but that it could often be identified in the family medical history, and did we wish to know whose side it was on. We both shouted "no" in unison, preferring to share the burden.

Life without you will be hell, Lou. No antidepressant and no therapist can ever bring you back. I loved our life together. I'm dreading the next part, without you, it makes me want to vomit, like I used to as a child when I was forced to eat cauliflower.

The day before yesterday, the procession was for you, from the church to the spot where they laid you to rest. This morning, the day after All Saints Day, the procession is for all of the deceased, from the church to that monument in memory of the sailors who have perished at sea. I've decided to skip it this year. When you're a newlywed, according to tradition, you're supposed to sit next to your spouse at the table for one year. When you're newly widowed, you have enough grief to deal with on your own.

"My condolences, Doctor."

The young solicitor gives me a firm handshake and looks at me sympathetically. His office is officially closed today, as yesterday was a bank holiday in France and he is making a long weekend of it. He opened it especially for us; our children have to be back at work in Paris tomorrow. I have a sunset-orange sailor's jersey draped over my shoulders.

This lad doesn't know us. He just sees a big Groix islander with spiky hair, a funny nose and an orange sweater. He sees the son, an urban, bougie version of his father although the physical likeness is uncanny, the suitable looking daughter-in-law who sports a carrot-coloured bob, and the gorgeous blond daughter leaning on a walking stick.

Cyrian has been stand-offish with me ever since you did a bunk, Lou. Sarah is made of stronger stuff. When people feel awkward at seeing her in a wheelchair, she taunts them by whispering that she is really a mermaid with a long fish tail instead of legs.

"Our father wishes to thank you, sir," begins Cyrian.

Damn, I'd better mark my territory right now, otherwise it'll be too late, he'll take my place and before I know it, I'll be in a care home too.

"I'm a widower, not senile, Cyrian. It was your mother who slipped away, not me. So, don't speak for me. Is that clear?"

He takes it on the chin. I bite my lip. Why did I say "slipped away"? I can see you right now, in your summer frock, with your long, tanned legs, your proud breasts, your full lips. Old ladies die, but women *slip away*. You slipped away, Lou, leaving me high and dry, with a broken heart.

The solicitor clears his throat. His jeans are impeccable, and his jacket has a small crocodile motif on it. He reminds me of your nephews from the castle. Your father bore a grudge against me for a long time for having taken you prisoner on my island. Though he was a mountain of a man, he collapsed like a ton of bricks when the time came, alone in his park, beside his swans and moat. He had good reason to insist that we live there. If we had, I might have saved his life.

Your solicitor has a posh accent. I used to put on that accent when dealing with posh patients, it reassured them. But deep down, I talk like an islander. You know this, you used to hear me talking in my sleep.

"The deceased," he announces pompously, "bequeaths her share of the flat on Boulevard Montparnasse to her husband, and her shares of the Groix house jointly to her two children."

We had made this decision together to encourage Cyrian and Sarah to return to the island. The house is big enough for us all not to be on top of one another and I'd keep it in a good state of repair for them.

"I'm now going to read you out her last will and testament," continues the solicitor.

Cyrian and his wife are sitting on the edge of their chairs. Sarah is leaning back in hers. Federico and Giulietta's faces proudly straddle the armrests. The solicitor raised an eyebrow when he noticed her tattoos.

"Joe, Cyrian, Sarah, please keep this family together and united, maintain our traditions, and preserve our family values. Please keep coming to Groix for the holidays."

Our children nod their heads obediently.

"We won't leave you on your own at Christmas and Easter, Grandpa!" declares Albane insistently. She still refuses to use my first name.

"No problemo," adds Sarah, giving me a conspiratorial wink.

The solicitor continues reading. "I would like Apple and Charlotte to learn how to bake my friend Lucette's *tchumpôt* cake?" says the solicitor in a questioning voice.

He pronounces the word phonetically, whereas the locals say "*tchoumpooote*". It's a cake made with salted butter and brown sugar that is so rich it makes the *kouign amann* cake— another butter-based Breton speciality—look like the low-fat diet option. You tried, Lou, but you botched your *tchumpôt* every time.

"Albane took cookery classes with a famous chef," said Cyrian. "She'll teach Charlotte."

I pity this great chef who had to put up with my miserable daughter-in-law. The *tchumpôt* is made with sugar and love, Parisian women don't always have much of those. The solicitor gives me a strange look. My smile freezes. A ventricular contraction shakes my chest. I discreetly test my pulse. It's racing, but I have no chest pain. Shame. Having a heart attack at the solicitor's would have added a bit of spice to the proceedings. I would have got half a column in the local papers, *Ouest France* and *Le Télégramme*. Your children are here, so why not *drop the pipe* now, as they say. In days gone by, a clay pipe was placed between the teeth of anyone who was sick or dying. When the person died, their lower jaw would sag, and the pipe would fall out and break. I open my mouth as if to drop an invisible pipe. Sarah stares at me. The look in the solicitor's eye worries me. You've set a trap for me, Lou, I know you.

"The deceased has added a special codicil for you, Doctor, with a bequest attached to it."

Here we go. What do I have to do, Lou? Bungee jump off the top of Port-Saint-Nicolas? Climb the church steeple and steal the tuna fish? Repaint the nursing home in blue polka dots? I have a feeling it's going to be comical.

"I have to read the first paragraph to all of you," says the solicitor. He pauses and shuffles his papers around, as if he's some reality show host, then clears his throat and begins.

"*For my husband, Joe.*"

I cringe at hearing this youth repeat your words.

"*We loved each other very much.*"

Okay, a sweetener to start with. I instinctively lower my head between my shoulders and brace myself for impact.

"*Yet you betrayed me, my love.*"

I reel from the shock. So you think you're funny do you? I've looked at other women, yes, I've fantasized and even desired some of them! But I never cheated on you. And, if what my mates say is true, I'm an endangered species, old school; still in love with my wife.

Cyrian glares at me and Albane looks disgusted. Sarah seems surprised.

"This is ridiculous," I say, forcing a smile.

"I haven't finished yet," says the solicitor. "*You lied to me, but I forgive you,*" he went on. "*I don't want our children to hear any more. It's our business. They must leave the room now. This is for your ears only, Joe.*"

The solicitor points to the door. Cyrian complies and gets up, turning his back on me. Albane follows him, staring at me as if I were the lowest of the low. Sarah leaves giving me a hard tap with her stick on her way out. I tremble with rage. Yet at the same time, I want to burst out laughing, because it's the most horrific bad joke you've ever played on me. It's terrible, Lou, but it worked. Congratulations, you're the best! And now how do we go about proving to everyone that it's a load of rubbish?

"*For your big ears only,*" continues the solicitor, unfazed. "*If you are listening to these words, it means I left before you, so it's true that people with Dumbo ears really do live longer.*"

You have a very warped sense of humour, Lou.

"*You are confused and angry, but I don't blame you, Joe. But you owe me, so I am entrusting you with a tricky mission. Let's call it 'your punishment'.*"

What, you mean you're not joking? You really think I was unfaithful to you? So you were already out of your mind when you went to see the solicitor? If I had known beforehand, I would have had a field day! Our friends' grandchildren had some hot babysitters. And there was that Swedish tourist I helped out once when her bike had a flat tyre. I had plenty of opportunities if I had wanted it! I wish I had now, at least then your accusations would have been justified.

"*This is your mission, my* piroche," continues the solicitor. "*Piroche?*"

"It's a family saying, go on," I say.

"*I am asking you to do what you can to make our children happy, as you've never really bothered with them. You were a wonderful lover and an amazing husband, but an absent father. Your father and grandfather were always out on fishing trips, and you followed the same model. Your ancestors were away at sea, you were permanently away at the hospital. Our children may have succeeded in their careers, but they are not happy. If my solicitor is reading this letter to you today, it means that I can't do anything more for them. So I'm handing them over to you. Cyrian is married and a father, and Sarah is footloose and fancy free, playing the field. Yet neither of them know anything about love. If you can resuscitate patients with flat electrocardiograms, I'm sure you*

*can bring a smile back to the faces of your two grown-up children.
I'm giving you carte blanche. Happiness is infectious. And there's
a surprise at the end for you."*

What is this nonsense, Lou? Undeterred, the solicitor goes
on.

*"Cyrian and Sarah mustn't know anything about this. I
forbid you to tell them. I also forbid you to talk about it with the
7 Gang. This is not mission impossible. You have as much time as
you need, after a two-month minimum sentence. No agency is
aware of your actions. This letter will not self-destruct."*

He looks up at me.

"Is this a reference to that Tom Cruise film?"

"Not at all, it's a reference to the series starring Peter
Graves and Barbara Bain. You weren't born at the time, it was
broadcast in the sixties."

"Do you understand what she means by the '7 Gang'?" he
asks.

I nod and ask what the surprise is at the end.

He says that Lou wrote a letter to me and the children and
that he can only hand it over to me once I have completed
her mission.

"Give it to me right now!" I roar. "Sarah and Cyrian are
adults, they live over three hundred miles away from here. They
were free to choose the lives they wanted to lead. Lou was ill,
remember? Her illness clearly prompted this preposterous idea.
I'm a doctor, I know what I'm talking about. You're a solicitor,
you're not qualified to judge other peoples' happiness."

"My role is limited to informing you of the deceased's
final wishes, Doctor. I will not pass comment on the manner
in which you are to proceed," he snaps.

"Who will then?" I ask.

"When I asked her, she told me she trusted you."

"Which is odd given that she has just accused me of cheating on her," I retort smugly.

The solicitor shrugs resignedly. "I see all sorts of things in this job. This testament makes more sense than many others. If you feel deep down, and in all honesty, that your children are happy, then come back and see me in two months' time. You can break the seal and read her letter. Good luck, Doctor."

He stands up to let me know our meeting is over. He is off home now to enjoy what's left of the bank holiday. As for me, I'm going to have to face our children.

"Hold on a second! You mentioned a seal. Do you mean that the envelope has been wax sealed?" I ask.

"There is no envelope," the solicitor replies. He then opens his desk drawer, grabs a small bottle and places it in front of me. It is sealed with wax. The label has been scratched off and the last two letters of the brand are missing, so that it now reads "Champagne Merci". It contains two folded pieces of paper. I recognize the bottle. The last time I saw it was one June, on a summer solstice evening. I was still an overworked boss at that time, and Apple was just a few months old . . .

Ten years earlier

Lou, Groix Island

It's the summer solstice tonight. We had decided to go on a picnic, so I lovingly prepared us some sandwiches. Even though I take cookery classes and have a whole shelf of recipe books at my disposal, everything I touch is a disaster. Knowing this, you had bought some crisps and Haribo to compensate. We take the moped to go and have our picnic on the beach. We are the only ones there, sat on a large towel, being spied on by a seagull who has his eye on our food. He has seen us before and knows we won't finish all the sandwiches, though you eat half of yours to please me. Sarah and her fiancé Patrice have just passed their university entrance exams. They are trekking across Corsica right now. They're getting married in October; the invitations have already gone out. Cyrian took the same exam but flunked it. He is seeking comfort in the arms of his new girlfriend, Albane. You said it will take him down a peg or two, but he could have been spared such humiliation. You're a wonderful doctor, my love, but you don't understand our son. When you wanted to become head of department, you gave it your all and succeeded. Cyrian has to live in your shadow; he's always afraid of disappointing you, sometimes paralyzed by fear. And he knows Sarah is your favourite. You don't like Albane, and you call her Eliane, Ariane, Morgane . . . You never get her name right. You prefer his ex, Maëlle, the mother of our little Apple, who is eight months old now and a real sweetheart. I'm such a mother hen. If my chicks are doing well, I cluck happily. And you can be the rooster, darling. To love a child is to let go of the child you dreamed of having and accept the one you've got, as they are, not as you want them to be. Cyrian isn't someone you would have chosen as a friend, but he is your son, Joe. Besides, he is the spitting image of you.

The Grands Sables beach is the only convex beach in Europe, and completely unspoilt too. The sea currents that skirt the island sweep up the sand and drop it further along. Storms have caused the beach to move several hundred metres north-westward over time, and it's starting to take over the rocky outcrop of the Pointe de la Croix. I've brought a half-bottle of Mercier champagne along and two champagne flutes, real ones, not plastic. You pop the cork just as the sun sinks into the sea. You have a bright red "Joseph" on your shoulders. All we need is Barber's "Adagio for Strings" conducted by Leonard Bernstein and we'd be in heaven.

"To love!" you yell.

"Look at me as we toast, Joe," I reply, "otherwise seven years of no sex!"

You obey instantly.

"Can you think of a song that would fit this moment, my *piroche*?" I ask. I expect you to choose Barbara, Reggiani, or Brel. You finally choose a song by Serge Lama but change the words, adding Lou, so it doesn't rhyme anymore.

"*An island between the sky and Lou! An island with no men or ships,*" you sing.

I then sing a song by Michel Fugain and his group Big Bazar, "Sing for life, sing … As if you're gonna die tomorrow!"

The tide goes out, leaving behind seaweed and seashells on the shore. Laughter erupts from an anchored sailing boat.

"Everything is symbolic on midsummer's night, Joe. We are halfway through the year and halfway through our lives."

"Yes, we need to live life to the full," you reply, "and make the most of every moment, *carpe diem*. You know your sandwiches are revolting, but your kisses are delicious."

You lean towards me; I push you back.

"I fell in love with you the very first time I saw you at my cousin's wedding, Joe. You were such a terrible dancer that I couldn't resist you."

"That's not true, I'm supple and graceful. Girls used to love it when I asked them for a slow dance," you retort.

"I noticed you because of that odd-looking sailor sweater hanging over your shoulders. I must have looked like a canary in my ridiculous yellow dress. I offered you my heart and you took it."

"It was the first time I had ever set foot in a château, Lou, and seen a bridegroom in tails, and women wearing hats other than Breton headdresses. I was impressed. Then I saw you and I knew . . ."

Growing up without a mother meant I was a badly dressed child. My father had a castle but no fortune, all his money went into the roof and the moat. I'm the fifth daughter; I wore my elder sisters' cast-offs that didn't fit them properly and looked hilarious on me. You came up to me at the wedding and said, "You have such deep blue eyes; I would love to drown in them." I told you that what you had just said made no sense. And that you danced like a bull in a china shop.

Back on the beach all these years later, I ask you to promise me something.

"Don't make me promise to eat those sandwiches!"

"I'm serious," I insist. "I want to be able to count on you."

I explain but you refuse to promise, so I keep on and on. We spend hours with the sea before us, chatting, bickering, hugging each other. We finish the bottle. The seagull flies off with the end of my sandwich in its beak. I ask you again. You still won't agree. We start arguing, so I move on to plan B and start to cry. You crack, and finally promise, as you hate seeing me cry. I give you a French kiss and whisper, "This is a 21st of June kiss, darling, never to be forgotten!" I borrow your penknife and trim the champagne cork. I take a piece of paper out of my pocket and write out an agreement which we both sign. I slip it into the empty bottle. I put my mouth around the bottle neck and whisper words that you couldn't hear into it. I push the cork in and scratch the label until the last two letters of Mercier disappear, leaving only "Merci": "thank you". We ride back to the village in the mild spring night air.

At home, two messages on the answering machine were to change our lives forever. The first one was from Cyrian, announcing his engagement to Albane, their forthcoming wedding and the arrival of a new baby in the family. The second was from Sarah, who was so distraught that I didn't recognize her.

"Dad, Mum, something is wrong, I can't walk properly anymore, we're ditching the trek and taking the first plane back to Paris."

I panicked and you reassured me that it would be okay, saying Sarah had probably pushed herself too far preparing for her entrance exams, and that you'd deal with it. You got her onto the ward of your friend and professor, Thierry Serfaty, the very best.

Thierry is quick to make the diagnosis and our world falls apart. Patrice broke off his engagement to Sarah, like a rat fleeing a sinking ship. You offered to make mincemeat of him, but I stopped you in time. Sarah never mentioned his name again and the wedding was cancelled.

2nd November

Joe, Lorient

I didn't see that bottle again, Lou, with your message and voice in it, until today. It now contains two folded up pieces of paper, the contract we made and a letter to me and the children. You sealed the bottle with wax. I'm finally beginning to grasp what you're blaming me for. I didn't betray you; I just didn't keep my side of the bargain. I feel dizzy, I hold onto the armrests of my chair. The solicitor looks worried, not about me, but because it's his day off. If I kick the bucket in his office, he won't be able to leave on time.

"Is there a doctor here?" I ask, tongue in cheek.

He doesn't look amused. "I'll go and get your children."

I tell him no, I'll be fine, and that I'm just a bit upset, knowing that my wife's voice is in that bottle.

This young fool takes me for an old fool and to top it all, he presumes you're dead. I know your voice disappeared along with you and that I'm not really going to hear it when I uncork the bottle. Yet I still hope I will, just as I used to believe my father when he made me hold a seashell to my ear so I could hear the sea. Spiral seashells are governed by the "golden ratio", like flower pistils, pyramids and cathedrals. You were my golden ratio, Lou. I'll honour your dying wishes because I love you and because I'm eager to find out what you wrote. I don't agree with you however. Our children *are* happy. Cobblers have the worst shod kids and doctors have the sickliest families. I got the full works with Sarah and Lou. Sarah hasn't got multiple sclerosis, but she suffers from a rare disease. You didn't get Alzheimer's, but you had a rare condition that affected your memory. It never rains but it pours. I wonder who will be next?

The solicitor has gone to get our children. There'll be bloodshed. You've just ruined the next two months for me, Lou. What legacy did you actually leave me? Two measly numbers? One double-digit for the number of years we spent together and the other a hundred digits long for the number of times we laughed.

The taxi drops us off at Lorient ferry port. The boat, known as the "roll-on roll-off", leaves the harbour and sails towards Groix. The locals sit inside, while tourists and part-time residents sit outside, staring at the ocean. The sea is calm, and the boat isn't rocking. Shame, it would have cheered me up no end to see Albane puke. Sarah takes the lift along with the elderly and pregnant women. She sits near a window in the main lounge and slides her stick under her seat. All male eyes are on her. She's used to it though and doesn't bat an eyelid. They scrutinize her long blond hair, blue eyes, slim-fitting jacket and jeans. My daughter oozes sex appeal. Cyrian and Albane climb up onto the upper deck amidst the tourists. Summer and winter, there are two types of tourists here: the hikers with their backpacks and walking poles, and the wannabe hikers sporting new oilskin jackets and deck shoes, who never make it beyond the harbour café. I don't fall into either category, so I stay on the lower deck, outside with the smokers. I gave up smoking twenty years ago to please you but now I scrounge one off a lad I know. I grip the handrail nervously, cigarette stuck to my lips, as I stare at the ocean and inhale the smoke. After a few minutes I go and sit beside

Sarah. The tourists think I'm some old idiot trying to chat her up and look at me with contempt.

"Tough day, eh, Dad?" she mutters.

"I did *not* cheat on your mother," I whisper.

She gives a disappointed laugh. "If I learned one thing from Patrice, it was never to trust anyone."

Your passing has opened up a can of worms, Lou. Yesterday, Cyrian and Maëlle actually sat in the same church, which I never thought I'd see. And today, Sarah mentioned her ex by name.

"What did Mr Lacoste say to you after we left?" she asked, sarcastically.

I reply that her mother entrusted me with a mission, but I can't tell her or Cyrian about it.

We watch the ocean through the porthole then Sarah turns to me. "Sorry Dad, for not helping you when Mum was ill. It was too much for me. If you put her in a nursing home, it must have been for her own good."

"I played no part in it, your mother insisted."

"At least she had you and wasn't alone," Sarah replies, "because loneliness is a terrible thing."

An alarm bell goes off in my head. Up until now, I had always thought that my daughter was quite happy being single. The boat blows its horn as it passes another boat on the way back to Lorient harbour.

"I'll come for Christmas, Dad, but I know Albane. She'll work on Cyrian till he gives in. She had no reason to hate you before, but she'll have a field day now."

You knew what you were exposing me to, Lou. My throat tightens. I think of how our children used to be, how close they were, how they enjoyed speaking *groisillon*, the dialect here. They were fond of their little island. Instead of using swear words, they used to finish their sentences with "*gast*" like the locals. They were tough Bretons, not soft Parisians. Cyrian changed during his teenage years. He became arrogant, while Sarah kept her natural, funny side. They would go out on Saturday nights to parties hosted by aristocratic and upper middle class families who sought to ensure their children married into the same milieu. When it was Sarah's turn to host one, your father opened up the castle orangery and we had a magnificent evening. Cyrian looked just the part in his suit, and Sarah was stunning in her ballgown. Then along came that damn entrance exam.

"Your brother still hasn't got over flunking it," I say.

"I know, and he's still mad at me for getting in. He's even worse since I've started working in film production, he says it's a waste."

"Well, you're a pretty wonderful waste," I joke.

"Albane doesn't agree," she retorts. "Do you know what she threw at me yesterday? That she's worried what Charlotte may have inherited from our sickly tribe, given that Mum and I have both been ill."

I can feel my hackles rising. Albane's grandparents were agricultural workers from Normandy who tilled the land passed on from their ancestors. Her father made his fortune by buying back plots of land from locals whose children didn't want to go into farming. He elicited sympathy, promising he would carry on their traditions. He conducted his dealings in secret and soon became the owner of a sizeable number of hectares. Then when it was too late to stop him, his neighbours discovered that he had secretly joined forces with a giant real estate investor. On this very land, tilled by their forefathers, that they had sold him in good faith for next to nothing, sprang up monstrous hotel complexes to accommodate Parisians on weekend getaways. Albane's father had so enraged the local farmers, that they had buried his Mercedes under a mountain of cow dung in revenge.

"Sorry to interrupt," says Cyrian. "We've decided to spend the night at the Marine Hotel. I've booked two rooms. We'll pick up Charlotte and be on our way."

"You decided, or Albane made you?" scowled Sarah.

"Stay out of it," snapped Cyrian.

"Does your wife think betrayal is contagious?" I ask in disgust.

"How could you do such a thing to Mum?" shouted Cyrian fiercely. "Packing her off to a nursing home so the coast was clear for you!"

I sink my fists deep into my pockets to stop myself from punching him. "Piss off," I yell. "I don't need your insults or your help."

Cyrian goes pale with anger. "Normally it's fathers who are meant to help their sons, not the other way round. If I'd wanted to go into medicine, you would have thwarted my every move. You have to be the boss, the dominant wolf, leader of the pack, the alpha male."

A phrase from the Apocalypse of St John springs to mind: *I am the Alpha and the Omega, the beginning and the end.*

Sarah starts laughing saying how her therapist would like the bit about the dominant wolf.

"Your therapist should advise you to start a family instead of banging every guy that crosses your path," shouts Cyrian.

"Watch it you!" I holler.

"Mum is dead," he shouts in a rage. "She didn't *slip away*, Dad, she popped her clogs. Six feet under in the local grave-yard of your precious island. We'll never see her again. It's all over. No more family Christmases, no more Mother's Days, no more love and affection. I'll never set foot on this shitty piece of rock again."

"Well I'd better remind you that your eldest daughter lives here."

"She'll come on holiday with us to the south of France."

"What, sever all ties just like that, a bit radical isn't it?"

Cyrian is lost for words. Albane leaps to his rescue.

"Grandpa, we're still shocked by what we learnt this morning from the solicitor," she says calmly.

"We need to take a break," adds Cyrian.

I have a job keeping my fists in my pockets. I think back to the sealed bottle, Grands Sables beach, the mission you have forced upon me and your warped sense of humour.

Taking a break is what you say during a separation, when you no longer love the person. This at least implies that we did love each other at one time.

The boat sounds its horn as it enters the port. Passengers gather their belongings ready to disembark. Cyrian and Albane walk towards the staircase. I wait for the lift with Sarah.

Apple, Groix Island

Joe, Daddy, Aunt Sarah and Albane have gone to Lorient. I would give my new watch to know where you are now, Lou. For me, Groix is paradise.

"Do you believe in heaven and hell?" I ask Charlotte.

"Mum does, but Dad says hell is other people," she answers with a shrug.

"Where do you think Lou is?" I ask again.

"Luckily not in the kitchen," she replies, spitefully.

Lou, you taught me that when people say mean things, it's because they're afraid or unhappy. Charlotte is lucky that she lives with Daddy and I am lucky that I live with Mummy, Joe and you. We may be sisters, but we've got nothing in common. Mummy is working late tonight. There's no school today, so I'll have to put up with my half-sister all day.

"Do you fancy going to the cinema?" suggests Charlotte.

"We can't," I snap.

"Why?"

I sometimes can't believe we're related. "We've just buried Lou!"

"What does that change?"

"It's about respect. Don't you miss her too?

"I only saw her three times a year. Dad said last month she didn't even recognize him."

"But he hasn't been to the island since August," I say in surprise.

"Yes he has, silly. He came every month when she was in the home. He used to go there and back in a day."

I'm reeling. So it appears that we don't have the same Daddy. She sees hers every evening and mine comes to Groix without even telling me.

"I didn't know," I mumble sadly.

"So now I hope you'll stop pestering us to come here. There's not even a pool!"

"You prefer a pool to the sea?" I ask, amazed.

She looks at me like I'm crazy. "The sea here is freezing! And Dad says that your mum is a limpet."

Limpets are small sea creatures with a cone-shaped shell that feed on the algae which grows on rocks. They carve out a circular groove in the rock and cling to it very tightly with their muscular foot to protect themselves from the waves. Mummy clings to Groix like me and Joe, so I suppose it's kind of true. I don't take it badly anyway. Plus I am on home turf, so I try to be friendly to her.

"Would you like to go for a picnic at the Pointe des Chats?" I ask. "It's just after the guest house at Sémaphore de la Croix, a rocky outcrop where there's a little lighthouse with a red top, and it's right in the middle of the François Le Bail nature reserve. The rocks there gleam in the sun, they shine under your feet."

"How will we get there?"

"By bike! I can lend you mine and I'll take Mummy's."

"I don't know how to do it," Charlotte says, looking embarrassed.

"What? You're joking!" I exclaim.

"It's true, I've never ridden a bike in my life."

"No problem, you can sit on the luggage rack," I tell her.

I prepare our food. Charlotte looks awkward stood there in the kitchen, I don't think her mother even lets her touch a breadknife, let alone make sandwiches.

"Do you like Guémené sausage?" I ask, as I throw a piece to Oskar the puppy who gobbles it up. My sister tries it and then takes another piece. If she knew that she had just eaten smoked pig intestines . . .! I put some in our sandwiches and grab a few apples and a bottle of water. Charlotte is wearing a pink polo neck and leather boots. I lend her a fleece, a warm jacket and an old pair of Converse trainers. We stroke Oskar and say bye to him. I climb onto my bike and tell her to get on behind me and to hold tightly onto the luggage rack and keep her feet apart so she doesn't catch them in the wheel spokes.

"Don't worry, I'll be careful, but don't move because if you do it'll unbalance me and we'll both fall off."

Mummy needs me so I'd better not injure myself.

There are no traffic lights in Groix, just crossroads with stop signs. I go slowly at first, then I get more daring. If Charlotte gets hurt, Daddy will hate me. It rained last night and the roads are still wet. The sun is shining, I go right through the puddles on purpose, lifting my legs up high out of the way. Charlotte copies me, and we laugh even though I still feel really sad that Lou has gone. We're getting along for the first time.

"We'll make a detour through Port-Lay. You can meet my friends," I say.

I have some friends who live on the island like me and others who come here just for the holidays. The twins are the same age as me, but they live in Paris. They are called Elliot and Solal. Their grandparents, Gildas and Isabelle, are friends with Joe and Lou. In the old days, there were tuna and sardine canning factories in Port-Lay as well as France's first fishing school. I pedal along the path, avoiding the mooring chains. The tide is out, and the boats are stranded. I leave my bike in the grass. We walk up to the white house on the water's edge. The twins are playing on the patio.

"Hey! We're waiting for Boy and Lola," shouts Solal.

"We think they'll be here in a minute," says Elliot.

They always say "we" instead of "I". They call their grandparents by their first names like me. They're cool.

"Who are Boy and Lola?" asks Charlotte, intrigued.

"Our friends," I say.

"Islanders or Parisians?"

"Neither," I tell her.

"'Boy' is English, have their parents got a house here?" she asks.

"They're homeless," Elliot tells her.

"My mum helps with a charity for the homeless in Le Vésinet where we live. Do your friends go begging?"

"No," says Elliot, "they've got everything they need. Look here they are."

Boy and Lola arrive as they do every day, starving hungry, at twelve o'clock on the dot. They circle above us and land on the patio.

"They're seagulls!" cries Charlotte in amazement.

"No, herring gulls," Solal corrects her. "Seagulls have a black beak and herring gulls have a yellow beak with a red dot."

"Their babies tap on the red dot and the mother gull regurgitates what she ate to feed them. It's yucky. The parents are white and the babies are grey," adds Elliot.

Johana, the twins' elder sister, arrives with crusts of toast covered in cream cheese. She looks like a mermaid with her long hair and willowy body.

"They also like sausages, prawns, fish, leftover cake, and anything fatty," she says.

Boy, the big male, grabs a crust with his beak and then steps back to let little Lola help herself, in a neat pas de deux. Johana goes up to them, but the birds screech and fly away at once.

"That's the special warning sound they make when they sense danger," explains Solal. "They make a different noise when they want to be fed and when they're chasing away the others, except for Julie."

"We thought Julie was a girl until Isabelle found out he's a boy," says Elliot. "Gildas feeds him out of his hand."

"There he is!" cries Johana, pointing to a grey-backed gull landing on the patio.

Boy and Lola move out of the way. Julie gives a shrill cry. The twins' grandfather arrives with some buttered bread. He holds out a piece and the bird catches it and then steps back, takes another piece and steps back, continuing his noisy ruckus as he does so.

"When we eat lunch indoors," says Gildas, "Julie taps on the glass with his beak. We open the window and put a stool in front of it. He jumps from the stool onto the floor to come and eat. If we forget his stool, he won't come in. We assume that Boy and Lola are his offspring."

I ask the twins to come with us for a picnic at Les Chats, but they've planned to go horse riding. I ask my sister if she wants to go with them. She refuses, saying she's scared of horses.

"Your grandfather was born here, so you're a Groix islander by blood," says Solal, in awe.

"I prefer the Côte d'Azur actually, it's more fun," replies Charlotte snootily.

I drag her away before things get out of hand.

*   *   *

We sit on top of a silvery rock to eat our picnic in the sunshine at the Pointe des Chats.

"Mum says the weather is always bad in Brittany," says Charlotte, surprised.

"That's not true, Morbihan has the same number of hours of sunshine per year as Cannes," I delight in telling her.

"Dad says that when there's a storm, they won't let the ferry cross, so you could end up stuck on the island."

"That hardly ever happens, and it doesn't last long."

"Do you know any famous people here, you know, like people you see in magazines?"

"I know some artists and two environmental activists."

"Did you ask for their autographs?"

"No, I don't want to bother them. Hey, Joe told me a riddle," I say to change the subject. "When there's no water, we drink water, when there's water, we drink wine."

"That doesn't mean anything, it's stupid," she says.

"Think about it," I say. "There was no floating dock in Groix in the old days. Fishing boats could only return to port when the tide was in. If they returned to port when the tide was out, the sailors had to wait in their boats, drinking water, till it came in. 'When there's no water, we drink water.' Get it? So when the tide came in, and the boats could return to port, the sailors got off their boats and rushed to the bars for a drink. 'When there's water, we drink wine.' I think it's clever!"

Charlotte couldn't care less about sailors and tides. "How did you get that?" she asks, pointing to the scar at the corner of my eye.

"Our cat knocked the coffee pot over and I burnt myself."

I told Daddy the same story and he believed me. When I touch the scar, I can't feel anything, Joe says the nerve endings will come back one day.

"My friends say I'm like Harry Potter except my scar isn't a lightning bolt."

"So you have friends too, like Grampy and Granny?" she asks, grabbing another slice of sausage.

"Of course! Don't you?"

"No. Just my mum. And my mum has me."

She picks up a pebble and throws it angrily. I feel kind of sorry for her.

"We could be friends if you like? We've got a head start, we're already sisters."

"*Half*-sisters," she says, "and we don't even know that for sure as Dad says your mum pulled the wool over his eyes and he didn't ask her for a paternity test."

I stare at her, frozen to the spot. Lou, if Daddy is not my Daddy, then you and Joe are not my grandparents. Does this mean you'll throw us out? Does this mean I won't be allowed to cry for you anymore? Is this why Daddy never hugs me and hardly ever comes to the island to see me?

"Mum says you're jealous of me," snipes Charlotte.

"How can I be jealous of someone who has a mother like yours!" I snap back, annoyed.

"We can swap if you want."

"Don't you like your mum?" I ask, surprised by her reaction.

"No one likes her except Oskar," she says. "I'll leave home as soon as I'm eighteen. Dad wouldn't even notice if I was gone."

And there was me thinking they were the perfect family.

"But you see him every day, don't you?" I ask, shocked.

"I'm in bed when he gets home at night and in the morning he's gone before I'm up," she says.

"But you at least see him at weekends?"

"Saturdays he's at the office, Sundays he goes jogging at the lake and when he gets back he reads and listens to jazz. I stay in my room watching films or TV series. I'm not even allowed to invite a friend round or go to other peoples' houses."

I can't get my head around this.

"I go to my friends' houses and they come to ours. I love reading, especially Jules Verne, Rudyard Kipling, and Enid Blyton. I raced through the seven volumes of Harry Potter and *Black Beauty*."

Charlotte just shrugs. "I have private one-on-one dance lessons. I go to youth theatre productions at the Comédie Française and the Salle Pleyel in Paris. Me and Mum go together. She says you don't need friends when you love your mum. She takes me to school and picks me up for lunch. I'd rather hang out at the canteen, but she won't let me."

"That doesn't sound like much fun!"

"I thought all kids lived like that. Do you prefer *your* life? There's nothing to do on your lonely little island."

I choke on her words.

"Nothing to do? Are you joking? Joe calls it our paradise. I swim in the sea all year round. I go to drama classes at the local theatre. I go dancing with the Celtic Circle Club. I collect driftwood at high tide. I go mushroom and black-berry picking with Joe. In the summer, I go to small outdoor concerts, where they bring the piano in on a trailer. There are midday drinks at George's Hangar, he's the one who makes amazing caravans and trailers. We have the Eco-museum. I help out with the rectory charity sale, the school fair, and Dojo's flea market. There's an adventure park where you can climb trees with huge safety nets under-neath. I was an extra in Laurent Morisson's video clip for his song 'Caballitos'. It was shot at night at the funfair and was super cool!"

"You're so lucky . . . Dad says you want to be a doctor like Grampy, is that true?"

I nod, surprised that Daddy even knows.

"What do you want to do when you grow up?"

"I want to get as far away as possible."

I feel sorry for her. "Would you like to see more gulls like Boy, Lola and Julie?"

In the spring you mustn't go too near the nesting birds at Pen-Men and on the cliffs because you'll disturb them. But you can in November, if you're careful. Charlotte gets back on the luggage rack and I pedal like mad to get us there. It's quite a way, but my calves are strong like concrete. We slow down so as not to scare them. I know the names of the different species: northern fulmar, seagull, brown gull, great black-backed gull, herring gull.

I tell her they stay in pairs for years and start nesting around April–May time and take turns sitting on their eggs. They fiercely guard them, attacking any idiots that dare get too near. Forty days after the eggs have hatched, they teach the hatchlings to fly. We walk towards the sunny rock where the birds have gathered. Suddenly Charlotte starts screaming and jumping up and down, holding her arms out, with a savage grin on her face. The seagulls take flight, flapping their wings furiously. They screech, nosedive and swoop low over her. She gets a shower of bird poo all over her arms. She freezes on the spot and stops screaming. The birds slowly settle down and watch her.

"Why did you do that?" I ask.

"It was just for fun," she says, as she wipes the bird poo off herself with a tissue.

"If the nests had been full of baby birds, you would have scared the life out of them."

"That would have been even funnier." She starts grumbling again. "Baby gulls are lucky. Their parents love and protect them, then teach them to fly so they can be free."

She sounds jealous of their freedom. Not surprising, given that Albane suffocates her and Daddy doesn't bother. They don't give her the tender love and attention I get from Mummy or our grandparents so that she has the confidence to brave the outside world. Charlotte has no one to teach her how to fly. Suddenly we hear a deep loud noise that shatters the peace. It's the ferry's horn. Time has really whizzed by today.

I pedal furiously to get us back home. Charlotte's weight makes it harder. Once we're back, I put my bike in the shed and open the door. Albane is standing there.

"Where were you?" she asks coldly.

"We went to the Pointe des Chats and then Pen-Men," I tell her.

I scan the room looking for Joe's reassuring eyes.

"Isn't Grampy here?" asks Charlotte.

"We're spending the night at the Marine Hotel; I've packed your bag. What is that awful smell? Is it your fingers, Charlotte? What on earth have you been touching?"

"We've been eating sausage," says my sister.

Albane stares at me as if I had given poison to her precious little princess. Then she looks at her daughter's clothes: fleece and saggy old Converse trainers. Where are her delicate pink polo neck and pretty boots?

"What on earth are you wearing? You look like . . ." She is briefly lost for words, seeing Charlotte dressed in my clothes. "So how did you get to the Pointe des Chats anyway?" she continues.

"On Apple's bike," bellows Charlotte.

Albane goes deathly pale, which Charlotte doesn't notice.

"You . . . rode . . . a . . . bike . . . on . . . the . . . road?" she says, separating each word.

"Yeah, Apple pedalled and I sat on the luggage rack," replies Charlotte proudly.

Albane rushes towards me, grabs me by the arm, and shakes me really hard. I am so surprised that I don't immediately react.

"You dared do that?" she shouts.

"You're hurting me," I yelp, finally trying to free myself.

Daddy hears the noise and rushes in asking what's going on.

"This little fool took our daughter bike riding on the main road!" screams Albane, digging her nails into my arm.

"All we did was go for a picnic. Let go of me!" I yell.

"Charlotte is fine, Albane," says Daddy. "She couldn't have known."

"Couldn't have known what?" asks Charlotte, looking worried.

"Calm down Albane, they are both fine," says Daddy.

"I should never have left her alone! My daughter's the only one who matters to me, I don't care about your daughter, she can go ahead and die!" she shouts.

Daddy goes pale. He grabs his wife by the shoulders and pulls her off me by force. I rub my arm. If Joe had been there, he would have kicked Albane out. If Sarah had seen what she did, she would have hit her with her stick. If Mummy had been there, well, she would have been livid.

"We just went for a ride," I say again.

Charlotte avoids my gaze and goes back to being a cry baby.

"She made me do it, Mum," she whines.

"My poor darling," Albane says, comforting her. Albane leaves the room and Daddy goes with her. I tell Charlotte she is a horrid sneak for dropping me in it like that.

"I have to live with her all year round, you don't. You don't know how lucky you are," she whimpers.

*   *   *

She goes off to look for her mother, keeping her head down. I let myself slide down onto the floor and my eyes start tearing up. Lou is dead. I don't know where Joe and Sarah are. Mummy thinks Daddy is here tonight, so she's spending the night in our house in Locmaria with just an electric fan heater, a quilt and her thermal underwear.

Daddy comes back and leans over me.

"Did she hurt you?" he asks.

He takes a look at my arm. He is starry-eyed, kind and loving for once. He speaks to me in a gentle voice. If this is what it takes for Daddy to be nice to me, then I'll let the old bag come back and hurt me again.

"I'm so sorry, Apple. She shouldn't have done that. She didn't know what she was saying. She was afraid. It won't happen again. We'll put some ointment on it. Here we go."

He helps me up, then rummages around in the first aid box for the ointment. When he finds it, he covers my arm in it. I can't stop thinking about what Charlotte said. So I ask him outright.

"Daddy, I am your daughter, aren't I?"

"Of course you are, what sort of question is that?"

"Are you sure?" I add.

"What a stupid question. Do you know where the key to the loft is?"

"On the laundry room shelf," I reply.

Joe is the only one in the family who goes up there. I hear Daddy climb up the steps to that horrible spidery, cobwebby room. I hear him shuffling about under the beams. My arm is stinging. He comes back, covered in dust and holding a black briefcase

"What's that?" I ask.

"It's Baz," he says, "I should have taken it back earlier. Your arm will soon be as right as rain. You must look after Joe, he's going to feel very lonely."

"He's like a limpet on his rock," I say.

He vanishes into the night. I stand in the hallway, my arm all numb, wondering what was inside the black case. A ventriloquist's doll maybe? I can just see Daddy sitting on a chair in front of an audience holding up a doll called Baz who says all the words Daddy doesn't dare say. I can still hear Albane's horrible voice in my head. She hates me. All she cares about is her precious baby, Charlotte. I may as well be dead for all she cares.

Joe, Groix Island

Sarah and I get off the boat. What an odd family we are. You held us together, Lou. Without you, everything simply falls apart. I can't go home, as Cyrian has to pick up his daughter and her things. I wish I could have kissed Charlotte goodbye. Just one last ordeal to go now, but if Sarah comes with me, it won't be as bad.

"I have to go back to the nursing home to free up your mother's room. Will you come with me?" I ask.

I did visit you every single day, Lou, even though you no longer recognized me at the end. I came to see the old Lou I used to know, not this woman staring up at me, wondering who I am, shaking with uncontrollable rage and frustrated love. When I took your hand, you just blushed like a coy teenager, or pulled away from me. I never knew what to expect.

We watched all your favourites together: *Out of Africa*, *The Fisher King*, *Babette's Feast*, and *House* the series, which made us howl with laughter. We even watched *Downton Abbey* again—it reminded you of growing up in the castle with your father. Though you only had old, moustachioed Jeannette the housekeeper to take care of the whole place, unlike the occupants of *Downton*. And when you just lay curled up in your bed, wallowing in grief and sadness, I would play Bach's Italian concertos, or Mozart's "Magic Flute" to you.

I thank the members of staff I run into, who are extremely devoted and do an amazing job, despite the constant budget cuts. I sign papers, I shake hands, I introduce Sarah to them. I'm a lucky man who had a beautiful wife and daughter. But my wife scarpered, and Sarah is never going to run the New York marathon.

I have to clear out your room as another family is already waiting. The room is bright, I brought your favourite furniture, some framed photos, fabrics in shimmering bright colours, your Tiffany lamp. It was your choice to come here, but once it was done, you went downhill. Doctors have a medical term for it, but in layman's terms, it's when you lose the will to live and let yourself get swept away, like a wave at low tide.

I tell Sarah that I don't want to keep anything in the room, but she is welcome to take whatever she wants.

She shakes her head. I leave everything to the staff who looked after you. On our way out, an elderly resident stops me. She tells me she was your Scrabble partner. I guess she means when you still had a good grasp on the French language.

She tells us to wait as she has something for us. After what seems like an eternity, she comes back holding a little pouch containing your leather diary, which covers the last five years and the current quarter.

"Lou gave it to me while she was still lucid. She told me to keep it for you."

When we get home, Apple comes running up to us.

"They're spending the night at the Marine Hotel. Did you have an argument?" she asks, looking worried.

"We are all on edge and I'm tired, my darling. I wouldn't be very good company for you tonight. I'm not hungry either. Why don't you go for dinner at The 50 with Sarah and Mummy?"

"You should come along too," Sarah insists.

"No, I need to be alone tonight."

I hug Apple, who is scowling. "Is your arm hurting? Can I have a look?" I ask.

"It's nothing, just a bruise," she says shyly.

"Did everything go okay with Charlotte?"

"It was heaven, Joe, Nirvana and Olympia, as you would say."

Lou, you've gone where we'll all go eventually. You'll hopefully be there to welcome me when I arrive. Don't go to the trouble of cooking for me though, or at least take some cookery classes up there while you're waiting, darling. Make them angel hair pasta, heavenly fish dishes, hellish roasts; poison the apostles, let the damned drink your broth. Yesterday, after the funeral, your friend Martine came round with her famous chocolate cake, that light as a feather flour-free chocolate delight, THE cake of all cakes. We devoured it this morning before taking the ferry to Lorient. I set a slice aside for you which nobody dared touch. It's so fluffy and light it's like sinking your teeth into a cloud. It's a delightful mixture of chocolate, love and laughter.

I eat your slice, while contemplating your diary. When I eventually open it, I discover various names, phone numbers, and addresses that you had noted and then crossed out. Why did you want this woman to give me your diary? I leaf through it and happen to see our wedding anniversary. Something else I'll be celebrating on my own from now on. I shall set the table for two, uncork a fine wine, put out our crystal glasses and get hammered. Good wine is excellent for the heart, something I've never failed to tell my patients, who have given me some nice wines over the years. We have enough to keep us going for decades, but it doesn't mean anything without you. I think of your letter sitting in the solicitor's drawer, and that song you loved by the Police. *I'll send an SOS to the world, I hope that someone gets my, I hope that someone gets my . . . message in a bottle.*

Apple, Groix Island

I'm at The 50 having dinner with Mummy and Aunt Sarah, at the round table on the right. They ask me about my day with Charlotte.

I tell them we went to Port-Lay, the Pointe des Chats and Pen-Men.

Mummy can read me perfectly and senses that something is wrong.

"Was there a problem?" she asks.

"Charlotte deliberately scared the birds away. Her mum doesn't let her do *anything* but she's nicer when she's away from her."

"That spoilt brat is like Janus," says Aunt Sarah.

"Who's that?" I ask.

"The Roman God with two faces, one sad and one smiling, one for the past and one for the future."

The happy Charlotte and the sad Charlotte . . .

Mum notices that I am holding my fork in a strange way. "Does your arm hurt?"

"I bumped it. I'm tired, I'm going home to bed," I mumble.

It's safe here, and I live about three hundred metres away. The sailors don't come to shore until late anyway and they are only a danger to themselves when they get back to their boats drunk and fall in the sea.

I cross the square, walking away from the church with the tuna weathervane. I pass in front of the Marine Hotel, several rooms still have the lights on. A man comes out of the bar door and I hide behind the baker's van. The man, whose face I can't see, is carrying a briefcase. He walks under a street lamp. It's Daddy! He skirts around the post office and goes into the covered market. Then he stops. My heart is beating so loudly it's going to wake up the whole village.

I slowly inch forward in the dark, terrified he might see me. He puts the briefcase down on the low wall and opens it. He turns his back to me, so I seize the chance to run over to the other side, hiding where the pizza van parks in the summer. He is making strange movements now. He puts something in his mouth, then he screws something onto something else. Is he loading a rifle? But he doesn't hunt. What if he's about to shoot himself? Or someone else?

I can't breathe properly. I don't get it. Daddy isn't a murderer. I see him take out of his briefcase what could be a rifle stock. He grabs another piece that looks too big for a barrel. He still has his back to me. He puts something around his neck and walks towards the middle of the hall. When he turns around I see him in profile, like a shadow puppet. Phew, what a relief. It's not a gun, it's a saxophone! He didn't come here to kill himself or anyone else, but to play. If my pounding heart hasn't woken up the villagers by now, his music certainly will.

I didn't know my dad played the saxophone; I just knew he was a jazz fan. So *that's* what was in the briefcase he got down from the attic. Baz isn't a person, he's a musical instrument. In the glow of a car's headlights, I can see Daddy with his eyes closed, elbows by his side, left hand on the upper keys, right hand on the lower keys. He doesn't blow into the saxophone, he just sways backwards and forwards. His hands are restless but his feet don't move. A cat meows, breaking the silence. Daddy's fingers wander over the keys, he dances, yet doesn't make a single sound. Then, suddenly, it dawns on me. He didn't dance with Joe and Sarah at the silent concert yesterday. He didn't join in because he was scared of Aunt Albane, or because he didn't have his saxophone with him, or because he was afraid of what people might say. But tonight he is all alone, and completely free. And he is playing for you, Lou. I move back into the shadows and go home. I can see light under Joe's door. I go straight to my room, and crawl under the duvet. Daddy is like Janus, he has two faces too. Happy Daddy and sad Daddy.

3rd November

Joe, Groix Island

Soaz is the cheerful young brunette who runs the Escale, the last café before Lorient. I say the last, because it's right at the end of the slipway, just a few metres from the quay where you embark for the mainland. She wasn't born here, she came over from the other side but she has long since been adopted by the islanders as one of their own. She gained her steadfast reputation by serving coffee to Groix residents travelling to Lorient for work during the cold dawn mornings, and standing up to drunken sailors and tourists on hot summer nights. I take a seat on the patio so I can see the first boat depart; I don't want to miss my son. It would be foolish to leave each other like this, all because of a misunderstanding. Last night, between two nightmares, I decided to give both our children a keepsake from you. You always wore your father's Jaeger-LeCoultre watch, and I think it'll look grand on Cyrian's wrist. I'll give Sarah your mother's pearls. I've kept your ruby and sapphire rings for Charlotte and Apple on their eighteenth birthdays. I'm wearing your watch, so as not to lose it, so I've got two on right now. People will think I'm losing my marbles. I do like your watch, but I prefer the ultra-thin one you gave me for our thirtieth wedding anniversary.

I greet the regulars who are already propping up the bar and watch the local newspapers being passed around.

"Coffee?" asks Soaz.

"Nope, champagne!" I reply.

I've decided to mark the occasion with your favourite drink, my darling. Me passing on your precious watch is indeed a big event.

"On my way," she says, unfazed.

She returns and places the glass flute down in front of me. There's a second flute on the tray, with just a tiny bit in.

"You shouldn't drink alone," says Soaz, raising her glass.

"To Lou," I proclaim.

"To Lou!"

Soaz used to have a great big dog called Torpenn, which some idiots decided to poison. I remember you emerged from your haze that day saying they should be poisoned too, an eye for an eye, that sort of thing. I suppose if you could reason like that, you hadn't quite lost your mind at that point.

A tourist comes in and orders a glass of Muscadet. Soaz serves him.

"That's a mini Muscadet, I want a proper one," he whinges.

She pours him a second glass telling him that the standard serving here is six centilitres.

"In Lorient, the glasses are bigger!" he cries.

"They contain twenty centilitres and it costs more," she retorts. "In Groix, wine is served in small glasses. This goes back to the old days when sailors used to go from bar to bar getting plastered; call it damage limitation if you like."

Lou, I'm sat facing the harbour hoping to catch our son. I listen to the wind blowing in the cable shrouds, other people's conversations, glasses clinking. Pedestrians walk along the slipway, locals slouch with their hands in their pockets, tourists are laden like mules. Cars disappear down into the inner depths of the boat. Passengers climb the steps. I can't see Cyrian. The roll-on roll-off moves slowly away from the quay. I pay for my drink and tell Soaz I'll be back later.

I've tied a golf club to the side of my moped. I must be the only doctor in the world who hates golf. I don't make a song and dance about it though or I could be fired from the College of Physicians. I don't understand the pleasure my colleagues get out of busting their backs and straining their shoulders and elbows. It's a perverse game that could easily provoke a heart attack. I can only think of one benefit: you let off steam. I'm alone on the cliff this morning. I brought some practice balls with me, so I can hit them as hard as I want. I go back to Soaz's café in time for the next ferry departure. I scan the harbour. Loïc, the "handsome butcher" to use your words, is sipping his coffee at the bar. He notices I'm wearing two watches.

"Cyrian is going to have the one belonging to Lou's father," I explain.

I've known Loïc since we were at school together and we were both knee high to a grasshopper. He raises his cup. "To this moment!"

That's Groix islanders for you: no mawkishness just real feelings, no bullshit just action, no loneliness just solidarity. We come into this world, then we die, and we spend the part in between sailing, loving, fishing, and fighting, all this in the midst of the sky and the sea . . .

Maëlle's apple-green Twingo stops in front of us. Sarah gets out. Her face lights up when she sees me.

"I was looking all over for you to say bye, I didn't want to miss you. I called you about twenty times! That oblong thing in your pocket is called a phone you know, and when it rings you pick it up and say hello."

I order two glasses of champagne. Too bad if it's not your favourite brand, Lou. One day, at a party when we were served a magnificent Dom Pérignon, you pulled a face and asked the waiter if he had any Mercier Blanc de Noirs. I thought the poor guy was going to have a fit!

Sarah spots her childhood friend, Morag, and says hi to her. She doesn't seem to notice how tired I look, and we make a toast. I can feel the hikers around us glaring at me, enthralled by my daughter and unaware that I'm her father.

I tell Sarah I have a present for her. I dip my hand in my pocket and bring out your necklace, the pearls sliding onto the table in an elegant stream. She smiles. On other young women the pearls would look out of place, but on Sarah they will be exquisite. I am proud, sat here surrounded by fishing and sailing boats, in the hubbub of departure, to be able to hand our daughter this heirloom passed on from generation to generation in your family. One of your grandmothers even asked to be buried with it, but the family lawyer refused to grant her request.

"When I was little, Mum secretly let me borrow them on my birthday, to wear to school, under my clothes," says Sarah.

"Really?" I reply in amazement.

That's you all over, Lou, letting a kid wear valuable jewellery to school.

"Can you help me Dad?"

Sarah lifts her hair up and off the back of her neck and I close the safety chain. She is as breathtakingly beautiful as you, Lou. I stiffen up, not wanting to break down in front of our daughter.

"You'd better board," I tell her. "I'm waiting for Cyrian. I want to give him your . . ."

"They've already left Dad."

"They can't have done; I was there this morning when the first boat left!" I protest.

Sarah said she went to their hotel this morning and found them arguing. Cyrian wanted to take the roll-on roll-off and Albane was insisting on the water taxi. Sarah had pointed out that the water taxi is supposed to be just for emergencies and Albane had said that it *was* an emergency as she had to get off the island right away.

I take your watch off my wrist and place it on the table.

"It's all yours, Sarah. Otherwise I'm so angry I might just throw it into the sea."

"I'll keep it until you decide you want to give it to him yourself," she says, slipping it into her handbag. "The silly sod isn't going to refuse it. It's best you give it to him."

Using her walking stick, our daughter boards the ferry, while our son is already racing back to Paris in his black tank. Where are you sweet Lou? Moored to what celestial dead body I wonder? The boat sounds its horn to announce its departure. The noise vibrates right through the island, which makes everyone look up and pause, before getting back to the task in hand. *Groix ahoy, feel the joy,* so goes the proverb. I find it quite moving to think that a beautiful young woman, wearing a string of pearls around her neck and holding a walking stick, is sailing towards the mainland grieving for you. I still can't get over the fact that she mentioned Patrice. I would have sworn blind that she'd forgotten all about him. Did *you* know that wasn't the case?

Cyrian, en route from Lorient to Paris

I'm driving, my hands clenched on the wheel, seething with anger. I tailgate the stupid little vehicles in the fast lane and flash them so that they'll get out of my way. "Go on, get lost the whole lot of you, I'm bigger and more powerful than you!"

I knew I would miss you, Mum, but I had no idea it would be this bad. I want to beat the shit out of everyone. But I'm not a fighter. The only time I've ever been in a fight was at one of your niece's weddings, when some pie-eyed bastard on the other side made fun of Sarah's disability. When this simpleton spotted Sarah, he started salivating, but then when he saw her walk, he began ridiculing her to a friend saying, "She's hot, but she walks like a deranged puppet. Lying down she'd be okay, but standing up, *no way!*" My fist suddenly had a life of its own and whammed right into the guy's nose. I could hear the cartilage crunching as blood spurted out. The wimp collapsed crying. I told his mate to remove him from the premises. I explained to him that I was Sarah's brother and that I had heard the disgusting remarks he had made about her. He left with his tail between his legs and a bloodied handkerchief under his broken nose. My hand hurt for a whole week afterwards.

I could do with punching someone today, it would relieve some of my tension. I regret taking the water taxi now. I gave in to Albane's nagging this morning. I won't ever forgive Groix for taking you away from me, Mum. *Groix ahoy, there's trouble ahead*, isn't that the proverb? When you lived in Montparnasse, we used to see each other once a week for lunch, I used to confide in you, you had such an infectious laugh. And then that bastard Systole took you away from me, to his rock in the middle of nowhere, full of fairies and witches, leaving me to fend for myself. Systole by the way, is the medical term for when the heart contracts, pumping blood into the aorta and the arteries that lead to the lungs. It's what I've called my father ever since I was a teenager. Systole is synonymous with a contraction, a fury, a gust of wind, in other words *my father*. Systole had everyone in his department wrapped around his little finger. Only the head nurse stood up to him, maybe it was with her that he cheated on you? He only ever loved you, Groix, his patients, his friends, Sarah, Apple and Maëlle. He has devoted his whole life to treating other peoples' hearts, but he doesn't possess one himself. I don't save lives like him; I sell high-end bathroom furnishings. I overheard him tell one of his friends once that his daughter inspires people with her films, and that his son gives them something to pee in. It hit me hard to see Maëlle in church. Apple looks so much like her. I will never go back to that island. I shall hold a memorial service for you in Paris every year. I'll put an ad in *Le Figaro* newspaper. I'll try and hold on to the happy times and forget Systole. How could he cheat on you? And how could you continue to love him knowing this?

My wife is dozing in the passenger seat. She's a good sort, loyal and reliable; she helped me get back on track when I was in the doldrums after failing my entrance exams. I never would have married her if she hadn't been pregnant. Albane was over the moon when she'd told me she was expecting a child. It was the first time I'd seen her smile since her brother's death. If I had told her to get rid of the baby, it would have destroyed her. Everyone saw me as the bastard who dumped Maëlle when she was pregnant, when in actual fact, I'd wanted to marry her and whisk her away to Paris. I wanted to be a doting father and husband, you know, a good man.

Charlotte is snoozing in the back. Oskar is dreaming, I can see his paws twitching in the rear view mirror. I start humming. *Oh Danny boy, the pipes, the pipes are calling, from glen to glen, and down the mountain side.*

Albane sits upright in her seat. "You woke me up, I was sleeping deeply. I remember you used to play that song in that smoky basement."

When Sarah, Patrice and I were preparing for our entrance exams, we formed a band. I named my saxophone Baz after the guy called Basil who sold it to me. Sarah was amazing on the piano, as was Patrice on the drums. We rehearsed in his parents' basement and smoked a lot of weed. The band broke up after I flunked my exams.

"I got Baz down from the loft," I announce, keeping my eyed fixed on the road.

"I know and it won't go down well with the neighbours."

To hell with the neighbours! Those on the right have a screaming brat and the one on the left is deaf and always has her TV on at full blast.

"I'm going to start playing again," I say.

"We hardly see you as it is," whispers Albane.

"Well, you'll hear me," I retort, spitefully.

What do I do now you've gone, Mum? In medical speak, systole is followed by diastole. Diastole is the opposite of systole and is when the heart relaxes after a contraction and fills with blood. This is synonymous with release, relaxation, calm, gentleness, in other words you, Mum. He is my systole, and you were my diastole. You were the only person I could confide in, I even told you about Danielle. I am very wary of my colleagues. If I don't hold it together, they'll be in there quick to replace me, they're just watching and waiting. No one likes the boss. I've been so busy with work these last few years that I've lost touch with my childhood friends. Even Oskar prefers Albane, the hand that feeds him. Apple looks up at me in awe when I speak to her. Charlotte doesn't seem to care. Sarah can't stand Albane. And now you've gone, my diastole. All I have left is Danielle and Albane. And I can't choose between these two women who both love me. I don't want to be a bad man, I'm just a man who wants to be happy.

5th November

Apple, Groix Island

The autumn half term holidays are almost over now. The island will go quiet again. The streets will be dead until Christmas, and all the visitors' footprints will be washed away by the rain. There will be fewer people at Loïc's for his famous *lard des thoniers*, a special kind of smoked bacon unique to Groix, and he won't have to explain to Parisians that black pudding is on Wednesdays and roast chicken on Sundays. Thierry the fishmonger will receive fewer customers, as will Sophie-Anne at her stall in the covered market, both bakeries, the post office, the three bookshops and the crêpe restaurants. There won't be so many people wanting Gwenola's cakes or Corinne's beauty products either. The village will go into hibernation.

Yves and Jackie are friends of Joe's. I hear a piano playing from behind the door, I wait for it to stop so I don't disturb them. Yves is the leader of the Tuna-Cats brass band; the name comes from the 'Chats', the 'Cats' lighthouse and the tuna fish weathervane on top of the church steeple. It's not the first brass band to exist on the island; there was one in 1895 and a second one in 1913. The piano stops. I ring the bell and Yves opens the door.

"Hello, Apple. Did Joe send you?"

I shake my head timidly. "I would like to have saxophone lessons."

"I can ask one of the teachers from the Lorient music academy who comes to Groix regularly, if you like."

"No, I'd like *you* to teach me."

Yves has a beard, wears checked shirts and jeans and his eyes are always full of laughter.

"Music is a big part of my life and I play several instruments but I don't teach," he says.

"Please, Yves! I don't have any money, but I can do odd jobs for you, I clean, iron, mow lawns. It's a surprise for someone."

"A surprise?" he says, visibly intrigued.

"My dad used to play the saxophone, but me and Daddy don't know each other that well so I'd like to learn so we can play together if he ever comes back to the island. But no one must find out, not Mummy, not Joe."

I think of Daddy playing in the night. Yves looks at Jackie.

"You really want to learn?"

I nod firmly. Yves's living room is full of musical instruments and the tables are covered in sheet music.

"Open that, Apple," he says, pointing to a worn-out case.

I lift the lid. Inside is a saxophone in bits, resting on velvet fabric.

"Is it broken?" I ask.

"No, it's just sleeping. Why don't we wake it up?"

He takes a small wooden stick out of a box and shows it to me.

"This strip of cane is called a reed. I put it in my mouth to moisten it. Then I lay it down on the flat side of the mouthpiece, facing this way, and line it up. Then I slide this round thing on, called the ligature, taking care not to damage the reed. And I tighten it up. Got it?" he asks.

I haven't, but I nod. He takes everything apart again and puts all the bits on the table.

"It's your turn now. The sound you make depends on how you set up your saxophone. Be careful with the reed, it's fragile," he adds.

I have a go, and get it all wrong, so he shows me again. It's really difficult, like learning marine knots at the sailing school. You just have to learn to get the hang of it.

"Next, the mouthpiece has to be mounted on the cork part of the crook. Like this, but no further. You see?"

I have a go.

"Perfect," he says.

Then he points to the two large parts. "Here we have the body and the bell. You fit them together and screw the crook on. The saxophone is a wind instrument and belongs to the woodwind family, even though it's made of metal. This one is called an alto saxophone."

He grabs a strap with a hook at the end, puts it around his neck and hangs the saxophone on it. Then he places his hands like Daddy did the other night, left one at the top, right one at the bottom, and blows into the mouthpiece. The sound sends a shiver down my spine. When Yves stops playing, I feel a bit sad and empty.

"That's the tune the band is working on at the moment, 'Mon amant de Saint-Jean'. Many of them had never touched an instrument before. Within a few months they were able to play this piece together," he says.

I'm impressed. Yves removes the strap, puts it around my neck, places my hands on the instrument and lets go. I stagger under the weight.

"You have to clean the saxophone each time you use it, before putting it back in its case," he explains.

"Like rubbing down a horse after you've ridden it?" I ask.

Maybe I shouldn't have said that. Yves might not like me comparing his precious instrument to a horse. But he and Jackie do have a cat, and they both love animals.

"You're the first to say that, but yes, it's the same thing," he reassures me.

He cleans the crook by stuffing in a piece of rag attached to a string, and cleans the body with a feather duster. He says that saliva seeps into it when you play.

"What are these pegs for?" I ask.

"These are keys," he says. "When you blow into the mouthpiece and press one or more keys with your fingers, you play musical notes."

He looks at his watch. "I've got rehearsal now I'm afraid."

"Do you agree to give me lessons?"

"That was your first one."

"What can I do in return to pay you?"

"I am entrusting you with a very important mission and hope you will be up to the task," he says.

I'm better at hoovering than ironing, and I can mow the lawn but Mummy won't let me clean the lawnmower afterwards.

"I want you to take care of your grandfather," says Yves seriously. "He took care of me once, I owe him a great deal. I'm worried about him."

"But that's not a favour, that's normal, he's my grandad and I love him!" I say.

"I'll sleep better knowing that you're looking out for him. It's a deal," declares Yves, shaking my hand.

7th November

Joe, Groix Island

There is no way I can miss dinner on the 7th. Being in mourning does not exonerate me from seeing my friends. If I'd just died, I bet you would have gone too, Lou. Fred's house is filled with her works and those of her family. She is an incredible artist and decorator. Everyone brings something. You always used to bring your favourite champagne. Your bubbly made up for your dry quiches and half-baked cakes. You couldn't have competed with Isabelle's spider crab canapés, Marie-Christine's chorizo and mint filled dates, Renata's tiramisu, or Monique's apple pie anyway. When you weren't looking, I would discreetly tip the contents of your baking into the rubbish and you were delighted to see your dish empty when we left.

"Hey look, Joe, they must have liked it, it's all gone!"

My friends shake my hand heartily to express their compassion, almost breaking my fingers in the process. Their kindness is overwhelming.

"You're family, Joe."

"Come to dinner anytime you want."

"Just turn up, as and when."

"My wife may not be as beautiful as yours, but she's a better cook," jokes one of them, trying to cheer me up.

You certainly were the most beautiful, Lou. And you taught me to be happy and at ease everywhere. Without you,

I'm totally lost. I didn't bring any champagne tonight; I didn't dare steal any of your bottles. You had an account at our favourite bookshop and I'm still putting my purchases on it. In some perverse way it's like you're buying my newspaper for me every morning. Crippling grief calls for a full-bodied wine, so I've brought along a Cairanne, Domaine de la Gayère, which should do the trick. Thanks to George and Geneviève who have supplied us with a good choice of Burgundy wines, I should be able to drown my sorrows. The men encourage me to drink and the women encourage me to eat. I look around for you, having forgotten for a millisecond that you are gone.

"How are your children coping, Joe?"

"Err, well, badly, as you would expect."

"Did you see the solicitor in Lorient?"

You can't keep anything secret when you live on an island. People see your car, they spot you on the boat, they know when you have people staying as you buy twice as much bread. They know whether you eat meat or fish or both, and which newspapers you read. Our friends' children also live off the island and return here for holidays, but it's complicated. The train timetable clashes with the ferry timetable; some local Breton sprite seems to have decided to deliberately mess everyone about. We rely on each other rather than on our families. We don't see each other much during the holidays, as we are all busy with our kids and grandkids, then it goes quiet again in September. We are sad when they go back but our normal routine then resumes and we start to meet up again.

"Lou chose a young man from the mainland," I reply.

"Do you need any cash, Joe?"

"You can ask us for anything, you know that?"

"I'm lucky to have such good friends, thank you all."

I'm dying to tell them about the trick you played on me,

but you told me not to tell a soul. Yet it would have been a hit, and I would have been the funny guy—or rather the funny widower—for the evening. So I ask my friends point-blank, "Do you think your children are happy?"

All conversations grind to a halt. An astonished silence follows.

"What a strange question, Joe."

"You really are a noodle," says Mylane affectionately, who likes to insult those she feels closest to.

"Good old Joe, never a dull moment with you!"

They want me to think that their children's lives are perfect, that the divorced son has met the woman of his dreams, that the elder daughter has found a job she loves, that the other son has moved to Spain and the youngest daughter is living in Dubai. So I turn the question around.

"What about you, are you happy?"

My question troubles them. They go silent, embarrassed. You're not meant to express any joie de vivre in front of someone who is grieving. Anne-Marie, who lost her husband, smiles at me without answering. Bertrand speaks of the happiness he felt when his sons turned up on the last lap of his pilgrimage to Santiago de Compostela. It took him months to reach his destination and the dedicated 7 Gang had even joined him there on his birthday. We would have gone too, if you hadn't lost your memory. How do you quantify happiness, Lou? I had a strange feeling when Sarah mentioned Patrice. Is that what you want, Lou, you silly sausage? For me to find Patrice and for him and Sarah to get back together again? Why didn't you ever talk to me about this? A guy who runs away when he finds out his wife-to-be is sick is rotten to the core in my opinion. Do you think she'd really be happier with him?

Lou, on the other side

Our children are unhappy. Cyrian is torn between two women. I don't want Sarah and Patrice to get back together. I gave you a clue, but you must accomplish this mission on your own.

There's no network, no connection, no battery. I would give anything just to be able to feel your cheek.

I saw you hesitating in the cellar, my *piroche*, you should have taken some champagne, what's mine is yours.

9th November

Apple, Groix Island

Yves and Jackie's cat is lying on the sheets of music when I arrive.

"What's his name?" I ask.

"She's called Miss Godin because she purrs like a Godin wood-burning stove," Yves tells me. He opens the worn-out case.

"Put the saxophone together, Apple."

I take a reed strip out of the case and suck it like an ice lolly.

"Your breath makes the reed vibrate, creating the sound. Place it on top of the mouthpiece. It has to line up and mustn't overlap. Now you need to position the ligature. No, the other way. And tighten the small screw."

I always thought a saxophone was all ready to use like a guitar.

"Now mount the mouthpiece on the cork part of the crook, without pressing on the reed."

I make a total hash of it; my fingers are too small.

"You're doing well. Mount the body and the bell. Put the mouthpiece in your mouth. Your upper teeth should be a third of the way down the baffle. The mouthpiece should rest on your lower lip, slightly bent over your lower teeth."

"What, I can't just make an 'O' shape with my lips and blow?" I ask, surprised.

"Relax your shoulders. Don't raise them. Don't puff out your cheeks. Now, blow."

"I'll never do it! I thought I just had to learn the notes, like with the piano," I say, disheartened. "I'll try one last time and if it doesn't work, I'm giving up."

Then just as I stop believing, a miracle happens and a sound comes out of the instrument and vibrates from the tip of my toes to the top of my head. I laugh excitedly. *Did you hear that, Lou?*

"You see? You did it!" says Yves, who is clearly happy for me too.

I shriek with joy, then try again, but this time, no sound comes out.

"I can't do it, Yves, it's too difficult," I say.

Yves doesn't try to persuade me. He takes the saxophone from me while I sit down on the sofa and listen to him play, his music tearing me into little pieces. I'm transported to Pen-Men, where I can see the baby herring gulls flying away from their parents who taught them to be free. I forget that I have a wicked stepmother, a two-faced half-sister, an unhappy father and a dead grandmother. I imagine I have two wings, and am surrounded by adults who want to protect me. I'm in front of the vast open sky. I'm like Julie, Boy and Lola. I soar over the cliffs and the ocean. The music is suffocating me. Then Yves stops playing.

"This piece is called 'Amazing Grace' and if you practise every day you should be able to play it by Christmas."

Joe, Groix Island

My friends Jean-Pierre and Monique have invited me to have dinner with them in Locqueltas. I accept so that Maëlle can have a break—I'm not particularly good company at the moment. You were at the nursing home from June onwards. I missed you terribly, but I imagined you would be home one day. That glimmer of hope kept me going. The only thing that keeps me going now is a message and your voice in a Mercier champagne bottle in the desk drawer of a solicitor young enough to be my son. The ocean roars behind the windows and the trees bend in the gusty wind. Their cat, Misty, wiggles its paws as it sleeps. Jean-Pierre stokes the fire. Monique has prepared your favourite meal. Their daughter, who is extremely attached to the island, comes to visit whenever she can.

"I used to be close to Cyrian and Sarah once, before I became head of department. Then my workload took off, and we drifted apart. You're lucky with Magali. How do you guys manage to get along so well?"

"She's our daughter and we love each other," Monique replies. "Try and take an interest in their work, their friends, their projects, anything."

"That's hard to do, they're as silent as the grave," I say, wincing at my own turn of phrase.

"You should set up a Google Alert to receive a notification by email each time one of their names circulates on the web," Monique suggests.

I hesitate, as this seems like spying, even though it's for a good cause. Jean-Pierre seems convinced of my noble intentions, however, and immediately switches on his computer to create two Google Alerts.

Jean-Pierre and Monique are lovely people, they are generous, discerning, kind and precious friends. Their guest house is a haven of peace. They share with me their garden, their homemade jams, their breath-taking view of the ocean. I leave them fed, watered and satisfied. You used to drive us home after evenings at friends' houses. I used to sit in your seat. I set off. The police do spot checks in the summer at strategic points, such as the famous local spot known as L'Apéritif. However, at this time of year, they stay at home in the warm. That's a shame, in custody I could have told them all about you. We're lucky to be able to get from one side of the island to the other in just under ten minutes. One day I calculated just how many hours of my life I had lost in Paris traffic jams. Thousands of hours I could have spent with you. I glance at the streetlamp lighting up the tiny square. Electricity first reached our villages in 1959, and the telephone arrived in 1965. Before the advent of television in the 1960s, villagers used to gather together outside in the evenings. Now everyone is at home in front of their screens.

I turn on the radio to stop myself falling asleep at the wheel. Renaud is singing. *Don't mess around, Manu, don't slit your wrists, don't crack. One woman lost means ten mates will soon come back.*

Maëlle has been waiting up for me. When she sees that I have had one too many, she says she could have picked me up. I tell her not to worry about me, I'm coping.

Sometimes I am completely overwhelmed by all that you are no longer able to enjoy. The waves crashing on the beach and battering the sand. The foam that blows into the gardens and clings to the hedges like whipped cream floating on Irish coffee. The books you can no longer read, the music you can no longer hear, the laughter you can no longer partake in, and Apple's sweet face you can no longer see. I retire to our room, *my* room, I should say. I look at the painting by Perrine you gave me, a sailor sweater on a bare linen canvas. And the one by Yannick that I gave you, an island with a red sail in the middle of the ocean. My iPad emits a lively sound to notify me that I haven't synchronized it with my computer for ten days, since your last night in fact. My heart fills with excitement at the absurd thought that you may have left me a message. Alas, no. I clean up my emails, sort through them, discard any ads for trips we will never take, beauty products you will never use, and a multitude of offers which will never risk tempting you. There is a huge pile of post for you in the hall, but I just can't bring myself to throw it away. You have been sent newspaper subscriptions, and advertisements for a hearing aid and a funeral plan. You've won a trip, a micro-wave oven and a tablet too; all the more reason for you to stay. Your jacket is still hanging on the coat rack, your psyche-delic patterned boots are still in the hall with ours. You did all your shopping locally and spread your custom equally between the shop owners. You bought bread from both bakers, books from all three booksellers, and groceries from all three supermarkets. You left us at the end of October, so you'll only have to pay tax for ten months this year. I sent the medical form filled out by the doctor who certified your death, to the social security office. A letter came back addressed to you, stating that the social security system would not be reimbursing you for this visit on account of the fact that you are dead.

11th November

Joe, Groix Island

It's Mimi's birthday today. Mimi runs the Ocean Boutique together with her husband, Pat. The table is set in front of the fireplace and it almost kills me to see that no place has been laid for you.

"You had a lucky escape from my wife's cake tonight," I say, trying to use humour to stop myself from going to pieces.

People who knew you politely refused your cake, but workmen or new friends would always accept eagerly. It was so hard and dry that even dunking it in coffee didn't help. Even the gardener's dog wouldn't touch it!

We reminisce about the great times we had with you, over our chicken in Coca-Cola sauce; we're guinea pigs in preparation for New Year's Eve. Every year, Pat and Mimi organize a fancy dress party. The walls of their living room are covered in photos of us dressed up. I catch sight of your blue eyes which pierce me to my soul. I quickly turn around. I remember that evening three years ago, when you were laughing your head off under your Stetson, with a Colt on your belt, standing next to Betty who was dressed as a saloon girl. Mimi's birthday falls on Armistice Day and also on the day that Alain Beudeff passed away. Alain owned the famous Ty Beudeff, a cult bistro frequented by mariners from all over the world; it's the most famous pub between the Scilly Isles and the Azores. The beer and rum were always flowing, full of friendship and adventure, and as a consequence many a sea shanty also flowed, while customers made merry and carved their names into the wood. Generations of drinkers have sat and debated and set the world to rights there. We had some unforgettable and fantastically boozy evenings at the bistro, just a few metres from the port going uphill. Captain Alain and Joe, his second in command, were life's flying buttresses, the life and soul of the party, the antithesis of death, one might say. After Alain passed, his daughter Morgan took over. I sometimes wonder why it is only our children who won't come back to Groix? What did I do wrong?

"I have to go now. Thank you for everything," I announce, as I get up.

"Black dog?" asks Pat.

That's what Churchill used to call it when he was down in the dumps. Pat knows me well enough to sense when the black dog is eating away at me.

"A quick train ride before you leave, old chap?" he asks.

We leave the others by the fire and I follow him into the room where he keeps his electric train set. We stoop to pass under the rails and position ourselves in the middle of the circuit. He switches the system on, and the locomotives light up and start. I marvel at the sight, filled with wonder like a child. For a moment, I forget you, Lou. Pat's locomotives help take the edge off my pain. I watch them chug by, listening to "Go West". I got on a moving train when I got with you and I didn't know where it would take us. I was onboard, Lou, and what an adventure it turned out to be.

I make my way home alone, smiling to myself as I pass the fishmonger's. I think back to the time when Albane used to come here, and I remember you telling me how you were stood in line with her once, behind some locals who were gossiping about various happenings on the island, births, deaths, accidents, work, boat schedules, neighbourhood quarrels and so on. Albane, behaving as if she was still in Paris, interrupted the fishmonger in her high-pitched voice to ask if he had any sea bass, saying that she wasn't queue jumping, but just wanted to know whether it was worth waiting or not, as she was in a hurry.

One of the local women looked at her in amazement. "Are you not on holiday here?" she asked.

Albane admitted she was but didn't want to waste any time.

"She means she doesn't want to waste any time talking to us lot," said another.

Albane then turned to Lou. "We're in a hurry because we have to get to the beach before the tide goes out, don't we Lou?"

Then in front of the islanders, who were by now in fits of laughter, you turned to your daughter-in-law and replied, "I don't know you madam; you must have mistaken me for someone else."

26th November

Joe, Groix Island

I have already received a few Google Alerts concerning my children. Cyrian attended an awards evening without Albane. Sarah went to a film premiere. Our kids look good in the photos illustrating the articles. You made me feel young, Lou; I remember being asked to show my ID because no one believed me when I said I qualified for senior rates. Now I'm practising the art of being a POW, a pissed old widower. Although I mustn't lose my dignity of course, on account of Apple. I'm conducting practical research on how to become the best drunkard of the year. My father used to drink to his heart's content after each fishing trip. I remember watching his crewmates drinking in his memory when his boat returned one day without him. I was Apple's age at the time. They drank to make themselves feel alive, while I drink to help me forget you're dead. I'm as miserable as sin in the morning, drunk by noon, and not fit to be seen by nightfall. On principle, I run on pure malts, small reds, dry whites, but never beer. I remember asking a patient once if he drank wine. He answered that he never touched alcohol because it was bad for the heart. He only drank beer, ten cans a day, and above all no cheap plonk, he valued his life too much. Our friends feel sorry for me, though deep down they are relieved it was you and not their wives, and I can't blame them for that. Maëlle forces me to get something in my stomach to limit the damage. I avoid Apple. Serge Reggiani sings "Paul's Song" over and over in my head. *I drink to those houses I left, to the friends who let me down, but especially to you who kissed me.* Am I really the only one who kissed you, Lou? Alcohol can make you paranoid. Let's take another look at your diary. What are these crossings out? Why are some words illegible? What had you noted for the 3rd of December? I can't make it out, it's too small, I'd need a magnifying glass. I get my phone, photograph the page, and stretch my fingers across the screen to enlarge the image. It says "9:30 brkfst Dan" with the address of a Parisian hotel located in rue Monge in the Latin Quarter. I understand "breakfast", but just who were you supposed to be meeting in that goddamn hotel? Dan? Who is this bastard?

30th November

Apple, Groix Island

Today is your birthday, Lou. Since you've been gone, Joe is starting to look like one of those lobsters in the harbour fish tank. He's alive, but trapped, as if he's waiting for the net to catch him so he can be gobbled up by a tourist. He is drinking too much and looks like one of those red-eyed albino rabbits. He shuffles his feet and his hands shake. Today, he comes into the kitchen at tea-time. He smiles a small, crooked smile. He opens the cupboard and fridge and takes out flour, salted butter, eggs, cream, yoghurts, and brown sugar.

He says Lou wants me and Charlotte to learn how to make the *tchumpôt* cake, and that his friend Lucette has given him the recipe.

I put the flour in a mixing bowl and add the salt, fresh cream, yoghurt and eggs. I spread out a clean tea towel on the table, then tip the contents of the bowl onto it and knead the dough. I put the brown sugar in the middle of the dough and add the butter. I fold the dough into the shape of a parcel that I place on top of the tea towel. I then wrap the tea towel over it in a square and tie a knot in each corner. Next I plunge the *tchumpôt* into boiling water.

"Can we all eat it together afterwards?" I ask.

His face lights up and he finally looks like the old Joe. "Yes, my little Apple Pie!"

I lean over the boiling saucepan to check all is okay.

"Mind you don't scald yourself."

He stops suddenly and looks at the scar near my eye. We have never mentioned it again. I remember he praised me at the time for having thought to put my face and your hands under cold running water. I remember him putting ointment on our burns. After that, the incident became a taboo subject in our house.

"The day the cat knocked the *grek* over . . ." says Joe, looking straight at me.

"That's all in the past," I reply.

"You and your grandmother both burned yourselves."

I tell him that Tribord saw a reflection in the coffee, which he thought was a mouse, and how much the whole thing still upsets me.

He doesn't insist. Mummy gets home from work just as we are taking the *tchumpôt* out of the water. It's so filling you can only eat it one small bit at a time, and Joe says it blocks your arteries, but it's still delicious. He says we can finish it off tomorrow, cut into slices dipped in hot butter.

Joe then sends me to the nursing home on my bike to drop off a piece of cake for that lady who played Scrabble with you.

Charlotte, Le Vésinet

After Mum picked me up from school, I put my schoolbag down in the hall and head for the kitchen. There is an envelope on the table with my name on it. It's from Groix, but I don't recognize the handwriting. Granny used to write to me, but Grampy only ever signed his name.

My dear girls,

Today would have been your grandmother's birthday. One of her last wishes was that you and Apple Pie learn how to make tchumpôt *cake. I have copied the recipe out for you. Big hugs and kisses, Grampy.*

I hand the letter to Mum.

"Your grandmother was getting rather fuddled at the end, sweetheart. Why don't you go and watch TV instead? How silly of her, she should know it's not safe to let children cook!"

"But Grampy said we have to do it *today*," I say.

Mum replies that we don't have any brown sugar, so I tell her we do, in the top cupboard. Granny brought it with her last time as Grampy loves *tchumpôt* cake.

Aware that she has been played, Albane backs down with a sigh and offers to make the *tchumpôt* while Charlotte watches.

"But Apple won't just watch, she'll make it herself," I protest.

"Have you seen that burn mark next to her eye? That's what happens when you let children play with the gas! You can open the butter for me. Fetch the round-ended knife and stay away from the oven."

Upset and frustrated, I watch my mum cook.

"Can we eat it together tonight? All three of us?" I ask.

"Dad will be home late and you'll be in bed. I can't digest butter, it's too rich for me, and besides, sugar gives you spots. You can have a tiny bit," Mum answers.

I can't believe I told Apple that we may not be sisters. Sometimes I say stuff just to make people hate me. It's like I want to hurt other people to make myself feel better.

I ask Mum when we are going back to Groix as I want to see Apple again. But she's still mad at her for taking me out on the road on her bike.

"She's a bad influence on you. You don't need friends when you've got me. You only have one mother, you know."

Lou, on the other side

It's my birthday today. I share my birthday with Winston Churchill. I would love to have tasted my granddaughters' *tchumpôt* cakes. You want to give me a present, Joe? There's no need to tell you my size or my favourite colour. Just stop destroying yourself with that stuff. Drink some water.

3rd December

Joe, Paris, rue Monge

The day after your birthday, I woke up feeling very unwell and spent the whole day in bed. My colleague, Alexis, reminded me that cirrhosis of the liver is not the most pleasant way to die. After he left, I opened your diary again, like a castaway clinging to a piece of driftwood. Much like my father, who hung on to a plank when he fell off his fishing boat before he drowned.

You still made me happy right up until the spring. You had begun to lose your memory in January, but I hadn't really been aware of it. And you behaved weirdly in March but I was in denial. You lost it completely in June and then you moved into the nursing home. We spent your first night there, lying next to each other in your new room. At fifty-six, you were their youngest patient. No one could understand why you had decided to go into a home, apart from your doctor and me. We listened to the overture to Verdi's opera, *The Force of Destiny*, while nibbling lobster pâté on toast. I begged you to come back home. You refused. Apple and Maëlle had moved back to Locmaria for the summer, so why didn't you come and stay with me in the village? You were very stubborn. In Italy, to wish someone good luck, they say, *in bocca al lupo*, which literally means "in the wolf's mouth". The other person then replies, *crepi il lupo*, meaning "may the wolf die". I don't speak much Italian so maybe I got confused and said, "may Lou die".

I've never cheated on you, Lou. Can the same be said of you though? I walk down the street to this damn hotel where you're meeting Dan at nine thirty this morning for breakfast. Who is this Dan guy? I couldn't just sit around on the island without finding out.

I enter a dining room with ochre coloured walls and a large buffet in the middle. Families are piling food onto their plates, and tourists hide croissants and pastries in their napkins to nibble on later. I find a table near the window, order an espresso and wait. Then a guy shows up, he's my age with slicked back hair, a slim-fitting suit and Italian shoes. I'd like to take him down a peg or two, but it wouldn't be worth it. He sits down, looks at his watch, checks his phone. Is he waiting for you, too? Does he not know you've gone? He's hungry and licks his lips as he stares over at the buffet, but the stupid rogue is polite and sits there waiting patiently. I see him send a text message. It's not like you're going to answer, is it! He pulls a face. It obviously gets his back up when women are late. He's probably going to yell at you. Where was this idiot a month ago when we buried you, eh? Anyway, how did you meet him? Is he one of your exes, a former lover who you meet up with every year at the same time in the same place? Does he make love to you with or without foreplay? In what positions? Is he silent, does he talk, does he grunt, does he comment? He's not wearing a wedding ring. Had you thought of dumping me for him? My hand shakes and I spill my coffee on the table and all over my trousers. The waitress rushes over. Your bastard lover doesn't care. I'm going to destroy him like he destroyed me, and I'll get a lot of pleasure out of it. I stand up, looking preposterous in my coffee stained trousers. My feet are leaden, I can hardly move. I eventually walk towards his table. I'm going to lean over him smiling sweetly and then press down hard on his carotid artery. That will slow down his heart and cut off the blood supply to his brain. I'll holler, "I'm a doctor, move out of the way!" and I'll catch him as he falls. And then I'll decide exactly what to do with him. Glued to his phone, the Brylcreemed imbecile doesn't see me approaching until suddenly a bony woman in a red coat with a pointed nose and a shrill voice walks around me and throws herself into his arms.

"Some idiot threw himself under the train, the whole line was at a standstill," she exclaims dramatically.

"I was about to go," grunts the slimeball. "My wife was being a pain this morning with all her questions."

"Yes, my husband was the same, asking me where I was going and why," grumbles the bony lady.

"People who kill themselves like that in public are so selfish, just thinking of themselves," Mr Brylcreem adds.

Famous last words. How could I have thought that you were cheating on me with this lowlife?

"Doctor?"

I turn around in surprise. A young woman with ample breasts, wearing a skin-tight dress and six-inch stiletto heels, smiles at me.

"My condolences, Doctor."

"Do we know each other?" I ask, intrigued.

"I was supposed to meet your wife this morning, I'm Danny. Danielle."

My neurones are racing. So Dan meant Danny all along! I accused you wrongly, my love. She points to an empty table nearby and asks if I'd like to join her for coffee.

I say yes, even though I still don't know who she is.

"How did you know who I was?" I ask, puzzled.

She points to the orange "Joseph" on my shoulders. "Your trademark. Plus, you're the spitting image of Cyrian— or should I say he is the spitting image of you!"

So she knows our son then. The waitress appears and whispers something in her ear.

"Problem with a client, I'll be right back," she says.

I ask the waitress if the young lady works here, and she tells me she is the manager.

I ask for her name. Then I take out my phone and type her name next to Cyrian's. Google offers me a link. I click on it. It's a professional think tank, which meets every month at this hotel. I scroll through pictures of men in suits and ties. A woman in business attire features in the meetings, and there is also another woman in the photos, in a figure-hugging dress and plunging neckline. It's Danny. I scroll from one photo to the next, and suddenly I realize. Danny has her leg pressed up against our son's. It wasn't you who had a lover, Lou. I look at Cyrian's face. He's a different person. So *that's* why you wanted me to read your diary? So I could help Cyrian leave Albane and find happiness with this Danny woman? And when I think of the song and dance he made when the solicitor said I had been unfaithful to you!

Danny comes back and apologizes, as she sits down. She has a beautiful smile and fabulous breasts. She and Albane are definitely not in the same league.

"Do you love Cyrian?"

"You're direct," she replies.

"I'm a doctor."

"Do doctors tend to pry then?" she asks.

"By definition they ask you questions about your private life. I'm a cardiologist, I specialize in matters of the heart."

"Are you shocked that Cyrian is cheating on his wife?" she asks.

"I'm surprised," I reply. "Can I ask you something?"

"You want to know if I'm a home wrecker?"

"No, I want to know if my son is happy?"

I would give anything for her to say yes, but she just shakes her head.

"He is torn between me and his wife. Married men have always had mistresses since the beginning of time. It doesn't actually make their lives any better, it just adds a bit of spice. I don't want to marry Cyrian or take over his home. I'm a free spirit. No strings attached, no promises, no commitments, and certainly no children. All I ask of him is that he be available for me."

"So, he'll just stay unhappy?" I ask.

"It seems to be a bit of an obsession of yours," says Danny with a seductive laugh.

"No, I'm on a mission," I reply, getting up.

Sarah, Paris, rue de Sévigné

My flat used to be a craftsman's workshop and is located in the fashionable Marais district of Paris. The bank didn't want to give me a mortgage deeming me high risk because of my illness, so I had to take out a special health insurance policy. I actually already make more money than Dad did when he was a top cardiologist, it's kind of embarrassing. I don't save either as I won't be having kids. I live on the top floor of the building. The lift is big enough to take my wheelchair. I welcome my father from my new customized glitter machine. It's not a good day today, I'm having trouble walking.

"I'm practising for my next video game night, look!" I say to Dad.

I point to the futuristic electronic keypad that I use to control the high tech wheelchair, an American-made prototype. There are only two of them, mine and one belonging to a famous American actor who has Parkinson's disease. When we see each other at the Oscars, we challenge each other to see who can perform the trickiest manoeuvres.

"You can't stay for dinner, Dad, I've got a date tonight."

"Your boyfriend?" he asks.

"No, safety in numbers. It's better to have several funny, charming suitors, than one jealous guy who is always on time," I say.

"So you don't like guys who are on time then?"

"No. I like the unforeseen, the narrow escapes, the close shaves. I'm serious, Dad, I never see a guy more than twice. And I don't say 'I love you'; you taught me not to lie."

"You can do what you like, you're an adult," he says.

Nevertheless, I can tell that he is shocked by my tight outfit. He didn't tell me he was coming so it's his fault. *You would never have done that, Mum.* I serve him a single malt that I was given by a Japanese producer.

"Did you know that Cyrian has a mistress?" he asks suddenly.

"How do you know?"

"I read Mum's diary and met the culprit, a certain Danny, this morning."

"Well she obviously cast him from a selection of brainy types and those in the public eye."

"What, men are *cast* these days, like for a film?"

"You did the same thing at the wedding when you met Mum. You just referred to it differently in those days. You basically scanned all the girls there and then you hit on Mum."

"*Oh, in what gallant terms these things are put!*"

"Courteline? Labiche?"

"Molière's *The Misanthrope*," Dad says triumphantly. "I wonder whether Cyrian is in love and if Danny makes him happy . . ."

"It's complicated. Cyrian didn't *choose* Albane as such, she happened to be there for him when he was in a dark place and then she got pregnant. He's grateful to her, but they don't have much of a sex life."

"Sarah!"

"You asked!" I retort. "Each woman gives him something he doesn't get from the other. Albane loves Charlotte but hates Apple. Danny doesn't want kids and couldn't give a toss about other peoples'. And Cyrian loves both his daughters."

"You'd never think so," he mumbles.

"He doesn't show his feelings, he's like you, Dad, a chip off the old block."

My father and I have never had such a frank conversation before.

"What about you, Sarah? Is it difficult for you too?" he asks.

"You've got a future, Dad. I just have the present and I'm coping."

"Yes, but are you happy in the present?"

I raise my glass and tell him my happiness is like this whisky: fashionable, sophisticated and costs a fortune. With Mum he had good old-fashioned traditional happiness, matured in oak barrels.

"I'm the darling of the French film industry at the moment, but once I fade, I'll be thrown away like yesterday's papers, so I'm making the most of it. This liquid gold in my glass is from a distillery with a pagoda-shaped chimney, you know."

"Okay, but you still haven't answered my question."

"You won't be happy without Mum. She took a piece of you with her. But though it won't be the same, you'll still have some good times. Patrice broke something in me. It's not him I miss, it's that giddy feeling, knowing someone loves you, and having someone to trust and believe in. Before he came along, I was light-hearted and easy going, now I'm just easy, full stop. My date will be here soon. He's invited me to dinner in this pop-up restaurant where you dine in total silence. You pay a fortune to interact entirely with your eyes. It's *the* place to be in Paris right now, you have to reserve months in advance."

"People are out of their minds," says Dad. "Does this chap work in the film business, is he an actor?"

"I don't go out with guys who sleep around just to get cast, that would be unethical."

"Your morals are impeccable, sweetheart."

4th December

Joe, Groix Island

On the train back to Lorient, I read that becoming a widower increases your chances of dying within a year. This is also true if you break your femur. I deduce from this that a widower who breaks his femur doubles his chance of kicking the bucket, so I'd better be careful.

My mobile phone rings while the boat is docking.

"Dad?"

"It's good to hear from you, Cyrian."

"Can I rely on you to not say anything to Albane?"

"Is that why you're calling me?"

"Yes."

I know him so well, I'm certain he took a sheet of paper, made two columns and wrote down a list of arguments for and against calling me. Clearly "for" won.

"You can rely on me. You can always rely on me, Cyrian. Your mother could always rely on me too."

He refuses to be drawn on the subject.

"My private life is none of your business, Dad."

"I couldn't agree more."

"You won't tell my wife about Danny?"

"Who?"

"The manager of the hotel in rue Monge."

"Who? Where? I've already forgotten."

He thanks me and hangs up.

*   *   *

In the Bible, Joseph, my namesake and son of Jacob, interprets the Pharaoh's dreams, while I can't even fulfil yours in reality. As I walk across the harbour, I am consumed by your absence.

Maëlle smiles when I arrive, and Apple rushes to hug me. There is a place laid for me. I eat the soup with gusto and refuse the wine. I tell them about Paris and the Christmas lights; I make it all up. A deep sadness pervades me and I know I'm going to have a bad night. When Apple is in bed, I take Maëlle aside.

"The day you feel you want to live somewhere else, in Locmaria or elsewhere in the village, don't ever feel you have to stay here just for me. Is that clear?"

"Do you want us to leave?" she asks.

"I don't want to be a burden. I am not your father and I'm not even your father-in-law."

"You're Apple's grandad. My parents are dead. You're all we have left."

5th December

Apple, Groix Island

I never thought I would learn to play the saxophone, but I'm finally getting the hang of it. I'm working on the mouthpiece. I wedge my teeth on the tip, I lower my shoulders, I don't puff up my cheeks. To make a sound, I put my lips in a "two" position and blow, pulling back my tongue. I know the notes at the top with the left hand—C, B, A, G—but still have trouble playing them. My teeth keep slipping, my tongue gets in the way, I grip too hard with my mouth, and I tuck my lower lip in too much. Sometimes the sound comes out, clear and bright, which makes me want to play over and over again. I dance home, feeling so happy, going through the graveyard, making "two" sounds so you can see how difficult it is. Singers use their voice. Pianists place their fingers on the keys. But saxophone players play with their whole bodies. I'm totally hooked. I can do this. When the sound comes out properly, I feel so excited, and bubbly, like the sea during an equinox tide.

Joe, Groix Island

Google Alerts pops up on my screen. A guy from Cyrian's think tank is under investigation. I hope our son is not involved. Sarah looks as stunning in the premiere photos as the actresses she casts. When you were little, Lou, and living in your father's castle, every year on Saint Nicholas Day good children were given sweets and disobedient children were given wicker whips. The story went that Saint Nicholas would arrive on his donkey down the chimney accompanied by his evil accomplice, Old Man Whipper. Your four elder sisters ate their gingerbread cookies while you threw the whip you were given in the bin, crying and upset. That same day, according to the tradition, you planted some lentils on cotton wool, and on Christmas Eve you placed them near the crib. Your sisters would water their lentils without spilling a single drop. But your saucer would always overflow onto the lace doily. The marquetry pedestal table got drenched and the water ran over the old parquet floor. You continued the tradition with Cyrian and Sarah, minus Old Man Whipper and his dreadful wicker whips. For safety's sake, our children used to plant their lentils on a chipped plate on the worktop. I take an old, collector's edition Breton plate off the wall and scatter Apple's lentils on it, just to provoke you.

I'm going to give meaning to this day. I have a well thought-out, feasible plan. Apple is at school. Maëlle is at work. It's foggy, the sea is choppy, the weather is rough, and not a good time to send a sailor out on the water. I am going to defy your God, challenge him, and make him an offer. Like a knight throwing his gauntlet at his foe. I'm sure God will accept. He snatched you and took you hostage. So, I shall suggest a swap, suggest he takes *me* instead. I shall surrender my pathetic existence to him in exchange for yours. This isn't suicide, I'm merely sacrificing myself. A one-way ticket is all I need, then you can come back here and get on with your life. When I made my marriage vows, I promised to protect you, and I shall keep my word. You're more useful to our family than me. They got it wrong up there, taking you instead of me. And I'm going to put things right. You are worth so much more than me, Lou. I was your knight in shining medical scrubs. But take away my stethoscope and I'm nothing.

I put on my boots and place a striped "Joseph" over my shoulders. If I jump overboard, the weight of the water will drag me to the bottom. I slip a plastic card with my name on it into my pocket for easy identification. A healthy adult normally lasts twenty minutes if the water is at eight degrees. My heart will slow right down as hypothermia sets in. Due to the currents and the shape of the coastline it should take nine to fifteen days for my body to resurface. I do want to be found. Not lost in the sea forever like my father.

I make my way to the port and deliberately park a good distance from the Escale café. I think of Jacqueline Tabarly's tribute to her husband in 1998, on the morning of the summer solstice, facing the ocean. *The sea is not evil, it took him, it didn't steal him*.

I chose my day and time so as not to run into the roll-on roll-off, or the local fishermen and sailors. The light is fading, the port is deserted, and the fog is spreading. I borrow a friend's canoe and slip some cash in an envelope with his name on it that I wedge in the steering wheel; no one locks their car here out of holiday season. The canoe pitches on the water, it'll be worse when the swell hits it. I look around to make sure nobody has seen me. I'm not one of those reckless fools who go out in foul weather conditions putting rescuers' lives at risk.

There's not a living soul around, and I'm not too sure if I still count. I scull towards the harbour exit. A yachtsman climbs up onto his deck as I pass on his starboard side. I hold my breath, hoping he won't see me. He pees on the port side and then returns to his berth. It was my father who taught me how to scull with the figure eight motion. And now he's waiting for me under the water. Once out of the safety of the

harbour, I battle with the sea. My canoe is nothing more than
a husk on the waves. I steer away from the seawall. The
current carries me out to sea off the coast of Port-Lay. I see
that our good friends, Gildas and Isabelle, are at home, their
windows are lit up and smoke is billowing from their chimney. I picture them in their living room, I imagine the big
armchairs and the coffee table with crab canapés arranged
on a plate. I can hear Isabelle's laughter and Gildas's music.
All this will go on, but without us, Lou.

I've seen some miracles in my time: silent hearts have
started beating again, patients I thought were doomed have
literally walked out of the ICU. Miracles do happen. I let out
a wild cry into the wind. Exhausted by the exertion and
stress, I start singing one of Barbara's songs. I shout over the
waves. *When those who are to go, finally go, those who didn't ask
for anything, but who were filled with wonder, at the fact that they
had been on this earth; We should let them at least choose the
country, as distant as it may be, in which they will spend their
final hour.*

I stop short, out of breath and panting. In the fog, my
flimsy little canoe hits a rock. I don't have time to react; I lose
my balance and fall overboard.

I'm not committing suicide. I'm making a deal with Him.
I just hope that up there they'll respect its terms and swap my
life for yours. My head surfaces. It's a typically freezing
winter sea. As a child, I used to wake up at night wondering
what happened to my father and how he must have felt in the
icy water. When I was an intern at the hospitals in Paris, I
treated those who had near misses in local swimming pools
and others who had thrown themselves into the river Seine
out of desperation. I prefer to finish things here in my ocean,
leave in style as it were.

Apple, Groix Island

Grandad was acting weird this morning. I am the first one out of school; I don't say bye to anyone and pedal home as fast as I can. We have to plant the lentils today. The plate is ready on the kitchen table. But Joe is nowhere to be found. His moped is there, but his car has gone. I head to the cemetery. You're here, Lou, but where is Joe? There are old ladies talking to their dead husbands who can't answer. There are mums putting flowers on graves of little ones who will never grow up. I scatter a handful of lentils on your grave and carry on looking for Joe.

I cycle to his favourite beach. There is not a soul in sight. I go down to the harbour. His car is there, that's a relief. I go to Soaz's place, but she hasn't seen Joe. I check at the ferry terminal, the harbour master's office, the tourist office. All the clothes shops, the ice cream parlour and bike rentals are closed. I go back to his car and notice the envelope stuck in the steering wheel. He has taken out his friend's canoe. If Joe isn't in the harbour, then he must be at sea. Oh no, I lost you, Lou, there was nothing I could do to help you. I've also lost Daddy, he won't be coming back here anymore. But I couldn't bear losing someone else I love.

The current is heading towards Port-Lay. I run to the end of the pier, squint with my eyes and scan the ocean. Nothing. Over there, maybe? No, it's a marker buoy. Over there? No, it's a bird. Yes, there! A canoe is floating in the distance. I don't see anyone in it. Did Joe collapse? Is he lying down, or has he fallen overboard? I rush to Soaz's café, but suddenly stop before going in. Joe would hate it if I ask them for help. The lifeguards are friends of his. Their speedboat, *Notre-Dame du Calme*, was launched the year I was born. I'll have to come up with something else. If I tell them, he'll never forgive me. And if he dies, I'll never forgive myself.

A shrill cry startles me. Two gulls are playing in the wind. Boy? Lola? They circle above my head and then fly towards the house where the twins' grandfather lives.

"Understood! Thank you birds!" I cry.

I cycle furiously, standing up on the pedals. I'm scared, out of breath and sweating. If my lungs explode, I won't be able to play the saxophone anymore. My thighs and calves are burning. I hurtle down the path that overlooks the harbour, I slide and skid, and narrowly avoid falling in the murky water or crashing onto the boats below. Panting now, I straighten up the handlebars with a sharp jerk and skid to a halt in front of the house. I bang on the door. Gildas sees me through the window and comes out.

"The canoe . . . Joe . . . Over there . . ." Too out of breath to say more, I point. Before I can catch my breath, Gildas and Isabelle are running towards their boat. It's getting dark, I can no longer see the canoe. The icy wind chills me to the bone. I sit down on the end of the seawall, my legs dangling over the edge.

Joe, Groix Island

I can't feel my fingers. My body is freezing cold. I remember the questions they asked us at medical school on drowning. The human body loses temperature twenty-five times faster in water than in air. The core body temperature drops. Blood vessels contract to reduce heat loss. Blood in the peripheral parts of the body flows towards the interior, raising blood pressure. The heart slows down to fight the high blood pressure. Blood supply to the brain is reduced and you lose consciousness. Afterwards, you either go into cardiopulmonary arrest and die due to submersion-inhibition—you go white as you drown. Or you swallow water and die due to submersion-asphyxia—you turn blue as you drown. Alone in the water, I think of my father sinking among fish that didn't speak his language. I push all thoughts of him out of my mind; I want my last thought to be for you, Lou. My fingers are so numb I can no longer grip the rock, they no longer do what my foggy brain tells them. I recall that wedding night I first met you and said I wanted to drown in your deep blue eyes . . . Yes, I will drown in them and you'll wake up in the canoe. I am only holding on to the rock with my thumb and index finger and can't hold on anymore. As I let go, my fingers skim the rock as though they were caressing your skin.

An engine noise blocks the sound of the raging sea. It's probably me hallucinating due to the low oxygen supply to my brain. I slide off the rock, and tumble down, delivering myself to the sea, my mouth flush with the waves, my salt-burned eyes fixed on the blue line of the water. The current will carry me away, my love. You'd better pack your bag and say goodbye to your new friends. Did you see my father? Or Jacques? What about your mother?"

"Joe, oh my God! Joe, can you hear me? Grab the boat hook! Catch it!"

What's that noise? It's not coming from the heavens. It's Gildas in his boat, with Isabelle who is trying to pass me a boat hook.

"Go away!" I yell with the little energy I have left.

Oh no, they're going to ruin everything, I can picture you about to step over the rail, the coast is clear, Lou, you can come now.

Gildas strips off and jumps into the freezing water. He joins me in two powerful strokes.

"I want to . . . save . . . Lou . . . I made . . . a deal . . ."

"If you resist, I'll knock you out, Joe!" he shouts over the waves.

He grabs me under my arms. I no longer have the strength to resist and flop like a rag doll. We've had it. You won't come back now, Lou. My offer was rejected. Gildas puts me back on the boat. I collapse on the deck. Isabelle wraps me in blankets.

They hold me up and help me off the boat and we stumble to their house. I fall asleep from exhaustion only to wake up lying on the sofa in front of the fire. I am wearing Gildas's clothes. Isabelle hands me a steaming mug.

"Here, drink this, it'll warm you up."

I obey. The grog brings my colour back. Apple is sitting next to me, her eyes so big they take up half her face. I ask her what she is doing here.

Gildas tells me that Apple saved my life by raising the alarm.

"I was so afraid, Grandad!" she sobs.

This is the first time she has ever called me Grandad. I reach out my hand to her and she snuggles up against my shoulder. Her innocent eyes anchor me to the present moment, and thoughts of you fade. Your God wasn't prepared to do a deal with me, Lou. I tried the impossible and failed. Ankou obviously had better things to do than recover my soul. I'm supposed to be a reassuring grandfather for Apple, just a normal retiree leading a quiet life and playing bowls. Instead, I've been a bad father and a terrible grandfather.

"Did you do it on purpose?" asks Apple in a hushed voice.

"No," I answer.

Gildas doesn't say a word in front of Apple. I know what he's thinking though. *You can't force someone to live. I could tell your children and call the family doctor. They'll put you on antidepressants and have you hospitalized. Then one day you'll come back and the ocean will tempt you again.*

"I wasn't trying to end it," I insist.

Isabelle's eyes scream at me silently. *It looked an awful lot like you were.*

I tell them that I had made a deal, and when they saved me, the deal fell through. You would have appreciated my sense of humour, Lou.

"Promise me that no one else will find out. Not my children, not Maëlle, not Charlotte. Can I count on you, Apple?" I ask.

She nods seriously. I turn to our guests.

"Nor any of the 7 Gang please. Is that clear?"

They nod.

Apple pipes up that Boy and Lola know, as they were the ones that warned her, but they can keep a secret. She makes me swear I'll never do it again though.

"I swear."

Apple, Groix Island

Gildas dropped us back in the village. I'll go back for my bike tomorrow. Joe warms up in front of the fire after taking a hot bath. Mummy isn't home yet. She's stocktaking till late tonight at the bookshop.

"You saved my life, Apple. I owe you," says Joe.

"Like the little boy in the Himalayas?" I ask.

The day Joe told me that story we were having dinner in the kitchen. He put his hands flat on each side of his plate and said, "I once saved a little boy your age with the help of something on this table."

"A knife?"

"No."

"A fork? A spoon?"

"No."

He held out his palms to me and explained. When I was a baby, he took you away, Lou, on a trip to Bhutan, the self-proclaimed land of "gross national happiness" (GNH), situated between China and India. You rode in a four-by-four with a driver and a guide. You stopped to watch a game of archery, the national sport. The Bhutanese in their striped kimonos, wearing modern trainers, had traditional bamboo bows and were shooting at distant targets. You stood back, admiring the archers. A bridge decorated with prayer flags was swaying over the dry river, a yak was watching you, and everyone was cheerful. And then disaster struck. A little boy got hit by an arrow in his chest. He fell backwards. The villagers surrounded him, his mother rushed over and reached towards the arrow in her son's body.

Joe shouted out, trying to stop her, but he was too far away for her to hear and she didn't understand French anyway. She pulled out the arrow. She should never have removed it because it was actually preventing the bleeding. She should have left it there and carried the child with the arrow in his heart to hospital, then the surgeon would have removed it on the operating table.

So Joe ran up to the child whose heart had already started bleeding. He plugged the wound with his fingers. The Bhutanese, who are Buddhists and believe in karma, shouted in horror. Joe managed to stop the bleeding. Then you stepped in, Lou. You spoke to the boy's mother and asked the guide to translate. You explained to her that your husband was a doctor, that he was trying to plug her son's heart to stop the bleeding. The mother told you her boy's name was Tachi and handed him over to you. You took him to the hospital in your four-by-four, with Joe's fingers plugging the hole in his chest, and he was rushed into theatre. The surgeon operated on Tachi and saved his life. Now every year you get a postcard from the Land of the Thunder Dragon. Tachi has just turned eighteen.

Today, I didn't save Joe with my fingers, I saved him with my legs by pedalling to Port-Lay at lightning speed.

Lou, on the other side

How could you, Joe? Others may have fallen for it, but I know you too well. A swap between heaven and earth, what utter nonsense! You're a doctor, you know how it works: blood coagulates, fluids drain out, flesh leaves the bones, everything falls apart. And you expect me to believe that you weren't trying to end it all? If I wasn't dead, this would have given me an ulcer! You took our friends and our granddaughter for fools. I gave you a mission and you bailed on me. You put your own misery and grief before our children's happiness. This is not proof of love, Joe. In Bhutan, you told me that I was your GGH, your "gross Groix happiness". No, I didn't slip away, I didn't step through a looking glass, I'm dead, Joe! This is my karma, my destiny, you can't change that. As for you, you need to go on living.

7th December

Joe, Groix Island

I lost my glasses in the sea. I go straight to Bruno and Florence, the multicoloured opticians that you used to joke about. Florence has bright red hair worn up on top of her head, and colourful glasses with one round lens and one square lens, and bright flashy clothes. Before they arrived on the island, we all had to go to Lorient for our eye problems. Since they've moved here, Groix islanders see life in technicolour.

I tell them I need to see them urgently as I lost my glasses in the sea. They'll assume I lost them swimming, but that suits me, let them think that. They reassure me they'll sort it out fast. Bruno lends me a spare pair in the meantime.

I caught a chill yesterday. I didn't die, but I caught a stinking cold. I flip through your diary. Something you noted in the spring makes my blood run cold. You drew a family tree to show the ties between you, me, our children and granddaughters. Was your illness really that advanced at that time?

You caught me off guard, Lou. I remember your memory lapses. You would forget where you'd parked the car. You paid the same bills over and over again and forgot to pay others. You didn't get on the right train for the Clara Prize jury deliberation in Paris. You told someone you had no children, and then, when you saw the look on my face, you suddenly came to and pretended it was a joke. And the rest . . . You moved away and became someone else.

I open your old diary and rekindle memories of friends we have lost over the years. I find our friend Jacques with his tongue-in-cheek humour. Beudeff is there, pulling pints again. Jean-Luc is going back on assignment. Jean-Louis is sorting through his postcards. Michel is painting his water-colours. Manu is adjusting a TV set. Véronique's father is steering his boat. Marion is crossing the village square. Florent is walking his dog. Jeanne's two husbands are busy doing odd jobs.

I turn the pages and take a trip down memory lane. Sarah hasn't spent Christmas Eve with us since she turned eight-een. She always joins us on the 25th. I've never asked her what she's been up to the night before. You probably knew though. Last year on this date you wrote "Sarah Princ" and circled it in red. Was Sarah spending the holidays at Princeton University in New Jersey? In a Prince of Wales checked suit? With a prince? I look at previous years. "Princ" again. Sarah never sees a man more than twice. Maybe at Christmas she makes an exception? In any case, it's not Patrice. On the 23rd of December, you wrote down "Cyr + Dan". On the 24th of December, you wrote "Cyr + Alb". Which one of them will make our son happy? You only get one life, Lou. He can't make up his mind. And I can't decide for him. I can't decide for Sarah either. What do you want me to do? Find Patrice? Get rid of Albane? At least, give me a clue!

I arrive at Fred's house with the others for my second 7 Gang dinner without you. JP asks me how I'm getting on with the Google Alerts. I tell him about my meeting with Danny. I discreetly return the clothes to Gildas. I eat, drink, and start getting on my friends' nerves with my questions again.

"How do you know if your children have met the right life partner?" I throw at them.

"What, this again?"

I tell them that I'm serious and I need to know. They get their heads together and come up with some answers.

"We don't interfere in their private lives," says one.

"We protected them when they were small, after that they lead their own lives," says another.

Someone pipes up that her daughter's husband is lovely. Then another says his son's girlfriend is delightful. Their children's partners are *tolerant*, *caring* and *generous*. Left wingers I expect. Then again, they could be on the right. They are not antisemitic or racist, basically they're not idiots. Fred brings in a dish of steaming curry. The conversation stops while plates are passed down. I think back to the way my father used to talk about his crew. He used to say the important thing was not to be the best fisherman, but to be someone others can rely on during bad weather, when there's no sun, no fish and no pay. I remember my internship. The important thing was not to be the most talented, but to be the most personable, that is to say the most compassionate, people-orientated. Is that what you want, Lou? For me to find out if Albane, Danny and Patrice are nice, decent human beings? Are you going gooey on me?

10th December

Danny, Paris, rue Monge

As manager of this hotel, I don't count my hours. It's been well worth it though, as our revenue has continued to increase despite the recession. I'm on social media, I organise themed evenings, I pamper and fuss over the clubs and charities that hold their meetings here. I work around the clock and I hardly ever take time off, but tonight is different; I'm meeting my lover in a sophisticated restaurant called the Molitor, which used to be an ice rink.

As I open the door out onto the street, I bump headfirst into a man standing there. I just about keep my balance, which isn't easy when you're wearing six-inch heels, but he falls over. I apologize and say I didn't see him. I hope that he's not a client who's going to sue me for damages. The guy is tall and skinny, with a beard; it's impossible to guess his age. His wet clothes stink. Oh, he's not a client, he's homeless. Phew! He lies listless on the wet pavement.

"Are you okay, sir? Can you get up please, you're blocking the entrance," I say firmly. I don't think he's had a bath for years.

"My leg hurts," he whimpers.

He stinks of alcohol. I tell him to try and get up. I step back so that my coat doesn't skim his smelly, shabby old raincoat.

"I can't put my foot down," he says.

I tell him in no uncertain terms that he can't stay there. My receptionist is busy. The hotel lobby is empty. Luckily the street is deserted in the heavy rain. Nobody saw us crash into each other.

Wincing in pain, he says he thinks his leg is broken. I tell him that he has merely sprained it and that there is a hospital right nearby. He says he can't walk, so what is he meant to do, fly there? I start to lose my temper; Cyrian hates it when I'm late. I tell him I'll call an ambulance to get him to hospital. But he wants to wait for it in the hotel out of the rain. I shake my head. His filth is nauseating.

"That's impossible, sir, this hotel is not a public space," I say.

I point out a restaurant a few doors down that is closed today and tell him to take shelter under its awning. He insists he wants to go inside the hotel and shelter there till the ambulance arrives. I tell him they'll say no and ask him to get up.

He gets back on his feet and stands in front of the door on one leg like a big, wounded heron. His piercing blue eyes unsettle me. I can't make out his features under that bird's nest of a beard, but he must have been quite an attractive man before he sank so low. He hobbles agonizingly slowly to the restaurant. I open my bag and take out a ten- and a five-euro note.

"Here, take this."

"I didn't ask you for money," he says, snatching it.

"It's for a taxi so you can get to A & E," I reply.

"They won't take me, it's too near," he mumbles.

They won't take him because he stinks and he's filthy. My little red Fiat 500 convertible is parked just across the street, but there's no way I'm going to let him dirty my seats.

"I'm lonely," he sighs. "I used to have a dog. But since I went into hospital, I don't know what's become of him. He's either been run over, or a lab has stolen him for some of those sick experiments they do."

Personally, I can't stand dogs, and it gets my back up when clients walk in dog excrement and then trample it through my lobby.

I tell him that dogs just dirty the streets and are full of fleas. "If you've just got out of hospital, then your leg isn't hurting because you fell. Are you taking the piss?"

"No, I was on the cardio ward, my heart is all over the place. They wanted to open up my chest and fumble around, so I told them to keep their hands off me. But I'm starting to have more and more episodes. Here, for example, I can feel it tightening . . ."

His face tenses up, as he grips the left side of his torso with his right hand.

"I can't breathe, I swear to you!"

He leans on the wall, sliding onto the ground. I step aside, rummaging through my bag.

"I don't believe you anymore. I have an important appointment. Look, here's another ten euros, I'm off now. Okay?" I say.

"My heart's racing, I'm scared, don't leave me on my own!" he pleads.

That game won't work on me. I put the money in his hand and tell him I'm not a doctor but I'll call the emergency services who'll be here very soon.

I turn around and cross the street, making sure he's not following me. I get into my car, lock the doors, drive off and take the first street on the right. I pull up in front of the double doors of a residential building, disinfect my hands with a wipe and call the emergency services.

"You have called the police, please hold."

"Good evening, a man has just collapsed on rue Monge. I'm in the bus, I think he needs the paramedics."

I give the location of the restaurant and then hang up. I'm on the bus—no one can sue me for failing to assist a person in danger.

I make my way to the Molitor, my conscience clear. I didn't just leave him, I called for help. Besides, the man isn't staying at my hotel, he was probably drunk and reeling with vermin. I'm not a charity and think I was extremely generous to give him twenty-five euros. I decide not to tell Cyrian about it. We're going to spend a lovely romantic evening together, respecting the rules we established two years ago when we started dating. I don't talk about my hotel, and he doesn't talk about his wife, daughters or parents. We're only interested in each other, in our own little bubble, oblivious to the rest of the world.

Thierry, Paris, rue Monge

The red Fiat 500 convertible has turned the corner. I wait another five minutes before getting up. I catch my reflection in the mirror of a shop window, I barely recognize myself with this lumberjack's beard. I walk away briskly, taking a yellow medical refuse bag out of my pocket and I remove my filthy shabby overcoat, that stinks of booze, and stuff it inside. I disinfect my hands with antiseptic gel. I bought this coat from a homeless man who was admitted for an epidural hematoma in the neurology department I head. He arrived in a comatose state, about to die, and left on his own two feet with the great big warm coat that I'd bought him. The head nurse thought I was crazy when she heard about it.

I step into a café a little further down the street. From the café window, I can see an emergency vehicle, with rotating flashing lights and siren on. I smile at the regulars leaning against the counter and hand the twenty-five euros to the barman.

"Get the gentlemen a drink on me!" I say, smiling to myself.

11th December

Albane, Le Vésinet

"Oskar, walkies time, come along!"

The young dog fetches his leash and brings it to me grinning. Charlotte is in bed. I'm hungry, but I'm fed up with eating alone every evening in front of the TV. It's not Cyrian's fault he has to work so hard. There's a recession on, and we all have to pull together and go that extra mile. But we are seeing each other less and less, just crossing like ships in the night. Last night, I was fast asleep when he came back from his meeting with the trade union representatives. He doesn't make love to me anymore either. I bought some expensive new underwear, and he didn't even notice. We'll just walk to the end of the street and back. Oskar is so well trained that I could order him to wee in the gutter in front of the house and come straight back and he would. Oskar, number two! But he needs some exercise. Cyrian should be back soon. I've put some retsina wine in the fridge to chill, like I used to. They were happy times; I hope it'll perk him up a bit. He's been totally lost since his mother died. A shadow of his former self. Something frightens me and I jump.

"Don't be afraid, little lady!"

"Oh, you startled me," I exclaim, turning around.

The man is tall and slim with round blue eyes like Smarties and a thick, dirty goatee beard. He obviously hasn't washed since God knows when. I volunteer at the local homeless charity, but I've never seen him before.

He tells me it's not safe, walking alone at night. His tone is not threatening, yet he makes me uncomfortable.

"Don't go near my dog," I say, "he bites!"

In reality, Oskar wouldn't hurt a fly.

He is leaning against the wall. He says he's hungry, to which I reply that I haven't got my purse with me. He tells me he's not asking for money but is hungry and lonely. Apparently, he used to have a dog, but then he had a heart attack and was hospitalized, and he hasn't seen his dog since. He thinks it was either run over or snatched by a lab for one of those disgusting experiments they do on animals.

The idea makes me shiver. "Doesn't he have a name disc, or a chip, or tattoo? Have you informed the animal rescue?" I ask.

He replies that his dog has lots of fleas, then asks me if I have any scraps of food for him. He pulls a face, wincing, as if in pain and puts his right hand on his heart.

"It hurts. I can't breathe, it's really tight!" he stutters.

He staggers, then slides down the wall into a sitting position.

"Are you alright, sir?" I enquire.

"My heart is really throbbing," he replies. "At the hospital they wanted to open my chest and fumble around inside me, so I told them to keep their hands off me."

His face takes on a look of sheer panic. His blue Smartie-like round eyes start to roll. I kneel down beside him, careful not to touch him, as he is rather repulsive. I don't have my mobile phone with me. I tell him that I watch the medical shows on TV till my husband gets home and know a bit about the subject.

"Did they not prescribe you any Trinitrine?" I ask.

"How would I have paid for it?" he mumbles.

I tell him I live nearby and am going to call the emergency services. He resembles a frightened little boy.

"Please don't leave me! I don't want to die, I'm scared," he pleads.

I tell him I'll only be a second and promise I'll be right back.

I hurry in the dark. I'll call the emergency services and they'll send the paramedics, then I'll go back and wait with him.

Thierry, Le Vésinet

As soon as she leaves, I grab the dog by the collar to prevent him from following her. I give him a snack from my pocket. The labrador sits on his hindquarters expecting more treats. I whisper to him persuasively, "Number one, Oskar! Number one, Oskar, good boy!"

He doesn't move. His mistress notices that he isn't following her. She calls him but she can't see I'm restraining him.

I try again, "Number one, Oskar! Are you deaf?"

"Oskar, come home at once!" orders his mistress.

Suddenly it comes to me. I put the words in the wrong order. "Oskar, number one! Now! Oskar, number one!" I order. The well trained dog obeys. I move closer to sit in the puddle of urine, swearing under my breath at Joe.

"Oh no, lady! Your mutt just pissed on me!" I shout.

"What?" she says, in horror.

She retraces her steps and sees the puddle. Oskar gets a good telling off.

I get up with difficulty. My coat is dripping with urine. Oskar wags his tail, staring at my pocket which smells of biscuit to him.

"My heartbeat has slowed down; panic over. I need to get out of here. Your dog clearly doesn't like tramps."

"I'm sorry, really, I'm going to make him apologize!"

Albane, Le Vésinet

This man is ill. He's all alone, and as lonely as me since my husband started neglecting me. I can't bring him into our house while Charlotte is sleeping but I can't leave him on the street either. I have no choice but to let him come and use our summerhouse.

"I live right next door, sir. Please come with me."

His disgusting coat stinks and is dripping in urine. I ask him if he feels any better. He says he thinks his angina pectoris is stable. I don't understand but apparently that's what they called it at the hospital. We walk slowly and painfully up to our garden fence. I open the gate; we bypass the house and I guide him to the little cabin.

I have trouble swallowing as I scan the room and see the old, broken armchair, the table, the sink in the corner, and Cyrian's hideous exercise bike in front of the window. I turn on the electric radiator. He collapses into the armchair.

"My head is spinning. I haven't eaten anything since yesterday," he says.

"I'm going to get you some food and a change of clothes."

I take Oskar in the house, and lock the door behind me. Cyrian's keys are not hanging up, so he's not home yet. I get his voicemail when I try and call him. I open the door to Charlotte's room, she's fast asleep. I open the wardrobe and grab a pair of sailing trousers I bought on Groix. I add a Barbour jacket that Cyrian no longer wears. I take a towel from the bathroom cupboard. I go into the kitchen and stuff a baguette, some butter, a chocolate bar, a banana and Cyrian's special Spanish ham into a bag. That'll teach him for not being here. I mustn't give the man any alcohol though, not in his condition. I open the cutlery drawer and hesitate whether to give him a knife in case he attacks me with it. I remove the butter from the bag, now he won't need a knife. I slip forty euros into an envelope and write an address on it.

"Oskar, come on, we're going back out!"

The dog follows me, intrigued by the contents of the bag. I cross the garden and knock on the cabin door.

"Hello?"

The man is still sat in the same position. He is trying to keep warm. I put the groceries, the clothes and the towel on the table and avoid looking at the bike.

"I apologize again for my dog's unacceptable behaviour. Here, you can change your clothes now and eat. I'll be right back. How is your heart?"

He says it's still ticking for now but won't hold out forever. I sit down in the garden on a teak armchair that cost a small fortune. In the early days, Cyrian and I used to take care of the garden furniture together, coating it with a special oil, and taking a break to kiss each other every few minutes. Then I took over the job, using a spray, before giving up on it altogether, a bit like our relationship. The garden chairs have been neglected and nobody bothers with them anymore. Just like our marriage.

I was stupid to let a stranger into our home, especially at night. Imagine the headlines: *Housewife and mother murdered at her home in Le Vésinet. No sign of forced entry.* That's me, a Le Vésinet housewife and mother who doesn't go out to work, preferring to take care of her daughter instead. Apple is also part of our family of course. I knew of her existence right from the start of our relationship. I found it touching that Cyrian was a young father. When I told Cyrian I was pregnant, he said, "Oh no, not again!" I went icy cold. My husband and Maëlle hate each other with the same passion as when they loved each other. I know he'll never love me as much as he loved her. We won't be going to Groix anymore which I'm glad about. Next summer, we'll take Apple to the South of

France with us. I could have strangled her when I discovered that she had taken Charlotte out on the luggage rack of her bike! She didn't know why I reacted like that of course, and just thought I was crazy, which isn't so far from the truth.

I return to the summerhouse. The man has started eating the baguette and the bar of chocolate. My husband's clothes fit him perfectly. If he shaved his beard, he would look like one of those contestants in a makeover show.

I apologize again, and tell him my dog made a mistake. Then it comes to me: the man's stench must have disorientated Oskar, and made him lose his bearings.

"Did he mistake me for a lamp post?" he asks.

"No, no," I reply. "Eat up."

Helping out at the local charity for the homeless, I have come across people from all walks of life, even former teachers who have lost everything. Tramps used to be marginalized for choosing to live outside of society, but nowadays it can happen to anyone.

"How's your heart?" I ask.

"Still alive so far."

He points to the exercise bike and says that it's an excellent workout for the heart.

"Is it yours?"

"I loathe bicycles of any shape or size."

"Did you fall off when you were small?"

I reply that the bike is my husband's, like the ham, which is a special one.

He tells me he eats kosher.

"I apologize!"

"You couldn't have known."

"Your dog has probably been taken in by someone who loves and cares for him," I say, trying to sound reassuring.

"You're a good woman," he replies. "Your husband is a lucky man."

I reply that he'll be home soon; I say the same thing to all electricians, workmen, postmen, or delivery men who come to the house, so they are aware there is a male presence here.

"Will he think I'm trying to seduce you?" he asks.

I shake my head. He obviously hasn't looked at himself in the mirror recently! In any case, Cyrian doesn't care enough about me anymore to be jealous.

"My father-in-law was in charge of a large cardiology department. You should get yourself checked out there. Here, I've noted down the address for you," I say.

I give him an envelope containing the money for the consultation.

"Is he a nice guy, your father-in-law?" he asks.

"He's a bit strange, but he loves my daughter, which is all that counts. He's a bit annoying, but a good man."

My eyes catch sight of that damn bike again and I shudder as I turn my head away.

"What happened to make you hate bicycles so much?"

I get a lump in my throat. "My little brother . . . he had a moped accident. He got hit by a lorry and was killed instantly. It was all my fault. Cyrian knows but not Charlotte and my parents refuse to mention Tanguy's name, as if he had never existed. There was a family gathering for my mother's birthday. Tanguy was just ten years old and I was fifteen. I had just bought a moped with the money I had saved up from babysitting. I was showing off and bragging about it to my elder cousins, who all had a go on it. I wouldn't let Tanguy go on it though as I was afraid he might damage it. He watched as I pulled the throttle to accelerate. I didn't realize it at the time, but I had left the key in the ignition and forgotten to put the steering lock on when we sat down to eat . . ."

I close my eyes in horror, as I relive the scene. My voice trembles, my eyes fill with tears, and I choke on my words.

"After the meal, the smaller children got up from the table to go and play. Cheese and wine were served, followed by birthday cake with candles. We called the children back in, but Tanguy was nowhere to be found. We looked everywhere for him. Then we heard sirens down the street. To this day, my mother has never forgiven me for killing my brother."

"But it wasn't your fault," he says.

"I should have removed the ignition key and put the lock on," I reply sadly.

"But it was an accident!"

"My mother needed someone to blame. I should have let Tanguy try it out like my cousins. I would have shown him how to brake. The lorry driver saw him accelerate and drive straight into him."

Describing this scene devastates me just as violently as it did then.

"I will never let my daughter ride a bike or a moped. My husband had a motorcycle when I met him, but he's sold it since. He works out here on this exercise bike. I refuse to let him bring the thing in the house."

Tanguy was my mother's favourite. We were close. On the evening of his funeral, my mother went outside with me in the garden and, with sheer hatred in her voice, she screamed at me, "I hope one day you will feel the same pain that you've caused me. I hope you will have a child and lose it".

I didn't tell my father; he wouldn't have believed me anyway. I see my parents as little as possible and I never let Charlotte stay with them. My mother lost a child, so I can understand how grief stricken she is, but at the same time I hate her. Charlotte thinks I'm an only child. I am overprotective of her, but the thought that something terrible could happen to her scares me so much. I could have murdered Apple when I heard they had been out on a bike together. The next night, at the Marine Hotel, I had a horrible nightmare. I was at the wheel of a lorry and saw Tanguy rushing towards me on a bright red bike, I wasn't even trying to avoid him. He was laughing his head off before he fell to the ground next to the red bicycle. My mother and Charlotte came running out of the garden. Charlotte ran towards my little brother's crushed body. My mother was screaming at her, "You killed my son, I told you not to lend him your bike, you deserve to die," and she strangled my daughter in revenge. I watched the scene from my lorry, petrified, my stiff hands clasping the steering wheel. This dream haunted me until we boarded the boat. I couldn't have stayed on that island a minute longer.

"Are you okay? You've gone awfully pale," says the man, offering me some chocolate from the bar I'd given him. "Eat a square of this, it'll do you good."

I break off four squares and munch them, and start to feel in better spirits. The man gets up; he seems to be feeling better too and is no longer staggering along.

"I'll be off now. Thank you."

I should be thanking *him*. He kept me company and I was able to confide in him knowing I would never see him again. For a while I was able to switch off my fear that Charlotte won't make it beyond ten years old, the age Tanguy was when he died. When I met Cyrian, I told him that my mother had put a curse on any children I may have. He just laughed saying what rubbish, he doesn't believe in that superstitious nonsense.

"Bye, Oskar," says the tramp and strokes him. No hard feelings there. I need to contact the dog therapist.

"My name's Albane," I call out, just before he closes the gate after him.

"David Anderson," he says, before wandering off into the night.

12th December

Joe, Paris

My best mate never fails to amaze me.

"David Anderson? Where on earth did you get that from?"

"If I had had a son, I would have called him David," he replies. "I love Hans Christian Andersen's *The Little Mermaid*. I panicked when your daughter-in-law asked my name. I almost dropped myself in it by using the term 'angina pectoris' though. I'd make a terrible spy."

"But a brilliant actor."

"I prefer neurology," says the eminent professor Thierry Serfaty, devouring the appetizer served to us at the Mini Palais. He points at my plate. "You don't want yours then?"

I let him have it. Life is unfair. He is stick thin, whereas I've spent most of my life depriving myself to avoid turning into a fat potbellied husband.

"She thinks you're 'a bit annoying, but a good man'," adds my friend, as he studies the menu. "Did you know about her little brother?"

I choose the creamy pumpkin soup with hazelnuts and porcini mushrooms. "No, it's the first time I've heard about this."

I order the egg purée with sea urchin mousse. Out of habit, I still scan the menu wondering what you would have chosen. A scallop carpaccio with oysters maybe? I still sleep on my side of the bed and I still leave the toothpaste cap off for you. Old habits die hard.

"Well, I got a Barbour jacket and some sailing trousers out of it but I definitely wasn't expecting the Spanish ham . . ." he says.

"I would have bet my retirement savings that Danny would prove to be the more compassionate of the two and Albane the more insensitive, but I was wrong. As for the ham, that's *pata negra* I'll have you know, the finest in the world."

Thierry and I met in Paris in the first year of our respective internships. I was from Rennes, and he was from Strasbourg. We discovered the French capital together. His round bright blue eyes drove the girls crazy, none of them could resist. We worked in the same department. Thierry ate kosher and observed the Sabbath, while I only had one thing in mind: saving all my time off to return to Groix. We covered for each other and helped each other out. We cheered each other up when we lost a patient and rejoiced when we saved one.

I bet you knew about Albane's brother, didn't you, Lou? And that Albane was a nicer person than Danny. So what do I do now?

"Forget about your family and enjoy the meal," says my friend.

So we drink, we eat, we talk about colleagues. One has just given everything up to go and live in an ashram in India. Another died while he was examining a patient. The ugliest guy in the class now has eight kids. The hottest girl in the class became a sex therapist. I order a pineapple mousse and Thierry chooses a rum baba.

"I'm seeing Albane in a whole new light since you told me about her brother," I say.

"It'll bring you closer to her and help you keep Sarah's illness in perspective. I can give you the name of a good osteopath if you like, you look like you're carrying the world's problems on your shoulders."

"I'm a doctor, having a sick daughter is like having a wound that won't heal. Not being able to cure her makes me want to scream with frustration!"

Do you remember, Lou, twenty years ago we went to see the film *Mr Holland's Opus* where Richard Dreyfuss plays a music composer whose only son is deaf? At the time, Sarah was bouncing around and full of beans. When we left the cinema, we thanked the heavens for giving us such perfect children. We obviously didn't thank them hard enough.

"What am I supposed to say to her when she's frustrated and resentful that her wobbly legs can hardly hold her up?" I ask.

"Tell her you love her."

"I'm not so sure she knows what love means after the way that bastard, Patrice, dumped her. I would love to rearrange that spineless moron's mug."

I now know where I stand concerning Danny and Albane. Who knows, maybe Cyrian is happier with someone selfish like Danny than with someone sweet and accommodating like Albane? You asked me to make them happy, not to change their lives. As a doctor I have to make choices such as prescribing antibiotics for a bacterial infection but not if it's viral. But right now, I must admit I'm at a loss. Cyrian and I grew apart when he hit adolescence. I get up.

"Number one or number two?" jokes Thierry.

I laugh with him, Lou. Yes, sometimes I laugh without you, but it doesn't compare with what we had.

Thierry returns to his neurology practice. I phone JP in Groix. He has just returned from karate. I ask him to set up a Google Alert for Patrice. I spell out his surname which was supposed to have been our daughter's new name. I walk past the Grand Palais where I reluctantly dragged you many a time. You only came along to please me. You loved people and stories, not exhibitions. I blame you for all the exhibitions you made me miss, and for your false accusations, not to mention this ridiculous mission you've forced on me. I'm really mad at you.

I have a white "Joseph" on my shoulders. When we met at that wedding, I was wearing a sailor sweater over my jacket. You gave me the phone number of your father's castle. In those days, mobile phones didn't exist. I took you for a banana split at the famous Renault bar on the Champs-Élysées the following week. You looked at my stripey sweater and asked me if I always wore one, and whether it was a tradition on my island. I didn't tell you that the evening my father's boat came back without him, I put his huge sweater over my shoulders. It comforted me then and still does now. It became my trademark.

We left the Renault bar together. I had come on my moped. You drove an old Autobianchi that you shared with your sisters, but that night you pretended to be on foot to avoid embarrassing me. We strolled aimlessly in the night, chatting about our childhoods. You started shivering, so I took off my sweater to put over your shoulders. I should have felt naked without it but I wasn't even cold; your gaze had thawed my heart.

Lou, on the other side

Nice work, boys. Hats off. What a class act! When you were interns, you ridiculed and played pranks on colleagues who you thought were cruel to patients. You poured laxative in their coffee, plastered up the wheels of a motorbike, slipped an ear you stole during dissection into a pocket. Thierry is a well-respected neurologist now, and a real gentleman. When you told him that we were moving to Groix, he was happy for us, like a true friend would be. Danny didn't know him. Albane has only seen him twice, at his wedding and at my funeral. She wouldn't have recognized him with that bushy beard and those rags. He went a bit over the top, but he got away with it. Cyrian had told me about Albane's awful mother, but not about her little brother. We all have our secrets. Maybe I would have understood her better and liked her a little more had I known?

I haven't forgotten the Renault bar, my *piroche*. You didn't play on your father's death to lure me into your arms. For years you hoped he would eventually turn up, wounded, suffering from amnesia. That sweater was your lifeline, your Superman costume, your Batmobile. You shared it with me and the patients you saved. You used it to protect our family.

Sometimes in life you choose not to take an umbrella when it rains; you don't want its protection, you just want to get soaked. That's how I felt when I moved into the nursing home. I took your sweater off my shoulders. I left you sheltering in its safety alone. I didn't want to lead you, Apple and Maëlle out into the rain. Don't be angry with me, my love.

14th December

Danny, Paris, rue Monge

Cyrian's father pushes open the hotel door as I walk through the lobby.

"Oh what a nice surprise, Doctor!"

"I wouldn't say that, I've got some bad news for you," he says.

I take him straight into my office and ask him if it's about Cyrian. He says that Cyrian is in great shape, unlike the heart patient he's been treating for years: an old art collector who lives in a castle in Denmark. People think he lives rough, but he's actually a wealthy arts benefactor.

"Do you want me to see if I've got room for him here? I'm flattered, but it's not the Ritz," I say.

He replies that I knocked the man over right here, in front of the door. I fiddle nervously with a paper clip.

"He wanted to take shelter in the hotel, but you wouldn't let him. He had a heart attack, and the emergency services brought him to my former cardiology department. I went to visit him and he told me everything."

"You didn't give him my name, did you? He can't prove it was me?" I ask, distraught.

He says my fingerprints are on the bank notes I gave him. This is just ridiculous! I'm not a doctor and it wasn't up to me to treat him. Joseph then says that since the Second World War, French law characterizes such situations as "failure to assist a person in danger", which technically makes me criminally liable.

I tell him I called the emergency services. He replies that I didn't wait with the patient until they arrived and refused to let him shelter in the hotel lobby.

"He looked and smelled like a tramp!" I cry.

"Why don't we just get rid of all the down and outs, and those who don't use deodorant, you're right, that'll clean up the streets," he retorts sarcastically.

"I was late for my dinner with Cyrian," I mumble. "How is the gentleman now?"

"Well enough to be able to recount the incident in detail," he says. "But the prognosis isn't good."

A crazy thought enters my head. If he doesn't make it, then he won't be able to testify against me.

"His children intend to bring charges. You'll be hearing from his lawyers soon."

"I thought he was a scammer, a fraud!" I yell.

"The fact that you didn't help him when he was injured is one thing. But abandoning someone who is having a heart attack is pretty extreme!"

I ask him to give me an alibi, and say I was with him at the time.

"You want me to commit perjury, against my own patient?" he asks with astonishment.

So I suggest that Cyrian testify on my behalf. This enrages him further, saying that his son would then be charged with aiding and abetting.

I rub my eyes in panic.

"I hope you didn't call the emergency services from your mobile?" he says then. "They log all incoming calls. You're in big trouble, Danny."

I am devastated. He's a doctor, so his patient will always be his priority. Cyrian has his priorities too; his mother took up loads of his time, and he always put her before me. His daughters and wife always come before me too. I've had enough, I'm going to put a stop to this.

Joe, Paris

God, what fun I had! I got the idea of Danny's fingerprints on the money from all those crime series we used to watch together. It was Thierry who told me that mobile phone calls to the emergency services are recorded. I plan my next move strategically. I'm going to raise the stakes. For this, I'll need help from your goddaughter, Esther. She has just turned eighteen and is razor sharp.

I check my emails on the iPad. What used to take private investigators weeks to do can now be done in three clicks. Humphrey Bogart wouldn't have to put on his raincoat to drink whiskies in sleazy bars, he could work at home in front of his screen and order sushi. I receive some Google Alerts concerning Patrice. I see pictures of him in a well-cut suit, elegant tie, salt and pepper hair, no wedding ring. He never smiles. In this one he's running a marketing campaign. Here, he's attending a cocktail party. And here, he's hosting a charity event. The last time I saw him in the flesh was ten years ago, and he was wearing a T-shirt and Bermuda shorts on his way back from their trek. I was supposed to walk Sarah down the aisle and lead her to him. I even started learning the waltz so that I could open the wedding dance with my daughter. I remembered this again at the silent ball in the covered market on Groix, as Sarah and I spun around together on the day of your funeral.

Now I'm tracking my ex-future-son-in-law online. I jump from one link to another, each showing me a different facet of his life. It looks like he campaigns for a children's charity.

Has he adopted a child I wonder? I click. This man, boss of a huge company inherited from his father, is a volunteer at a charity which helps children keep in touch with their parents while they're in prison. This kind of attitude doesn't resemble that of the CEOs I know. I wonder what's behind it. And what motivates him enough that he devotes what little free time he has to this cause? What Patrice did to Sarah was disgusting. Is he trying to redeem himself by helping these kids? I remember a conversation we had in the car once travelling between Paris and Groix. He wanted to have several children so that they wouldn't have to experience the loneliness he did, as an only child. He used to talk beautifully about his love for Sarah, and like a fool I was taken in.

15th December

Joe, La Défense

I arrive in front of a tower constructed entirely out of glass and metal. At reception, I ask to see the managing director. When the receptionist asks me if I have an appointment, I show her my doctor's ID; that always works. Not this time though. The sunny young employee transforms into a rottweiler, and she's suspicious.

"What is the purpose of your visit?" she growls.

"I'm Patrice's ex-father-in-law."

It works. Her face lights up. I'm family, that's good enough for her.

Patrice frowns when he recognizes me.

"Joseph? I thought it was my real ex-father-in-law, my ex-wife's father. I'm obviously not cut out for marriage."

Then he remembers that I'm newly widowed. "I heard about Lou. I really wanted to write to Sarah but I thought she would just throw my letter away."

I don't contradict him.

"Lou was a great lady."

"Do you have five minutes?"

He looks at his watch. "No, but seeing as it's you, yes."

We sit in black leather swivel chairs, with a breathtaking view of the Grande Arche.

"Still wearing your famous sweaters I see," he remarks. "I

hope Sarah hates me, that she's moved on with her life and is happy."

"Yes she does and yes she has. What about you?"

"I married an English woman who bears a striking resemblance to Sarah. We have a son; she divorced me and took our son, John, to London. My family business is here, so I only get to see John once every two months. My son calls his mother's new boyfriend 'Daddy'."

"Don't hold it against me if I can't sympathize."

His foot twitches nervously as if he were in a job interview.

"I loved Sarah, you know. I didn't have the strength to cope. I wanted a family, but she didn't want to risk having kids. It was a deal-breaker. I could have accepted the wheelchair part."

"You could have *accepted* it?" I repeat angrily.

"It wasn't her disability that made me back out. I needed an heir to take over the family business, it's a long tradition in my family, that's how I was raised."

"I understand, I raised my daughter to do wheelchair racing."

"Enough of the cheap jokes."

"You just didn't love Sarah enough, and proved yourself to be a spineless coward. I can never forgive you for dumping her when she needed you most. A real man would have stayed, not bottled out when the going got tough."

"So you just came here to insult me after ten years?" he asks.

I shake my head. "You owe me one."

"What do you want?"

"I want you to invite Sarah to dinner. Drink, eat, insult each other, confront each other."

"She'll never accept. Is she married?"

"No, she lives alone," I reply.

I hand him Sarah's business card. He grabs it eagerly. "I've often wanted to see her again," he admits.

"Especially after your wife dumped you, no doubt," I can't help adding.

I get up. "I will deny ever having met you, even under torture. If you ever tell Sarah about this conversation, I'll beat the shit out of you."

"What if she asks how I got her contact details?" he asks, meekly.

"The Internet, social networks, the university alumni association, you're spoilt for choice. By the way, why are you so involved in that children's charity?"

"It's not the children's fault. They shouldn't be punished for their parents' mistakes."

"Do you know someone in prison? Why are you so invested in this particular cause?"

He sighs. "The law over in England has deprived me of my son. So I help other fathers, who don't have the option of the Eurostar, to see their kids."

16th December

Sarah, Paris

My brother has invited me for lunch at the Polo Club. He doesn't play polo, but he meets clients there regularly. Sitting at the balcony bar, he likes raising his hand nonchalantly to greet an acquaintance. This is his natural habitat, like Daddy in Groix harbour or me on a film set.

The taxi drops me off. Cyrian gave my name at the front desk. I walk in slowly; it's a good day today. My walking stick could easily be mistaken for a fashion accessory. My brother has chosen a nice table for us, at the edge of the grounds. I'm wearing a conservative-looking jacket and he nods approvingly. Sometimes my outfits are too wacky for his taste.

"I've got a present for you," I say.

"I don't have time to go to premiere parties, but it's sweet of you. Would you like some coffee? The croissants are exquisite. Anyway, what did you want to see me about?"

I'm too hot, so I take off my jacket. He helps me, the perfect gentleman that he is. Cyrian opens car doors for ladies, he walks into public places first, but knows how to stay in the background in a private setting. My bare arms expose my tattoos. Cyrian stiffens up.

"You can pretend you barely know me. Do you have the time?"

"Yes."

"Well you'll have it twice now," I say, taking out the watch Dad asked me to give him.

He strokes the gold dial and asks if it's Mum's watch. I tell him it was her father's.

"Systole gave it to you then, you're lucky," he says.

"He wanted to give it to you before you left Groix, but you left without saying bye to him."

"Did Mum want me to have it?"

I shake my head. "Dad wants you to have it."

"I won't take anything from Dad," he says, even though I know he loves this watch.

"Stop acting the fool," I say and place it firmly in his hand. The waiter arrives and we order.

"So, where do you stand with your two women?"

"I'm torn. I don't want to hurt either of them."

"What, you're still screwing both of them?"

"Albane isn't bothered about sex anymore; we have separate bedrooms."

"Whereas Danny is a sex maniac?"

"She's insatiable and imaginative."

"And she doesn't ask you to walk the dog, call the plumber, or attend parent-teacher meetings," I add.

"She's dreaming about dancing with me all night long on an exotic beach. She wants me to take her to the Maldives for Valentine's Day."

"Little girls believe in Prince Charming but they all get disillusioned as they grow up. They go backpacking with a hippy at eighteen, then marry a fashionable middle-class lefty with a good job. Meanwhile boys never stop fantasizing about Jessica Rabbit."

"Danny looks up to me, Sarah. I feel like a king when I'm with her, Leo at the helm of the *Titanic*. With Albane, I'm a responsible man, a family man, just an ordinary guy. I got married too young. You only get one life. I want to live life to the full, climb volcanoes, swim in waterfalls. I have the right to be happy, damn it!"

His spiel would move me, if it wasn't so cliché.

"Well, I hate to tell you that Di Caprio dies at the end of the film, and your dream resembles a chewing gum advert. I'm not lecturing you; you know how I feel about Albane. If you're happy with someone else, I'd be over the moon," I say.

He finishes his croissant. "There's just one snag with Danny. She hates children, so if I leave Albane for her and we move in together, I won't be able to have Charlotte over and would have to meet her somewhere else. Danny also hates dogs, so I would have to leave Oskar with Albane."

"She sounds truly delightful," I say.

"She's been putting pressure on me to leave Albane. I feel sorry for Charlotte, but she's none the wiser, tucked up safe in her own little world. If I leave her mother, I'll be able to spend quality time with her, just the two of us, it'll make our bond stronger."

"You've forgotten someone."

"Oskar prefers Albane to me, anyway, she's the one who feeds him."

"I don't mean your dog!"

"Oh, Apple's very happy living on Groix."

"The poor girl has been pretty unfortunate having you for a father," I say, getting into my stride now. "You blame Dad for being an absent father, but he took better care of us than you ever have of your daughter, Cyrian! What you blame Systole for, you've done a hundred times over to poor Apple."

"I'm a good father," he protests, "I make a point of seeing her every Christmas, Easter, and birthday, and if she fell ill I would jump on the first train to be with her."

"Is that what you call being a father?" I ask him accusingly.

"It's not my fault that Maëlle refused to come and live in Paris with me. Anyway, you hate Albane, why are you defending her?"

"I'm not defending anyone, but in eight years' time, your daughters will be adults and will go their own way, and you won't get those childhood years back."

My mobile phone rings, cutting me short.

"Excuse me, Cyrian, I'm waiting for a casting call. Hello?"

My hand shakes when I hear the voice on the other end of the phone. My left hand is a clenched fist, ready for battle, after years of pain and suffering. I often wished he could be in a terrible car accident, wheelchair bound for the rest of his life, dependant on twenty-four-hour care, fed and changed like a baby, with me grinning at his misfortune. Since then I've moved on and though the wound is no longer fresh, it still hasn't healed. We were supposed to continue the trek together, get married, have kids, take a sabbatical on Groix before beginning our careers as proud young graduates. But my fiancé did a runner, his tail between his legs. Now my free time is dedicated to boyfriends, seeing Apple, parking for free in disabled spaces and skipping queues.

Cyrian, Paris

My sister has gone white.

"Yes, you *are* disturbing me, what is it you want?" she yells down the phone.

I pretend I'm not listening, but I can hear every word.

"How did you get my number?" she asks.

". . ."

"Well I'm snowed under right now, I'm extremely busy," she says.

". . ."

"Just a drink at happy hour in the Marais, then. I live near there."

"Seven o'clock. You'll easily spot me, I'll be the one in a wheelchair."

She hangs up and beckons the waiter. She orders a cognac. I raise an eyebrow. It's an unusual order at nine o'clock in the morning. Sarah looks like she has just emerged from a nightmare.

"It was him," she says.

18th December

Apple, île de Groix

Joe is back from Paris, he missed Groix. I helped the vicar set up the nativity scene in the church, with figurines, hay, running water and stones. Shopkeepers have decorated their shop windows, it looks really festive. Mummy said it was probably best not to put a tree and lights up in the house, it's too soon, Joe is grieving. We've had no news from Daddy so I guess he won't be coming. Aunt Sarah normally spends Christmas Day with us, but this year she won't get here until the beginning of January, as Joe is spending Christmas with friends in Lorient. He'll be better off with them than here.

Aunt Sarah always buys my Christmas outfit. This year she sent me a pretty black H&M dress and sequined ballerina pumps. I went to collect the parcel from the ferry terminal. All parcels arrive at the port here. When tourists or people with holiday houses order stuff on the Internet, they wait for delivery at home until someone tells them that they have to go and pick it up themselves. I haven't told Aunt Sarah that Mummy and me will be in Locmaria at Christmas with no heating. I'll put on her dress, send her a photo of it and then put my fleece, leggings and furry boots back on. I really miss you, Lou, you loved Christmas and made the house look so Christmassy. I'll make sure I celebrate it for both of us this year. My saxophone lessons are going well. I love playing, it makes me feel so good. I get all excited and happy like I'm going to take off and fly. The left-hand notes, C, B, A, G, are getting easier now. I'm also getting the hang of the right-hand ones, F, E, D, and the lower C. I loved it when Yves played "Fly Me to the Moon", it was beautiful.

You used to help me with my Christmas shopping, I'm on my own now. Daddy sent me a cheque. I would have preferred a surprise, but it was useful. I spent it on gardening clogs for Joe, a toiletry bag made from recycled sail cloth plus a notebook with pictures of Groix for Mummy, and a fleece for Charlotte. I gave Daddy something homemade. I painted two clock dials on a board and glued paper hands on them. One shows high tide and one shows low tide.

When I get back from school, Mummy and Joe are kneeling down in front of the kitchen sink. Joe has his toolbox open. I crouch down beside him.

"That's where the leak is," he says. "Mummy will reopen the valve. Take the cloth, Apple, to stop your fingers from slipping. As soon as you see water spurting out, press hard on the spot where it's leaking. Got it?"

Mummy turns on the tap and water gushes out of the pipe from a hole so small you can't see it. I press as hard as I can. She turns off the tap and we drain the water. Joe repairs it and Mummy turns the tap back on. It's not leaking anymore.

She laughs, saying she'll make a donation to SAWIH, the Society for Aiding the Wives of Inadequate Husbands.

"Daddy isn't inadequate," I say instinctively.

Taken aback, Mummy and Joe look at each other. I should have kept my mouth shut.

"You're a good handyman, Joe," I say, feeling awkward.

"Cardiology is like plumbing; it's all about pressure and leaks, flaps and valves. Cardiologists are paid less than plumbers though," he sighs.

Lou, on the other side

Where's the Christmas tree, Joe? The baubles, the fairy lights, the gingerbread cookies, the Advent calendar with its twenty-four chocolate surprises? Where's your Christmas spirit? I leave and you let everything slide!

People are ordering their turkeys, fishing for scallops, buying chestnuts, ironing their Christmas tablecloths, chilling champagne. Everyone except Sarah of course.

24th December

Joe, Groix Island

You took Christmas with you, Lou. We haven't put up a Christmas tree in our house this year. Apple and Maëlle will be spending Christmas in Locmaria by the fire, roasting marshmallows in the hearth. I don't want to spoil their fun, so I pretended I've been invited to a friend's house in Lorient. I'll take the ferry tonight, spend the night in a hotel and return tomorrow. Maëlle didn't seem convinced and said a place would be laid for me at the table should I change my mind. Dear little Apple slipped a present inside my suitcase.

I check my emails. I have a Google Alert about Cyrian attending a Lions Club meeting, and another one about Sarah. To my amazement, I finally find out where our daughter is spending Christmas Eve. I imagine you knew, since you used to write "Princ" in your diary every 24th of December next to her name. The link directs me to a group of volunteers who organize Christmas celebrations at the local hospital. I click on it and discover a picture of our daughter in a wheelchair, wearing a red nose. Our little princess is spending Christmas Eve in Le Vésinet, avenue de la Princesse. Not with friends, but in a building dating back to the Second Empire, originally used to accommodate convalescent workers in the region. She spent time there herself for rehabilitation and physiotherapy after a serious flare up one year. I remember it well; we spent Christmas there by her bedside.

Cyrian stayed with Albane, who has a phobia of hospitals, even though he doesn't live far away. I remember you prepared a Christmas meal for us, Lou; it was completely inedible but it's the thought that counts. We sloshed it down with the champagne that you had stashed at the bottom of your bag. Volunteers came to each ward to cheer up the bedridden patients. Sarah vowed she would return one day, on her own two feet, to thank them. She kept her word.

I log on to the hospital website hoping to find a colleague I know. Bingo! I send an email to Thomas Defyves, a spine specialist with whom I worked as an intern at the central emergency services in Paris. I remember the foam fights we had with fire extinguishers in the hospital corridors, our summer barbecues on the helipad and the barbecue skewers we made out of medical equipment, not to mention the babies being delivered, bodies crushed under trains, or hanging from a noose, or squashed to a pulp, those we resuscitated, those who died, and those who survived . . .

Thomas replies in a jiffy.

"Hello old chap, are you still on your island?"

"Yes, I am, I need a favour," I reply.

He is not working today but promises to make enquiries for me. He has three children, two of whom are medical students and one is a vet. Why didn't I encourage our kids to follow my path? I wonder if Apple really will become a doctor?

He gets back to me an hour later. Sarah is hosting a cinema evening tonight at Le Vésinet. I get a seat on the boat to Lorient, but all the trains to Paris are full. I call the 7 Gang for help. Some of them leave a spare vehicle on the other side for emergencies. A friend lends me an ancient BMW. I drive to the port, make the crossing, and then sit behind the antique wooden steering wheel. Le Vésinet here I come.

Joe, Le Vésinet

I feel at home in hospitals. A bit like pilots in airports, chefs in kitchens, lawyers in court. The antiseptic smell is familiar and reassuring to me.

There is a party atmosphere in physio. Patients' doors are wide open, comedies are blaring out from TV sets, nurses are wearing party hats, and there's a Christmas tree on the landing.

Cheerful faces smile at me as I walk past. Everyone is getting into the Christmas spirit, that time of year which resembles a truce, a fleeting respite from reality illuminated by colourful fairy lights. Volunteers wheel patients to the chapel for the evening service before serving the chestnut-stuffed turkey. Miniature Father Christmases are perched on bed rails, and staff have snowmen pinned to their gowns. Zimmer frames are decorated with tinsel. There are no children on the wards, just elderly adults. Defyves tells me he found out that Sarah chose to spend Christmas here, with the frail and ailing. Some of them have no one except tonight's volunteers to chat with; they hand them their empty plates filled with turkey bones.

They have a small TV set in their room and there's a giant screen in the common room. This is where they gather to listen to Sarah. I recognize your distinctive voice from afar, which some men would describe as sexy. How would I know, Sarah is my baby. I watched her take her first steps, I taught her how to ride a tricycle, then a bicycle, how to tie her shoelaces, and how to tell the time. She is sat there in her wheelchair decorated with tinsel and tinkly bells, dressed in the same leather suit that Diana Rigg wore when she played Emma Peel in *The Avengers*, except that Sarah's is red. Her long sleeves hide her tattoos. She is wearing your pearl necklace, Lou. She is on the stage, to the right of the big screen, in front of a laptop. The room is jampacked; I sneak to the back without her spotting me. The carers are standing there, watching, eager, and alert. The patients are lying down or sitting stiffly in their chairs. They all take in every word she says.

Sarah asks them if they have heard of *Cinema Paradiso*. It's her favourite film. Some hands go up, but fewer than I expected. Sarah steers her MacBook as skilfully as her wheelchair. The film poster pops up on the giant screen accompanied by Ennio Morricone's music, which sweeps through the room, taking the audience hostage in its wake. Even the hard of hearing are moved. The film trailer conveys heartfelt emotion. Time stands still, eyes gleam. Hearing aids make acoustic whistling sounds. Nobody cares, it's party time.

"I have a surprise for you," declares Sarah. "Not a Rolex or a Ferrari, something a bit more personal. You're here for physiotherapy. We're all in this together, sharing the same struggle, a united front."

I hold my breath. Our daughter has never broached this subject in front of me and Lou before. I feel like a peeping Tom, an intruder, but I can't sneak out now or she'll see me. I stoop down low behind a woman with white hair. The stranger asks me if I'm okay. I pretend to have a crick in my neck and say I'm fine. A man asks in an Italian accent if I'm alright, and if I'm about to faint. He's clearly not a patient and appears to be helping an old man in a lumberjack shirt who I guess is his father.

If ever I'm hospitalized, Cyrian won't visit me. At least it'll make us quits for all the times I was busy working instead of watching his swimming competitions. You went on behalf of us both, Lou; I thought that was enough.

The music stops and Sarah picks up the microphone. "The film is set in the late 1940s. A little boy named Toto makes friends with Alfredo, a projectionist in a cinema in southern Italy. Alfredo, played by Philippe Noiret, makes cuts in the films, censoring the kiss scenes that he considers too racy. When he dies, he bequeaths all of these pieces of censored film to Toto, by now a grown man, who watches them in a cult scene. Take a look!"

She starts the clip. Jacques Perrin who plays Toto is sitting in a modern cinema and has discovered his legacy. The ailing patients assembled here in the Le Vésinet hospital common room crane their necks to see what the beautiful fairy in the red leather suit and pearl necklace has chosen for them. Film kisses follow in black and white. I recognize some of the actors: Vittorio Gassman, Silvana Mangano, Charlie Chaplin, Vittorio De Sica, Totò, Jean Gabin, Marcello Mastroianni, Maria Schell, Cary Grant, Clark Gable, Alida Valli, Farley Granger, Anna Magnani, Gina Lollobrigida, Greta Garbo, Ingrid Bergman, and Gary Cooper, unless I'm mistaken. I plunge my face in my hands without covering my eyes so I can keep watching. Jacques Perrin does the same. I can relate to the guy on the screen just as my daughter relates to the frail and damaged people gathered here today.

At the end of the clip, the light comes back on. Everyone is talking at the same time. Sarah gives them a few minutes before she takes the floor again. "We are all superheroes in this room. We've got something the able-bodied, the marathon runners, the common mortals haven't. We have deadly weapons: walking sticks, wheels, walkers or crutches. We have an ace up our sleeve, a tremendous opportunity! We have the courage and strength to move mountains, brains and arms. We won't let a spinal cord injury, a narrow spinal canal, a replacement knee or a wobbly hip get us down. Have you ever been in love? Have you ever kissed someone like those stars did on screen just now, and was it beautiful? You don't need legs to kiss!"

Weary faces light up.

"Cinema is a big part of my life," she goes on enthusiastic-ally. "We are all protagonists of the most unlikely scenarios, whether funny or tragic. Normal people, by that I mean those *unfortunate* people with legs, shoot their entire lives using a Steadicam. We, on the other hand, shoot tracking shots, we are on our wheels, travelling to our destiny."

The crowd is enraptured.

"In life, you only get one shot. We got through the casting of the broken, the crumbling, the dislocated. We made it. What we have gained is greater than any prize, we have gained our independence!"

She stops. The crowd clap enthusiastically, and the applause swells. There is no standing ovation as this is physically impos-sible for the majority of them, but their faces are beaming and they continue to clap. My heart explodes with emotion.

"I have put together a few excerpts for you tonight from films where the heroes have some form of disability or are in a wheelchair. Take a look . . . Action!"

The room once again plunges into darkness. Able-bodied actors are sat in wheelchairs for the entire shoot. James Stewart in *Rear Window*. Tom Cruise in *Born on the Fourth of July*. Daniel Day-Lewis in *My Left Foot*. Gary Sinise in *Forrest Gump*. John Savage in *The Deer Hunter*. Jack Nicholson in *One Flew Over the Cuckoo's Nest*. Mathieu Amalric in *The Diving Bell and The Butterfly*. Denzel Washington in *The Bone Collector*. Fabien Héraud in *The Finishers*. Sophie Marceau in *Cartagena*. Sam Worthington in *Avatar*. François Cluzet in *Untouchable*. Each time, Sarah has chosen a powerful scene which really feels like a punch in the gut. It ends with the cult scene from *Awakenings*, based on a true story, in which Robin Williams plays a neurologist who brings his patient, Robert de Niro, back to life after years of being in a comatose state. He helps him rediscover the emotions of fear, joy, friendship and love.

The lights come back on and the audience is brought back to reality, after being catapulted into the past by Alfred Hitchcock. They can still taste the sweets which used to be sold during the interval.

"I have one last gift for you," says Sarah.

The room goes dark once again and excerpts from classic Christmas films appear on the screen. Comedies and dramas such as *Santa Claus is a stinker* and *The Christmas Tree* with William Holden, Bourvil and Virna Lisi. *It's A Wonderful Life* with your idol, James Stewart, *White Christmas* with Bing Crosby, *Home Alone* with Macaulay Culkin, *Miracle on 34th Street* and *A Christmas Carol*. The selection comes to an end with *Joyeaux Noel*, which stars Guillaume Canet, Diane Kruger and Danny Boon, and is set in the trenches. The film is based on the true story of the Christmas truce in 1914, and speaks to patients whose grandfathers lived through the First World War.

The lights come on again. These poor people who were suffering behind closed doors are now sharing their feelings like roommates.

"I used to go to the cinema in the centre of Paris with my wife," remarks one.

"When I was a kid, we used to sneak in through the exit!" says another.

"To buy a ticket for the cinema was the ultimate dream . . ."

"And it was the only place where we could kiss in the dark!"

"My husband proposed to me at the cinema."

"Since I've been widowed, I can't bear watching love stories."

"I can't stand films starring young handsome actors now that I'm old and ugly."

"We were young and handsome too!" protests the man in the lumberjack shirt.

The young Italian guy who thought I was fainting laughs. He has a sweater on his shoulders; it is such a rare sight that I notice it's the same green as his eyes.

"Now, let's get on with the music!" says our daughter before wheeling herself off the stage. A woman with a grey bun replaces her. She sits down at the piano and starts playing the chorus to "Petit Papa Noël", but it's not the same. The golden-haired beauty in the red suit has gone.

"Get rid of that old dear and bring back the horny blond," grunts an idiot in a wheelchair with foul breath. "I wouldn't kick her out of bed!"

"That's my sister you're talking about," says the Italian with the green jumper on his shoulders.

"Shit, how could I know? She's a fine bit of . . . I mean she's sexy!" the man replies lecherously.

"You obviously weren't brought up to respect women!" says the Italian.

The idiot manoeuvres his wheelchair and leaves.

"Is she really your sister?" I ask the Italian.

He shakes his head. "I've never seen her before but I have a twin sister so I can sympathize."

I nod in agreement.

"I've never seen such an irresistible woman," he whispers. "If she wasn't hospitalized, I would invite her to dinner!"

"She's not a patient here, she's a volunteer," I tell him.

He is mesmerized and repeats how gorgeous she is.

"My wife was beautiful too," sighs the lumberjack.

"And mine was superb," I add with conviction. Lou, it helps me to talk about you to strangers. You should be here with me, tucking into turkey instead of pushing up the daisies in Groix cemetery.

"My name's Eric," says the lumberjack.

"I'm Joseph."

He introduces me to his sidekick, Federico, his next-door neighbour, who lives in Venice and comes to Paris regularly for his work. He says they don't wish to intrude any longer as I must have things planned.

"I'm joining some friends in Chatou," I lie.

Eric tells me he fell in the stairwell and broke his hip. He stayed there alone in the dark until Federico found him. I tell Federico he has the same first name as Fellini.

Apparently, it's not a coincidence. His grandfather was an extra in a Fellini film, and his father worked in the Cinecittà studios. His twin sister is called Giulietta. The whole family are film buffs and Federico runs the film club at the university where he teaches.

I wonder if this is one of Lou's jokes?

I ask if his wife goes with him on his travels. He says he is not married and splits his time between Italy and France, which wouldn't be much fun for a spouse.

"Merry Christmas, Federico," I say. "The *donna stupenda* who you want to ask to dinner has tattoos of Fellini and Giulietta on her forearms. If you tell her that your family knew them, I bet you anything you like that she'll accept your invitation."

Joe, Le Vésinet

I can't go back to our flat in Boulevard Montparnasse if you're not there, Lou. Christmas television is a rip-off. The presenters dressed in their Christmas garb pretend to be celebrating Christmas live with us when we all know that the show was recorded weeks ago. They're cheating us, like I'm cheating our kids by not telling them about the mission you gave me.

The main door of the building opens. Sarah finally comes out. She can't see me. I parked the old banger of a BMW in the shadows. Looking like Mother Christmas in a scarlet coat, she nimbly steers her wheelchair over the ramp. Federico follows her, talking with his hands as Italians do. She unlocks her car with the electronic locator, stands up, and under Federico's astonished gaze, folds up her chair. He helps her put it in the boot. She gets behind the wheel and he gets in next to her.

I shan't go to Midnight Mass, Lou. This is my first Christmas without you, I feel totally lost. No one teaches you how to become a widower, you just get thrown in at the deep end—sink or swim.

Federico, Chatou

The Via 47 is fully booked, but I manage to persuade Antonio, the restaurant owner and a fellow Italian, to add a chair and a place setting at our reserved table. My friends give Sarah a warm welcome, saying such a beautiful woman is a delight for the eyes and the soul.

"How do you know each other?" asks Milan.

"The *maestro* introduced us."

"Which one?" asks Paola, his wife.

I glance at Sarah knowingly. "Fellini," I reply.

"How old were you at the time?"

I work out that Fellini died in 1993.

"I must have been around ten years old. Right, Sarah?!"

Sarah plays along and we toast with Prosecco and savour the truffle risotto. My friends crack jokes that Sarah can't understand. I'm worried that she may be feeling left out, but then an idea comes to me.

"1 2 3?"

Milan raises his eyebrows but Sarah catches on right away.

"1 2," she replies, completely unfazed.

"1 2 3 4?"

"1 2 3!"

Paola, thinking she's misheard, tilts her head towards us.

"1," I call out, confidently.

"2?" she says, pointing to the green sweater on my shoulders.

"Wearing your sweater like that is so last year."

"1 2 3 4," I reply.

Fellini used to teach his extras to role-play like this, counting out loud, and then real actors would dub them. It feels so familiar, it's as if we've been speaking this language all our lives. We already have a special bond, a certain complicity thanks to several numbers; I can't tear my eyes away from her. Dinner continues around us amidst general laughter. We recognize each other. We just know. We don't need words when we've got the *maestro* and his code, which brings us as close together as any embrace.

Apple, Groix Island

This is the first Christmas I've ever had without my grandparents. We go to sleep in sleeping bags in front of the fireplace and roast marshmallows on the fire. Mummy took a picture of me in my party dress which we sent to Aunt Sarah and then I changed back into warm clothes. We have a Christmas Eve tradition. Every year, Lou would put on Frank Capra's *It's a Wonderful Life*. I know the lines off by heart. Me and Mummy watch it again. I'm not cold, as she gave me a red fleece hoodie, red because it's Christmas and red to pay tribute to the courage of Groix women in the olden days. In 1703, English ships led by Captain Cook were cruising offshore, planning to attack and plunder Groix. In those days, the men were out fishing, so only women, children and the elderly remained on the island. But the vicar of the island had a great idea. He ordered the Groix women to dress in red, roll up their skirts, and grab pitchforks and stakes. From their boats, the English thought they were a troop of French soldiers in uniform. So they changed their course not wanting to be attacked and the island was saved.

Joe, Paris

I'm not hungry. I was always hungry when I was with you, Lou. I am listening to Bach's "St Matthew Passion". I rip the paper off Apple's gift. Every year you used to give me a new sailor sweater. No matter how many times I told you that my wardrobe was full of them, that my father only ever possessed three of them which was more than plenty, you always protested that I didn't have one in that particular shade. You used to say that the colour of my eyes changed according to what I was wearing and that you liked to look at my eyes so it was for your selfish pleasure. I wasn't expecting one this year, but Apple drew me a picture of one with rainbow-coloured stripes.

"Merry Christmas, Apple Pie!" I call out down the phone.

"And to you too, Joe! Have you opened my present?"

"Yes, I love it! It goes with everything!"

"You can't put it on your shoulders, but I thought . . ."

She pauses mid-sentence. This little girl is kindness personified.

"It was an excellent idea, sweetheart. And I've got a surprise for you too, which I've hidden outside your house in Locmaria."

I can just see her putting on her jacket, her hat, her furry boots. It's only a knick-knack, but I deliberately went there yesterday to hide it.

"Are you outside? Go around the house to the right. Stop under the gutter. Count three steps diagonally towards the hydrangeas. Are you there? Then four steps to the low wall. You should be able to see a tree stump. Your present is inside, in a plastic bag."

"I've found it!" she yells.

She laughs with delight at discovering a small bracelet with a red clasp. I sent Charlotte the same one with a blue clasp. The small metal oval has the shape of the island hollowed out on it.

"I love it, thank you!" cries Apple. "We watched *It's a Wonderful Life*. Angel Clarence has got his wings again. I felt sad because of Lou and then realized how lucky we were to have had her, as without Lou, I wouldn't have been born, nor would Daddy or Charlotte."

"That's true, without Lou I would have had no friends and in turn I would have hated everyone. I would have named my dog 'Imbecile' and people would have turned around in the street when I called out, 'Hey, Imbecile! No, not you, I'm talking to my dog!'"

She giggles. "Whereabouts in Lorient do your friends live? Can you see Groix from their house?"

"I can see you, I'm waving at you, can't you see me?"

She bursts out laughing. I hang up and stop waving manically at the stream of cars beneath the windows in Boulevard Montparnasse. You loved Christmas so much, Lou. I bet Father Christmas has made a place for you next to him on his sleigh, the old devil, and that you're helping him deliver the presents tonight. I hope he at least pays you double for your time.

"Merry Christmas, Sarah!"

"Merry Christmas, Dad, where are you?"

I lie through my teeth. "With friends in Lorient!"

"We really do miss her, don't we," says Sarah.

"But we're eating better, that's for sure," I reply to cheer her up.

Humour always makes bitter pills easier to swallow.

"I'm having dinner with an Italian whose grandfather was an extra in Fellini's films, how incredible is that!"

She sounds ecstatic.

"Oh really?" I say.

I must have sounded curious despite of myself, as she replies straight away, "Don't get carried away, Dad. Remember my rule: safety in numbers."

"*Buona sera*, darling," I say, smiling down the phone.

I practise saying "Merry Christmas, Cyrian" over and over again and then I dial his number.

Voicemail, blast, I should have known. Never mind. I'll leave a message.

"Merry Christmas to you all son, you, Albane, Charlotte and of course Oskar. Your mother would have called you, but as she is no longer around, I'm doing it for her . . . Give me a call if you like. Right, well, big kisses to all of you, except Oskar of course, and I really hope you all have a wonderful Chris—"

Biiiiiiip! The damn thing cut me off!

As soon as I hang up I realize that telling him I was doing it for Lou was the last thing I should have said. And telling him to get in touch was daft; if he wanted to he would.

Blasted answering machine! I feel like throwing my phone out the window. When I dropped my ancient iPhone in the sea last year, you set up the new one for me. It arrived in the post and I wasted hours getting worked up about it. You just said, "If you don't validate your card, it won't work", you typed in the security code and hey presto. Like the day I met you, Lou. You typed in the security code and we connected. Without you I'm obsolete.

That's my phone ringing. It's Cyrian's number, he must have accepted my Christmas truce.

"Cyrian?"

"Merry Christmas, Grampy! Thank you for your present, I got it this morning!"

"I'm delighted to hear that, my little apple Charlotte."

"My parents got me an iPad mini, it's amazing!"

"You'll have to show it to me," I say.

"When? Mum says we're not going to Groix anymore."

I try to hide from her the fact that those words pierce my heart.

"Next time we see each other," I answer. "Are you in Le Vésinet sitting round the fire?"

"Yes but the fire isn't lit because Mum says it's dangerous."

I would have been surprised to hear anything to the contrary.

Someone is talking quietly behind her.

"Mum and Dad wish you a happy Christmas," says Charlotte.

I ask her to put her Dad on.

She transmits the message and then tells me he is busy.

"Enjoy the rest of your evening," I say and then hang up before my voice gives me away.

Merry Christmas, my beloved! I hope you hung the star on top of the tree without falling off the top of Jacob's ladder and that you are able to get your favourite brand of champagne up there in the heavenly supermarket. And that no silly archangel is hitting on you. Beware, Lou, those guys are smooth talkers and then they just fly away leaving you high and dry. What you need is a solid, reliable guy like me, with his feet on the ground, even if that ground is an island.

Lou, on the other side

My loved ones are all listening to music. Apple and Maëlle are singing "Silent Night" beside the sea. Cyrian, Albane and Charlotte are listening to Barbra Streisand's "I'll Be Home for Christmas", sat next to the hearth of the unlit fire. Oskar is savouring the sound of Albane dropping a turkey leg into his bowl. Sarah is listening to "Bianco Natale" performed by Mina in the Italian trattoria where she is celebrating Christmas Eve. Boy, Lola and Julie are listening to the waves crashing against the Port-Lay harbour wall. The 7 Gang and Pat and Mimi are popping corks. My friend from the nursing home is putting Scrabble letters on a triple word score. And my friend, Gilles, who hates Christmas, is playing Barbara's "Le Soleil Noir" over and over again. It's midnight everywhere and the bells ring out. Everywhere except here, where there is total silence.

Federico, en route from Chatou to Paris

Sarah offers to drop me off on her way back to Paris. I accept and we continue the game in the car.

"1 2 3," she sighs, as we cross the Chatou bridge.

"1 2," I say, on the A86 motorway.

"1," adds Sarah, when we reach Porte Maillot.

"2," I say, giving her my address. I teach at the University of Padova, the French call it Padoue. I live in Venezia, which the French call Venise.

"I live in Paris, which Italians call Parigi. I work in the film industry here. Do you always have a sweater draped over your shoulders or is it just tonight?" she asks.

"1," I say, smiling.

Sarah parks in a disabled space in front of my house. I point out that it's not allowed.

"1 2," she says, pointing to the badge stuck to her windscreen.

If I invite her up, will she accept? I have some Barbera d'Asti in the fridge, it's not champagne but it's rather good.

I lean over and kiss her fiercely—a greedy, passionate, playful Christmas kiss. She thinks we're going to spend the night together. I stroke the inside of her palm slowly. Then I shake my head.

"1," I say, to explain myself.

She raises her eyebrows, incredulous that I'm capitulating there and then. Her face falls which makes her look even prettier. Our cosy little game has put up a wall between us, but we can't go back now. If I use words instead of numbers, the magic will be broken.

"1 2," I say again, by way of an explanation.

I get out of the car; I close the door. She drives off without looking back. I tell myself I'm a bastard, a *stronzo* as we say in Italian.

25th December

Joe, Paris

I wish it would either snow or rain, instead of being a beautiful sunny day. When it's bright like this, most families go out and walk off their festive feast. I'm sad that you're not here to see the blue sky, Lou. I'm at Montparnasse train station. Then my phone vibrates, it's Sarah.

"Is the weather good in Lorient?"

"It's always sunny when you call," I reply, avoiding the question.

"My Italian date last night wore a 'Joseph' on his shoulders, that's unusual these days."

"Women use make-up, men wear sweaters, and if your cashmere matches your eye colour, so much the better."

"How do you know that his eyes were the same colour as his sweater?" she asks, surprised.

Damn, I've nearly dropped myself in it, quick what do I say now?

"Just a coincidence," I say, "and I bet he has blue or green eyes? Girls love that. Your mother wouldn't have looked twice at me if I'd had brown eyes."

"Rubbish!"

"At the wedding where we first met, there was a lad hot on her heels. He had spiky hair, wore a signet ring and danced the waltz perfectly, but his eyes were a brownish colour, so she chose me!"

She laughs. Phew, she's no longer suspicious.

"My Italian is called Federico after Fellini," she says. "We talked all evening, speaking in numbers like the *maestro* himself; we were like a deaf and mute couple communicating in sign language in front of people who could hear and speak normally."

"What do you mean, speaking in numbers?" I ask.

"Dad!" exclaims Sarah, appalled by my ignorance. "Fellini chose his extras based on their appearance. They weren't professionals; they couldn't memorize their lines like actors. So he devised a system, whereby he made them count out loud, as if they were talking. Then professional actors would do voice overs. Everyone knows that!"

"Well, I didn't. Are you going to see him again?"

"No more than twice. You know the rules."

26th December

Sarah, Paris, the Marais district

I deliberately turn up late, though in some ways I've been waiting ten years for this. I want to get back at him, insult him. No one has ever hurt me as much as he did, the person I thought I would spend the rest of my life with.

I'm not in my wheelchair today, I just have a walking stick. I am wearing my skin-tight red leather catsuit again. The bastard stands up. His salt and pepper hair is too long in the neck, his suit is elegant but his shoes need polishing. He's not wearing a wedding ring. He has deep lines around his eyes and mouth. Life obviously hasn't been kind to him. Good. We made love so many times that now my hatred is visceral, I feel it vibrating through me, from my toes to the roots of my hair.

"You're still just as beautiful, Sarah," he says.

The first film I ever saw as a kid was *101 Dalmatians*. Dad was working, as usual. My brother fell asleep, but it gave me nightmares for weeks. I shall enjoy playing Cruella de Vil tonight.

"Champagne?" he asks. "They may not have your mother's favourite brand though."

"She's dead," I say, straight to the point.

"I know. I wrote to you."

"That's odd, I never received anything."

"I didn't send the letter in the end, I thought you'd just rip it up," he says.

"Too right!" I reply.

The waiter brings us two glasses of champagne.

"What should we toast to?"

"Our break-up? I want to thank you, Patrice. Thanks to you legging it, I have a career I absolutely love and a full, exciting life. If you hadn't been so spineless, we would have got married and I would have led a dull, bland existence as your wife. My pride took a hit, but now I'm actually grateful for your astounding cowardice."

He starts to laugh. "Dull and bland. My wife would agree with you there. That's what she said to me in front of the lawyers the day we got divorced."

"Let's toast your wife!" I suggest.

As I raise my arm, my sleeve slides down, baring my left forearm and revealing Giulietta.

"Is it real?"

I roll up my right sleeve to show him Federico.

"Was it painful?" he asks.

"Less than you copping out. Sorry, I couldn't resist that! They give you a local anaesthetic beforehand. I didn't get it done in some filthy tattoo parlour. It was in a Tuscan garden by a Californian tattoo artist. I didn't feel a thing when he drew the black outlines, but it was excruciating when he applied colour to do the red scarf and the jersey stripes."

"Do they mind you having tattoos at work?"

"It's pretty mainstream in the film industry, which is what I do for a living. Did you take over your father's company?"

"Yes, I didn't break the mould," he replies. "Are you with someone or do you live alone?"

I pretend to have a boyfriend.

He wants to make a toast to me; we finish our champagne and order another glass. The waiter thinks we're a couple.

"Thank you for coming tonight," he says.

To be honest, I was wondering whether he would be able to look me in the eye.

"I was just a kid. I got cold feet," he explains, by way of an explanation.

"What about me?" I whisper fiercely. "My whole world fell apart! I was counting on you. But no, you wanted a perfect fiancé with a guarantee and a warranty, in perfect working order, with two arms, and two legs!"

The waiter arrives with the champagne and I propose a toast to the children we never had.

"I was never happy without you, Sarah. I married a girl from London who looked just like you. I married her in England to please her. We lived in Paris but our son, John, was born in London, my wife wanted to be near her mother. We got divorced there too, it was simpler. My wife ended up going back, taking John with her, and the judge ruled in her favour. My son calls his stepfather 'Daddy' and calls me 'Patrice'. It's worse than a life sentence, it's like I don't exist for him."

"I feel sorry for him but not for you," I say. "If you're nasty to disabled people, it'll come back and bite you on the arse. It's a major sin; the heavens punish the able bodied for inflicting pain on us wobbly ones."

Patrice pushes his chair back.

"Do you feel better now? Now that you've got that off your chest? The champagne is on me, let's leave it there."

He picks up the bill and gets up.

"You're not running away from me again!" I say as I grab him by the wrist.

He sits back down and gulps down the rest of his champagne. I do the same.

"You look just as beautiful as before, but you've changed," he remarks.

"I've toughened up," I say.

"You're lucky."

We order a third glass; I know him, it would have been better to order a bottle, it would have been cheaper.

"When you suggested we go for a drink, I knew where you had ranked me, Sarah. You may have changed, but you still have the same habits. You have dinner with your loved ones, they're your priority. Next come your friends, you see them for lunch. And the others, the least important ones, are relegated to drinks status."

"You *were* my priority at one time," I retort, "but you chose to give up that status of your own free will."

"I was young and stupid."

"Getting older doesn't seem to have made you any smarter."

We clink glasses and drink every last drop.

"Do you want to stop there or have another?"

"Stalling already?" I ask.

He beckons the waiter, who is hovering nearby.

"How's your brother?"

"He had a delightful, charming daughter with an awesome Groix local, but then went and married an idiot and together they've got a spoilt brat, who's getting more obnoxious by the day. Can I see a photo of John?"

He shows me a photo on his phone of a sweet little boy with freckles, who looks very English.

"We've drunk to my ex-wife, your current boyfriend, the children we never had. So who do we toast now, Sarah?"

"We'll toast our last drink together," I say. "We shan't be seeing each other again after this."

"How about our last evening instead?" he suggests. "Let's spend it together, end in style."

I'm dying to see my Italian film buff again tonight. I don't understand why he didn't ask me up on Christmas Eve. I mean he's not married or anything, but I always seem to attract unavailable men. He likes me, I can tell. Some men are embarrassed or, on the contrary, turned on by my disability. Not him though. I can easily spot the perverts. So why then? It's a mystery. Talking in code was unexpected too. When we were children, me and my brother were really close; when we attended the Groix sailing club we even invented a language so no one else could penetrate our little bubble.

I prepare to send Patrice packing, telling him I am meeting Federico, but suddenly and to my astonishment, I find myself saying, "Okay, let's drink to our last night together."

He is just as surprised as me.

"You'll leave first thing in the morning and that will be the last time we see each other," I clarify.

"Is this your way of punishing me? Kind of sadistic, isn't it?"

"I have a golden rule, I never see a man more than twice," I say, putting my glass down carefully.

"You'll never forgive me?"

"No."

He hesitates. The atmosphere between us is electric. It's like an aphrodisiac.

"To our last night," says my bastard ex, downing his fourth glass.

While he is paying for the drinks, I grab my phone. I click on Federico's name. My thumbs are all over the place. The champagne has made me tipsy and I can't type properly. Plus the automatic corrector is playing up too. My finger slips and sends the text before I can reread it. Damn, I meant to say, "Sorry about tonight, I'm stuck with someone in a meeting." Instead I sent, "Sorry about tonight, I'm stuck with someone."

Federico, Paris, the Marais district

I got here early and chose a bar with a heated patio where I could read the *Corriere della Sera* with an espresso. I discover Sarah's text message just as she walks by on the opposite side of the street. She doesn't see me.

The couple enter the inner courtyard of a fancy old residential building. Sarah is leaning on her stick and up against a man with salt and pepper hair. They've clearly been drinking something stronger than apple juice. The heavy door closes behind them. Disappointment engulfs me. She was far too attractive to be single. She lied to me. I'm not offended, just sad that she's not *my* girlfriend, not *la mia fidanzata*. I wanted her so much on Christmas Eve, but was afraid of ruining things by taking advantage of the fact that it was Christmas. I want to make love to her on a normal day, a day just for us. In hindsight, I may as well have taken advantage of her. If I had, I would be in that guy's shoes right now instead of sat here.

I'm a single, eligible university professor, with no lack of female admirers, but I have one important rule: no students. I sometimes sleep with Chiara, one of my colleagues who's a physics teacher. We're not together, we're just close friends who care a lot about each other. Her partner was transferred to Sicily recently. I keep my feet on the ground, yet my head is often in the clouds. Galileo taught for twenty years in Padua. He timed the swing of the chandelier in a Pisa cathedral using his heartbeat, and then spent the rest of his life with his head in the stars. My heartbeat is regular but I like to daydream. I reply to Sarah's text. "Enjoy being stuck."

Apple, Groix Island

The island is full of tourists and holiday home owners who park where they shouldn't. The restaurants are heaving, so the shopkeepers and business owners are happy. Once the holidays are over it'll go quiet again. Then the only people left will be the "real" Groix islanders: the residents who were born here, those who have retired and settled here full-time, newcomers looking for a peaceful lifestyle, the poets and the hikers.

I rummage through the box of Christmas decorations that we didn't open this year and take out three pieces of tinsel. I go into the cemetery and walk past the memorial for those who perished at sea. I say hello to the large stone lady, who is kneeling down and crying beside the drowned sailors and fishermen. The ones who died a really long time ago were laid to rest in the old part of the cemetery and those who died more recently are in the new part, where people have left items such as a sculpted guitar, a little boat, and photos. It makes me sad. I carefully place my tinsel on the headstone where your name and the names of Joe's parents are engraved, even though Joe's father was lost in the Irish sea. I show you my new Groix bracelet and red fleece.

Mummy and I are enrolled on a course where we're going to learn all about life on the fishing boats during the last century. I have to do a presentation on it for school. I'll read it out to you here beforehand, so you can let me know what you think. I'm doing well with the saxophone. I've learnt the sharps and flats now. The note I like best is C sharp; to make the sound you don't have to press on anything, it's cool. I'm sure you can hear me, but it's not fair because I tell you everything and you can't answer.

Danny, Paris, rue Monge

Paris is a sought-after destination for the festive holiday season, so the hotel is full. Cyrian has invited me out for dinner tonight. He told Albane that he has a meeting, and she fell for it. How daft can you get, believing he has to work right in the middle of the Christmas break. I'm feeling good; the plunging neckline on my silver dress would give a seasoned climber vertigo! I don't know where he's taking me, I just hope it's as far away from here as possible, I've had it up to here with badly dressed foreigners and my staff calling in sick. Edith Piaf's distinctive voice can be heard coming out of my bag. I grab my phone.

"I'm double parked, are you ready?" says Cyrian.

"On my way."

I put on my fur coat. It's real but I pretend it's fake, it's more politically correct. I give my instructions to the night receptionist. A customer eyes me up in the lobby, then looks away as soon as his wife gets out of the lift. She has a mouth like a duck and a bum like a carthorse, serves him right. I prepare for the biting cold that has descended on the capital. I stop short when I see a teenager with psychedelic hair loitering in front of the hotel entrance.

"You can't stay here," I tell her angrily.

The girl has pink, green and blue hair and black lipstick. She is wearing jeans, a thick winter jacket and Doc Martens. She has that cocky charm of youth. She has put a small bag featuring a skull and crossbones on the ground, in which I can make out a few coins. And she is drawing some stupid white bird on a dirty blue background right here on the pavement. Passers-by move aside to avoid stepping on her ugly scrawls.

"The street belongs to everyone," she retorts.

"You're putting people off coming into my hotel!" I shout.

"Making them dream more like," she replies nonchalantly, and carries on.

"You're disturbing my customers and you're messing up the pavement," I say.

"I need money to pay for my studies. I hope your customers are nicer than you are and that they'll respond to my art."

"What, so you intend to stay?"

"Are you nice and warm wearing that murdered animal on your back? It's freezing cold today. Tourists feel guilty seeing me shiver in the romantic City of Lights. I need some nice kind sponsors."

"If you don't move now, I'm calling the police."

"They are already swamped. Your clients were children once, I'm sure they read *The Little Matchgirl* and cried when they saw her imagining the fireplace and the roast goose before she froze to death. I'm no different from flower sellers on Valentine's Day or chocolate sellers at Easter. I have a job to do. You're in my way."

This brat is starting to get on my nerves.

"You're going to clean up my pavement or I'll kick you off myself," I say threateningly.

She looks up, surprised. She is quite pretty despite looking like a parrot.

"If you lay a finger on me, I'll sue you!" she exclaims.

Ever since Cyrian's father first warned me, I have been worried sick, expecting a phone call from his patient's lawyer any day. I can't sleep, I have red eczema patches on my neck, a cold sore on the corner of my mouth and heartburn. This is the last straw. I go into the hotel, grab the vase of roses from the middle of the lobby, take out the dripping flowers and hand them to the dazed receptionist telling her to put them in another vase. I go back out into the street holding the vase full of water. In my anger I forget all about Cyrian who is watching the scene through his tinted windows. He gets out of his car and walks over.

"What's going on?" he asks.

"I'm going to force this wannabe Picasso to take her artwork elsewhere. She deserves a real gallery, not my humble pavement, it's not up to her standards."

I hurl the vase of water over the chalky coloured mess. The blue sky or sea in the background blurs and then runs into dirty gullies. The white bird trembles for a second before vanishing. Petrified, the girl doesn't move. I grab her chalk and throw it into the street under the wheels of a passing bus; the chalk is crushed and scatters all over the road. The tarmac turns into a rainbow.

"Did you read *Jonathan Livingston Seagull* as a child? That was him, wasn't it?" Cyrian says to the girl.

Then he turns to look at me. "You're mad, what the hell did you do that for?"

"I want her gone!"

The girl wakes up from her stupor. "So, the stupid bitch should just fuck off, is that it?" she shouts. "Get rid of the street scum. Who the hell are you, to order someone off rue Monge, do you think you own it or something?"

I am submerged by an overwhelming wave of anger which has been building up for a while now. I have eaten dirt and crawled through mud to get to where I am now. It's been sheer blood, sweat and tears. I've had to sleep with people, starve myself, cut ties with my family, abandon my dreams. I pretend to be the chic Parisian but I'm a country girl at heart. My parents had a tough time making ends meet and no time to love me. My father wanted a son and always referred to me as "good for nothing" throughout my childhood. Now I can afford to eat in palaces they can only dream about, but I have no one to have breakfast with wrapped in a soft fleecy bath-robe. And Cyrian is about to go on holiday with his family. I walk up to the girl, who is hardly a candidate for a heart attack given her age, and scream at the top of my voice, "CLEAR OFF!!"

"What is wrong with you?" asks Cyrian, before apologizing to the girl and telling her she should leave.

His politeness infuriates me.

"You'd better not be here when I get back, or I'll throw you under a bus!" I scream at her again.

Cyrian drags me to his car.

"I feel sorry for you if she's your wife, sir," shouts the girl. "And I hope, for their sake, you don't have any children!"

I turn around, beside myself with rage, but before I can respond, Cyrian pushes me into the Porsche and slams the passenger door shut.

Cyrian, en route between Paris and Levallois

Here I am driving, my jaw clenched, sat next to this gorgeous woman who normally has such a calming effect on me, but who now appears to have turned into some kind of ogre. If I hadn't intervened, they would have ripped each other's throats out. Danny is *not* my wife I'm relieved to say, and we won't be having any children, thank God. She's just shown her true colours. Richard Bach's *Jonathan Livingston Seagull* was the jolt I needed. I don't believe in coincidences, Diastole. You gave me that book for my tenth birthday. I loved the story of the bird who was different from the others, who had a passion for flight that led to his quest for self-perfection. I used to be as free as him. Then I crash landed, losing both my feathers and my illusions in the process. I meant to give it to Apple for her birthday, but it's still in my office. I was going to ask my secretary to post it the day Systole phoned me to tell me you'd died. He was in a state, despite having dumped you in the nursing home, like Danny wanting to get rid of that street artist. I don't feel like eating or sleeping with her tonight. I want to be a kid again, the kid who dreamt of getting on a boat and following the migrating birds. When Sarah was ten years old, you gave her *My Sweet Orange Tree* by José Mauro de Vasconcelos. Each one of us had our own book, our own place to dream. Systole didn't read, he didn't have time, he spent his life poking around inside strangers' hearts, strangers who meant more to him than his own children.

"That kid was dirtying my pavement. Thanks for rescuing me," says Danny.

"It was her I was worried about, not you; you were like an evil harpy screeching at her like that!" I reply, not taking my eyes off the road.

She strokes my thigh and slides her hand towards my crotch.

"Please take your hand off, I don't want an accident."

"You're not going to make a big deal out of this, I hope. I could have lost revenue because of that girl. Let's just forget her."

How can you desire a woman in the morning and find her a total turn off in the evening?

"Your reaction was completely over the top," I say.

"She was being a public nuisance, besides her art was ugly," she retorts.

"I thought it was beautiful."

I think of the barge in Levallois where I booked a table for tonight. I think of the sailing school in Groix where I used to go with my sister, Sarah, who said I was a bad father. I think of my two daughters who I hardly know, despite them being the best things in my life, and I think of Systole who cheated on you like I'm cheating on Albane.

"Are you sulking?" asks Danny in a cajoling voice.

"What?"

"I asked if you were in a sulk," she says again.

This woman has hijacked my mind for the last two years. I would dream about her breasts as I ran my business. I would think about her bum as I was lying in bed next to my wife. Danny made me horny and high on life; I had needed that lift, to stop myself from imploding. I pull myself together. Right, we're going to drink, eat, shag, and forget all about this unpleasant incident.

Our table is right on the water's edge. A contented-looking man is fishing on a small boat a stone's throw away. Danny's beautiful eyes catch the glow of the fire in the hearth. Her skin is like gold satin and her silver dress shows off her figure to perfection. I'm a lucky man.

"Have you read *Jonathan Livingston Seagull*?" I ask, gently placing my hand on hers.

"I'm not keen on birds, they make so much mess everywhere," she answers.

Suddenly, the mirror cracks. Her skin-tight dress is vulgar. She has a cold sore on the corner of her lip. Her tan is fake. She hates children, chalk drawings, dogs and birds. The only thing she likes is herself.

Joe, Paris

We didn't know when Cyrian would see Danny again. So your goddaughter decided she would plant herself in front of the hotel every night. Yesterday, no show; she waited in vain. Today, she hit the jackpot.

"Mission accomplished!" she cries.

"How did it go?"

Esther has extraordinary eyes, a subtle sense of humour and a razor-sharp wit. She was a fan of the rock band Tokio Hotel. She had wanted to be a surgeon then a vet then a journalist. She has owned rabbits, guinea pigs, dogs and cats. She has just passed her baccalaureate exams with flying colours. She is interested in philosophy, sociology, and people.

"I pushed her over the edge, she went ballistic!"

"Tell me all about it!" I say, intrigued.

"I drew a seagull on the pavement right in front of the hotel entrance. She totally lost it. I used multicoloured hair chalk—washable hair colouring—and I wore gothic black lipstick. There was no way Cyrian would have recognized me, I haven't seen him in years. The last time was at Marie-Albéric's wedding, when I was ten years old. I wish I had been at Lou's funeral. I really liked her."

"I know you did," I reassure her.

Lou, your goddaughter put her heart and soul into the part. She did it for you, as a farewell.

"As for Danny, well she was trembling with rage. If her eyes had been loaded, she would have blown me to bits. She chucked water all over my drawing and threw my chalk under a bus. She would have thrown me under too, if Cyrian hadn't stepped in."

I can visualize the scene. Danny's blood pressure goes up. Her pulse increases. Her hypothalamus is stimulated. Her amygdala, the part of her brain that manages emotions, goes on autopilot for a quarter of a second. The blood flowing into the frontal lobe of her brain causes the fight or flight response. Cavemen used to respond in this way, it's nothing new. Then she regains control of herself. The brain's reaction to a fit of anger takes two seconds. But, in those two seconds, you can commit murder or flee after running someone over, or you can get a grip and respond rationally.

"I'm sick of Paris, I want to be on the beach at Cape Ferret," continues Esther on the other end of the phone. "I drew a seagull flying over the ocean. Cyrian asked me if I'd ever read a book by Jonathan somebody or other when I was little, but it didn't ring a bell."

Jonathan? That doesn't ring a bell for me either. My job as department head took up every minute of my time. Cyrian and Sarah enjoyed reading their children's books. You monitored them closely, and I had complete faith in you. When Cyrian was a child, he was fascinated by migrating birds. I remember you gave him a copy of *The Wonderful Adventures of Nils*, the story of a little boy who flies on the back of a gander. He must have remembered it when he saw Esther's seagull.

27th December

Patrice, Paris, the Marais district

We did live together once, so I know what Sarah likes. I push the door of her room open with my foot. "Breakfast is served, madam!"

She stretches and sits up in bed. She looks beautiful with her tousled hair. I put the tray on her lap. We are both stark naked. I won't go to the office this morning.

"Tea, toast, salted butter, marmalade."

"That's nice. I haven't drunk tea in years."

I had been hoping for an all-nighter, acrobatic, hot, steamy, and fun, but Sarah had drunk too much and collapsed like a dead weight. I just watched her sleep; I find her even more attractive than before.

"Forgive me," I say.

"For the tea, yes. For the rest, no."

She is fabulous. And I let her down.

"How are you, Sarah?"

"Okay, how are you?"

"I mean your health. How are you health-wise?"

She laughs mockingly. "Didn't I tell you? The idiots got it wrong. At first they thought I had a neurodegenerative disease that would worsen over time, a serious illness with no known cure. It turned out to be less serious than they thought. I just have a stiff leg, hence the walking stick, and I don't even use that unless I really have to. I'm as fit as a fiddle."

"But on the phone you said you were in a wheelchair!"

"I was joking, Patrice."

"So you're not ill, and you actually never were?"

She smiles sweetly. "No, I'm not ill."

I walked out on the woman I loved out of fear and cowardice. I dumped her for nothing! Our lives were ruined for nothing! I stare deep into her eyes.

"You could have told me."

She covers her toast in marmalade. "Why, would you have come back?"

"Of course. Does that mean you can have children too?"

"Yes."

"And no paralysis?"

"Nope."

I grab her tray, and put it on the dresser. I kiss her passionately. She pushes me away. I think it's a game, so I kiss her again. She pulls away.

"Fuck off, Patrice."

"Are you joking?"

"Do I look like I'm joking? Get out."

"Is this a joke, like with the wheelchair?"

"No."

"But now that you're not ill, we can get back together again, start a family, have a brother or sister for John . . ."

She lets out a horribly loud cackle that makes her look distinctly less appealing than a moment ago.

"You make me want to throw up, get out!"

She opens the drawer of her bedside table and takes out a pepper spray gun. She tells me that she will count to five and if I'm not gone by then, she will fire it at me.

"You're stark raving mad!" I shout.

"One . . ."

"So it was a trap, you just wanted revenge."

"Two . . ."

"Let me explain . . ."

"Three . . ."

I hastily pull on my clothes, underpants, trousers and shirt, tearing off a button in the process. I stuff my socks in my pockets. Where are my shoes?

"Four . . ."

She wouldn't dare would she?

"Five . . ."

She aims the pepper spray at me and pulls the trigger. I am blinded as I run for the door.

Sarah, Paris, the Marais district

"Your father is fucked up!" he shouts, slamming the door behind him.

I put the pepper spray down. I didn't actually pull the trigger, but I bet his eyes are stinging. I'm shaking but I feel liberated, happy to have unmasked this drooling slug that I mistakenly believed to be a decent person. What has my father got to do with any of this? If it weren't for him, or you, Mum, I wouldn't be here now. Thanks for bringing me into the world, Mum. Even though I have wobbly old legs and even though your friend, Thierry, didn't get my diagnosis wrong.

I go to the window. I see him running into the courtyard barefoot, foaming at the mouth. Dad says we catch colds through our feet. I grab Patrice's superb hand-stitched English shoes from a famous shoemaker and hurl them out the window. I'm rubbish at darts, or indeed at throwing anything, I've got a terrible aim. The right shoe lands on the concierge's roof and the left one hits Patrice on the head, causing him to yelp in pain.

"You are stark raving mad!" he roars as he picks it up. "Where's the other one?"

I point to the roof. He tries to jump up and reach it, but it's too high. You'd have to climb up through the skylight window from the inside. He bangs on the concierge's door. Nice try, but Josefina and Evaristo are in Portugal over the Christmas period. I close the window and chuckle to myself.

I look down at my carved wooden walking stick, my faithful friend through thick and thin; *we* won't betray each other.

I check my phone, no news from Federico. I start typing. "Are you free tonight? My meeting has finished, phew." Then I change my mind, and delete the message. "Are you free tonight? It wasn't really a meeting, more like a hostage situation." I delete it again. "I want to see you." Then I delete "to see" so it now reads "I want you." I delete that too. "When are you leaving?" I delete my message one last time and end up typing "1 2 3?" I press send. For the first time in years, I'm waiting for a man to respond.

31st December

Joe, Groix Island

Something unexpected came in the post this morning. Our son is a bright lad who doesn't beat about the bush, Lou. He couldn't be bothered to write himself, so he dictated a letter to his secretary. His letter doesn't start with "Dear Dad", "Dear Father", "Old fool", "Doctor", or even "Annoying old man". It simply starts "Dad". No term of endearment when he signs off either, just his signature. And it destroys me.

> *Dad,*
>
> *Pursuant to Article 815 of the Civil Code, no one has to remain in joint ownership against his will. I do not wish to retain the share of the house in Groix which I inherited from my mother. We shall not be going back there. I have discussed this with Sarah who has agreed to buy me out. We'll sign on the 3rd of January at the offices of Mum's solicitor. As he is the administrator of the estate, he already has the necessary documents. We will stay over in Lorient. I shall use the money from the sale to buy a studio flat in Paris for when my daughters go to university. Mum would have approved. I didn't have to tell you, but I thought it was only fair.*

And then the snotty-nosed upstart signs his name. Well, he's wrapped that up nicely. If he were here now, I'd show him what I think of his neat little plan. Conniving, pretentious, preposterous, grotesque, pathetic, sneaky, deceitful little idiot. You trustingly left him half of your share, Lou, not imagining for a second that he would want to part with it. That's what pisses me off. He doesn't need the money but he's pulling out anyway. He won't come back to the island to see Apple anymore. He is severing all ties with Groix with the surgical precision of a scalpel. How dare he say it's with your posthumous approval! The islanders refer to city dwellers who trash their beaches and pathways as "Colorado beetles". Your son is a Colorado beetle, Lou. Please tell me that this scumbag is not my flesh and blood, and that you cheated on me, my love. Please tell me that he is the postman's son.

My phone starts ringing.

"Hey, where have you got to, we're waiting for you in Port-Lay to start the party!" says Jean-Philippe, sounding worried on the other end of the phone.

He is an actor. He looks like D'Artagnan, and has an unusually deep and seductive voice. I was always afraid that you would fall for him, Lou. I just stand there, holding my phone. Is it that time already? The day has flown by. Maëlle and Apple are seeing in the New Year with friends. The house is silent.

"We've already opened the champagne. All that's missing now is you. Gildas and Isabelle, Bertrand, Fred, Jean-Pierre and Monique, Gus and Silvia, Renata, and Anne-Marie are here. Where on earth have you got to?"

"Tell your beautiful wife that I'm very tired and that I'm going to have a quiet night in . . ."

Jean-Philippe is not having it and threatens to haul me to the party by the scruff of my neck if I'm not there in ten minutes.

I jump into the shower. I pull on the first clothes I see and place a yellow "Joseph" on my shoulders. I am ashamed of our son, Lou. Your father was a decent, upstanding man living in his castle. My father was also a decent, upstanding man, living in his fisherman's cottage. Two honest, worthy men; I was honoured to follow in their footsteps, or rather in their riding boots and fisherman's waders. Cyrian has hurt me where I feel it most, my heart, my most vital organ. If you were here, Lou, you'd calm me down, you would plead his cause, saying how unhappy he is. I would say he's not a child anymore. He is cutting Charlotte off from her roots and spitting on the graves of her forefathers.

"Aaaaah, at last! Jo-seph! Jo-seph!"

The members of the 7 Gang welcome me with open arms. It's always so cosy and nice at Mylane's house. In Paris, where she was a pharmaceutical sales rep, her lab's drug sales went through the roof because of her smile. She was born on the island like Gus and me. She met Jean-Philippe at an evening do and happened to tell him that she didn't like big ostentatious parties because she was born on a small island off the coast of Brittany. He asked which one and she told him, convinced he wouldn't have heard of it. He replied immediately, "The island of Yann-Ber Kalloc'h?" He had recently seen a show performed by Kalloc'h about the poems of the famous bard of Groix who died in 1917 during the war. Jean-Philippe then recited some lines from memory, "*I was born in the middle of the sea, three leagues offshore, I have a small white house there, gorse grows by the door and the moorland covers the rest.*" Mylane was unable to resist.

We eat, we drink, we laugh together. When midnight strikes, couples kiss and friends embrace. Anne-Marie watches me. Lou, I hope you wished her Jacques a Happy Celestial New Year.

Sarah, Orly airport

My taxi stops in front of the terminal. I reread the text that
Federico sent me this morning for the twentieth time: "Meet
me at Orly terminal 3. Bring passport, cabin bag, red underwear and a warm sweater. Return tomorrow morning." The
first time I read it, I thought it was a joke. The second time, I
laughed. The third time, I was intrigued. The fourth time, I
cancelled my New Year's Eve party, put on some red underwear and packed my bag.

Standing there with a royal blue "Joseph" on his shoulders,
he takes my bag from me. "I've printed our boarding passes."

"Where are we going?" I ask, intrigued.

"It's a surprise," he says, grinning.

"I feel like I'm on a gameshow."

"Excuse me?"

"You know, like on those TV shows where the host takes a
guest to some far-off land without telling them where they're
going."

"I'm taking you somewhere iconic," is all he says.

I travel a lot for my work: Venice for the Film Festival,
Cannes, Deauville, Berlin, Toronto, Sundance, Utah. I
wonder if he's taking me to one of these cities . . .

"Will there be many of us there?" I ask. "Is it a traditional
New Year's Eve, with oysters and foie gras? Or some boho
gathering, with ethnic fare?"

"You'll soon find out," he says.

The pilot welcomes us aboard and announces that we'll
soon take off for Rome. Will we be seeing in the New Year at
the Colosseum, I wonder? In front of the Trevi Fountain? In
the ruins of the historical part of the city?

Apparently I'll be leaving on the seven o'clock plane back
to Paris in the morning, while he'll take the train to Venice for
a conference at the university in the afternoon.

"You're working on New Year's Day?" I ask, surprised.

"It's a New Year's resolution, but it won't last," he says.

The passengers around them are in a good mood and already asking for white wine.

"We have to look each other in the eye when we drink a toast," I whisper, making sure not to add "*or else no sex for seven years*", as you always used to say, Mum.

The cab drives us through the Rome night. I gaze at the billboards, the trees, the flashing lights. It is not as cold as in Paris.

"Are you doing an all-nighter?" I ask the driver.

"No, you're my last customers. I care too much about my taxi!" he exclaims.

Federico explains to me that at midnight tonight, Italians will throw old things out of the window to symbolize getting rid of the old year. This causes accidents, damages cars, injures people, knocks them unconscious. Not to mention the idiots who burn themselves with fireworks.

"Why the red underwear?" I ask.

"It's the tradition, all women wear it."

The taxi stops in front of an ochre coloured building bearing nine letters that cause my pulse to go haywire. We are right in front of the Cinecittà film studios, built in 1937 by Mussolini who intended to rival Hollywood! All the great directors have filmed here: Visconti, Rossellini, De Sica, Leone, Bertolucci, Scorsese. Fellini shot his films here in the famous Teatro 5 for over twenty years. The studios are closed of course. I expect the taxi to drive on, but it stops here. A tall young man who is built like a gladiator and looks like a film star comes to greet us, holding a bunch of keys.

He introduces himself as Rio and welcomes us in. Federico whispers to me that he is the grandson of Serena, Bertolucci's assistant director.

*   *   *

We walk in the dark, guided by Rio's flashlight. A giant head looms out of the ground, its bulging eyes level with the grass. It's a prop from the *Casanova* film set. Then we finally arrive at the place where it all began.

It's a mere hangar with a corrugated iron roof. A number five is stencilled inside a black circle above the door, and *TEATRO No 5* is written on the dirty wall. Rio hands Federico a basket from which the neck of a bottle protrudes. He takes a key, unlocks the door, goes inside, and turns on the light. The legendary *maestro's* studio is a shell, an immense icy hangar and a bare floor, lit by rows of spotlights. Its walls have seen the birth of magic, iconic actors loving and dying, snow falling, ships sailing, trains rolling, priests roller skating, the Trevi Fountain flowing. Arising out of one man's dream to wreak havoc with our emotions on the big screen, the films unspool, buzzing with intensity: *I Vitelloni, La Dolce Vita, 8 ½, Satyricon, The Clowns, Fellini's Roma, Amarcord, Fellini's Casanova, Orchestra Rehearsal, City of Women, And the Ship Sails On, Ginger and Fred, Interview.* I walk around reverently, clutching my stick, breathless and heady, surrounded by painted shadowy ghosts. Mastroianni doffs his hat to me. Anita Ekberg is stroking a small cat. Anthony Quinn is grumbling. Giulietta Masina wraps herself in her cape. This empty hangar should be full of extras walking back and forth reciting numbers. When the *maestro* died, his fans flocked here over three days to kneel in front of his coffin, which was carefully guarded by two policemen. They all came; Mastroianni, Scola, onlookers, extras, spectators, actors, producers, neighbours from Rimini, Rome and Fregene.

"1 2 3," says Federico, spreading a rug on the ground.

"1," I reply. This must be the most insane New Year's Eve I've ever had!

It's freezing in Teatro 5; thank God I'm wearing this thick sweater. Rio has gone now. Federico takes a bottle of fresh

Prosecco from the basket, plus two glasses, a panettone, two pieces of fruit tart, a steaming Tupperware dish and a plate covered with aluminium foil. He removes the foil and announces the menu.

"*Vitello tonnato*: cold veal with tuna in caper sauce, aubergine roulades, and chicory patties. And in the hot dish, there's *cotechino*, sausage with lentils."

I laugh and ask what's really in the Tupperware. He opens it. He was in fact serious! This is what Italians eat on New Year's Eve, they believe it brings them good luck for the year ahead.

He sets the volume on his laptop to maximum and places it on the floor. Nino Rota's music floods the abandoned warehouse.

"Would you like to dance?"

He's worried I may not be able to. I reassure him with a nod and tell him I can't dance the rock, but we can slow dance. We twirl around to the *La Strada* soundtrack. The last time I danced was with Dad in the covered market on the day of Mum's funeral.

"Thank you," I say, tilting my head back to stare up at the rows of spotlights in the rafters.

Firecrackers and fireworks go off at midnight. We make our way through the Cinecittà studios, travelling back in time. We hurry through the streets of Broadway with the *Gangs of New York*, wander through the ruins of ancient Rome, and discover the city of Florence during the early Renaissance. The cardboard scenery is lit up in blue, red, yellow, and green. We kiss each other passionately, like we did in my car on Christmas Eve, as the grand finale lights up the sky.

The Prosecco bottle is almost empty. The meal was delicious.

"Everything comes from my aunt Mirella's restaurant, Al Cantuccio," explains Federico. He then tells me about his

family. He is one of eight children, four boys and four girls.
He and his twin sister are the youngest. He teaches in the
north of Italy in Venice, while Giulietta teaches in the south
in Puglia. The other siblings are all named after famous
actors. He is only half Italian. Their mother was Irish; she
died four years ago. I tell him that we lost our mother recently,
and describe the house in Groix. I explain that I am buying
back my brother's share to pass on to my nieces since I won't
be having any children of my own. I don't want to risk passing on my illness.

"Do you regret being alive, Sarah?" he asks me.

"I wouldn't want to pass my condition on to an innocent
person."

"An innocent person is the opposite of a guilty person,
right? A guilty person has committed a sin. Is being ill a sin?"

"It's a sin to risk making someone you love ill," I reply.

"Maybe Teatro 5 will collapse. Maybe your plane will
crash, or my train will derail. Maybe we'll never see each
other again, or maybe we'll spend the rest of our lives together.
Who knows? Life is a risk," he says.

His words unsettle me. I tuck into the pear, almond and
ricotta tart. Federico puts his hand into the basket and digs
out some boxes with numbers on them.

"Tombola! It's a cross between bingo and the lottery.
Everyone plays it tonight."

What a strange New Year's Eve this is. I think of my French
lovers in their tailored suits nibbling their foie gras on toast
while sipping vintage champagne, checking the countdown
to midnight on their Swiss watches. While I'm sat on the floor
in a freezing cold hangar wearing red underwear and a giant
sweater, getting tanked up on Prosecco and playing tombola
after a meal of salted pork with lentils. Yet it is the best New
Year's Eve I've ever had. The temperature is far too cold to
make love though. I wonder whether Fellini, Mastroianni and

Gassman also played tombola? And if Claudia Cardinale, Gina Lollobrigida and Sophia Loren still wear red underwear and serve pork and lentils on the 31st of December each year?

He has ordered me a taxi for five o'clock in the morning as my flight is at seven. All later flights were full. Maybe the air hostesses also wear red underwear beneath their uniforms. I hope my flight won't be diverted to Mastorna due to turbulence.

"Perhaps Marcello left his cello there," he says.

Federico is clearly an expert on the subject. After triumphing with *8 ½* , Fellini dreamed of shooting a film called *The Journey of G. Mastorna*, but it was never made. All that remains is the script, written with Dino Buzzati, and a few test shots in which Mastroianni plays the cello in his shirt sleeves, wearing a hat, with a cigarette stuck to his lip. A few props and photos remain including the remains of a plane and trains as tall as buildings.

"Some films seem to have been cursed," I say. "Marcel Carné shot a film on Belle-Île that never saw the light of day either. It was called *La Fleur de l'âge*, and starred Arletty, Anouk Aimée, Martine Carol, Paul Meurisse and Serge Reggiani."

"Yes, Carné mounted twenty-five minutes of it, but the reels got lost."

"Wow, you know everything!" I say.

"I run the university film club which is full of film buffs; their enthusiasm is contagious."

I remember you always used to say that happiness was contagious, Mum.

1st January

Apple, Groix Island

We saw in the New Year with Mummy's colleagues and their families. We danced and we sang; it was really fun. I pour milk on my cereal. Tourists think that people from Brittany only eat crepes and that the women walk around all day long wearing headdresses. Joe joins me in the kitchen, with a purple "Joseph" on his shoulders.

"Are you coming to the beach to listen to the New Year's concert from Vienna on the radio, Apple Pie?"

I nod. You two always used to put on thick coats, hats and boots and you used to go together, Lou. The phone rings. Joe sounds relaxed.

"Happy New Year, Sarah!"

". . ."

"You were in Rome? Fantastic!"

". . ."

"We can't wait to see you, try and get here asap."

". . ."

"To Apple? That's very generous of you."

". . ."

"Your brother will be staying in Lorient. It's better that way, I would have had trouble stopping myself from throwing the little shit into the sea."

*   *   *

Aunt Sarah is coming, great! But what is she being generous about? Why won't Daddy be sleeping here? And why is Joe so angry with Daddy?

Charlotte, Le Vésinet

I heard them talking yesterday. They printed out the reservation for the hotel in Lorient. Dad went out for a jog. Mum is having a bath; she'll be ages.

I switch on the computer. I connect to the website and click on "Manage your reservation". They have booked a "Deluxe" room with twin beds and an adjoining children's room. The room comes equipped with Internet, a flat screen TV, a separate lounge area, and a safe. Dogs are accepted, so Oskar can come. The room is non-smoking and refundable with no cancellation charge, and breakfast is included.

It only takes one click to cancel the reservation. They send me an automatic cancellation confirmation. I move it to the trash folder and empty the trash in secure mode. Perfect. We no longer have a room reservation and I've covered my tracks.

2nd January

Joe, Groix Island

I always enjoyed having a tipple with you, Lou. Any occasion would do, whether to celebrate good news or drown our sorrows after bad, a candlelit dinner, a visitor dropping by, or family get-togethers. I place my annual order with the amateur wine club founded by our friends Georges and Geneviève. Some widowers buy small bottles so they drink less. But my grief knows no boundaries. I miss you every hour of every day; that gives me the right to drink for us both. But only in moderation. I've learnt my lesson.

A New Year's Day swim has been organized for today. If you were here, we could have gone for a paddle together. The Groix islanders are never idle, they organize events and create clubs and charitable associations for a range of causes including painting, cleaning fountains, protecting black bees, caring for and sterilizing stray cats, singing, playing music, saving *The Deer*, Groix's last tuna fishing boat with sails, and *The Raven of the Seas*, the last sloop lobster boat and a symbol of the resistance of Breton fishermen. We were also volunteers at the Groix International Island Film Festival, which takes place at the end of August every year. And now, like a buffoon, I'm all alone manning the Lou appreciation society: president, treasurer and member all rolled into one. Groix is known in Morbihan for its sculling race in Port-Lay, its swimming race across the Courreaux, the shallow waters separating Groix and Lorient, from Port-Tudy, and the annual January dip in the ocean organized by Jean-Louis, the owner of The 50 restaurant and his friend, Jacky. They came up with the idea after braving the water one New Year's Day. They chose a particular beach which is sheltered from the prevailing winds. It takes place on the second day of the year, so that we have time to recover from the New Year's excesses. We meet at noon. If it's not too cloudy, I'll go and cheer on my friends. If not, I'll stay here in the warm next to the fire. The sun comes out at quarter to twelve. Apple turns up, holding her bathing suit and towel.

"Are we going swimming, Joe?"

"No, not this year."

She stops, looking disappointed.

"Oh! Well I suppose you have to be careful at your age."

"Are you suggesting I'm old?" I ask, offended.

"You're always saying you're not twenty anymore," she says.

"I'm not eighty either," I snap.

I grab my trunks and a towel, and search for the keys to my moped. I hand Apple her helmet. Who does this cheeky rascal think I am? The beach is crowded. I spot the lifeguards with their triangular torsos, broad shoulders, slim waists and abs resembling one of those Lindt tablets of chocolate. Children are chasing each other, dogs are scampering, teenagers are smoking, their glowing cigarette butts sizzling in the cold. A Belgian tourist, Françoise de Mol, has taken a dip every morning since Christmas Day. Children have to be supervised by an adult. Jean-Louis and Claire have brought mulled wine. The bathers undress. Apple is shivering in her bikini. To warm up, we do exercises that boost our heart rate.

"Do mermen exist, Joe?" she asks me.

"I'm more of a sea god. An old-aged sea god," I reply.

Even if I drown, you will never be a widow, Lou. They give the signal and I run towards the sea holding Apple's hand. I go in up to my neck without letting go of her. The cold takes my breath away.

"Once you're in, it's not that bad!" shout the bathers, frozen stiff.

"Get in line for the photo!"

We hold each other by the shoulders, our teeth chattering. I feel empty without you, Lou, but standing together in a bunch warms me up. Brigitte from the local newspaper *Ouest France* and Bernard from *Le Télégramme* are snapping away at us. The mulled wine burns as it goes down. Apple dips her lips in it, then I rub her with my towel to warm her up. I wish you were here, Lou, you would have rubbed me down tenderly as if I were a quivering horse, while I whispered dirty words in your ear. Shivering, I pull my clothes on and place my sky-blue "Joseph" over my shoulders. I am one big mass of goose flesh and wet hair. I can just hear you now, whispering that I'm going to catch my death, and how daft I am. But Lou, I need to have stuff to focus on, otherwise I'm screwed.

I tell Apple I'm going to buy a boat and call it *Lou of the High Seas*. This winter dip has given me a new lease of life. *Lou of the High Seas*, yes I rather like it. Now, I need to repair myself, heal myself, rid myself of this leaden weight I've been carrying. I don't like golf or hunting, the obligatory leisure pursuits of every self-respecting cardiologist. I don't need to pretend anymore. I'll donate my rifle to one of my friends who hunts. I inherited it from my father, but I won't be using it again. The last time I touched it, I was trying to wrestle it out of your grasp.

3rd January

Cyrian, Lorient

I enter the hotel with Oskar at my heels.

"Hello, I've got two rooms reserved for tonight."

The young receptionist looks like a rabbit caught in the headlights.

"Err, I'm afraid we're fully booked."

"You can't be!" I say.

I show her my reservation. She taps away on her keyboard.

"Your reservation was cancelled, sir."

She tilts her screen towards me to prove it.

"There must have been some kind of mistake!" I protest.

"We did send you a cancellation confirmation," she says.

"I never received it. I am a regular customer of your chain, please sort this out."

"We have no free rooms, sir."

"Well then find me two in another hotel!" I snap.

"Many establishments are closed for the holidays, and there is an event taking place at the submarine base," she says.

A taxi stops in front of the hotel. My sister took the boat over to meet me here. She gets out of the car and I go outside.

"They've messed up our booking. We're on the streets tonight," I tell her.

"Come and stay in the village then, there's room at the inn," she says.

"No way!"

"Dad isn't going to bite your head off."

"Why, do you think I'm scared of him?" I ask.

Maybe the island isn't such a bad solution after all. I could pop to the cemetery to see Diastole while I'm there.

"Okay, we'll stay at The Marine Hotel then," I say.

"It's closed for the winter. There's nowhere to go but the house. Hope you don't regret selling it to me?"

"On the contrary, it's a relief."

We get into my car with Oskar and drive to the solicitor's office.

"Groix was once our little paradise. What's changed?" asks Sarah.

"Mum is dead. The island is her tomb. And Systole killed her. I see her everywhere I look. Besides, it's not like I'm selling my share to some shady developer, it's staying in the family."

"I'm gifting it to Apple by paying the inheritance tax up front," she says.

"Do as you like," I reply. "How's Dad?"

"Gutted," she says.

"That's impossible," I say. "The man is indestructible. He looks like a big, soft teddy bear, but remember that bear is a fierce creature with no scruples."

"How's Danny?"

"We're taking a break."

"Whose idea was that?"

"Mine. Danny went ballistic and started screaming at a young street artist who was sketching with chalk on the pavement in front of her hotel. She really showed her true colours that night."

To top it all, Albane gave my Barbour jacket away to a tramp because Oskar pissed on him. I don't believe for one second that Oskar was involved, but I prefer her benevolence to Danny's violence any day.

I would rather die than admit it, but I'm actually pleased to be spending one last night in my childhood home. I shall make sure I stay in touch with Groix via Anita's blog, where former islanders can log in when they're feeling homesick. I'm not quite in the same boat though because I'm technically now an ex-islander living in exile.

Apple, Groix Island

Here I am, waiting at the port. I see the boat in the distance, a white oblong on the grey sea. I say "Happy New Year" to the antiques dealer who has the same name as my grandfather.

The boat docks. Marie-Aimée gets off first with her grandson, Como. Charlotte is walking calmly beside her mother, but her eyes seem to crave adventure. I wonder if Albane has forgiven me for the bike episode? Daddy and Aunt Sarah are going to the solicitor's office this afternoon. Charlotte insisted on seeing me. We wish each other all the best for the New Year. Joe gave us the same bracelet but in different colours. I'm looking forward to seeing my sister again. Albane mouths hello to me with her lips. My arm tenses up when I see her.

Joe welcomes us in the kitchen. He is acting all weird today. I run to get the Christmas present I bought Charlotte. She tears open the paper and unwraps the orange fleece that matches her carrot coloured hair.

"You can leave it here, that way you'll have it every time you come, and you won't ruin your other clothes," I say.

"It's so cool, I love it!" she cries. "I'm going to take it back with me and wear it to school."

"I doubt a hoodie will go down well in your class, especially in that material," says Albane curtly.

Does she hate me because I'm Daddy's daughter, or because I'm Mummy's? Mummy says you don't have to like someone, but you have to be polite to them.

"Hey, open mine now!" says Charlotte excitedly.

I pull off the Sellotape and fold up the pretty wrapping paper decorated with stars, thinking of all the poor trees that were cut down to make it. It's an iPad, that's way more expensive than a fleece!

"It's amazing!" I shout.

"I wanted to get you a phone, but Mum said your mum wouldn't be able to pay the monthly bill because she's poor," says Charlotte innocently. Joe raises his eyebrows and Albane looks embarrassed. I look her right in the eye, making the most of my advantage in this situation.

"My mother works and looks after us without owing a penny to anyone. Can I go for a walk with Charlotte? On foot, I promise. We'll be home early, and we'll be extra careful crossing the road."

Joe smiles.

"I would prefer you to play quietly here," she says.

"They're safe enough," says Joe. "Their father grew up here and nothing happened to him. If you trust them, they'll prove themselves to you."

Albane glares at me. "Okay, I'm leaving Charlotte in your care," she says.

I nod and rush to go and put on a blue fleece. Charlotte puts her hoodie on and we set off.

I am alone with my sister for the second time. It feels like I have a new friend. Maybe one day we'll be a real stepfamily.

"We were supposed to spend the night in Lorient, but I cancelled Dad's hotel reservation," laughs Charlotte. "I hope we'll be sleeping at the house. Shall we take your bike?"

"I promised your mum we would walk."

"What's the big deal? She won't find out!"

"I gave her my word. Why was she so angry last time? Did you two ever talk about it again?"

"We don't talk; she tells me what to do and I do it to keep the peace."

I took her to the Pointe des Chats and Pen-Men last time. Today, we could walk to Port-Saint-Nicolas, the Pointe du Grognon, the Black Hole or the Hellhole.

"Is there really a place called the Black Hole?"

"Not officially, but that's what Joe calls the neighbourhood overlooking the harbour, where many of his former colleagues have had modern houses built."

"Who lives in the Hellhole, the devil?"

"Legend has it that once upon a time a monstrous sea god with a man's face lived there, he used to scream at night so that boats would break up on the rocks. He was redheaded, like you, and his chest was covered with scales and his back was covered with mussels and clams. He ate tons of fish and used to belch while napping. When he opened his mouth, seagulls would clean his teeth. His legs were fins, and his nails were shells. He used to mimic the captains' voices to sink ships."

"Have you ever seen him?"

I wonder what on earth they teach them in Paris schools.

"It's just superstition," I explain. "The real story is that in the olden days, after a wedding, the groom would have to prove himself by jumping over the Hellhole's rocky crevasse. If he failed, the bride became a widow on her wedding day. She had the choice between marrying a coward or grieving a brave man for the rest of her life."

"Do you think Dad jumped over it?"

"He got married in Normandy."

"Were you there?"

She may be top of her class, but she doesn't half ask some daft questions.

"I was only eight months old and I doubt very much that Mummy was invited. Do you want to go to the Hellhole?"

Everything is easy to get to in Groix. The island is only five miles long and two and a half miles wide. Hikers can do the whole thing in a day if they start early. I set out a few ground rules before we go.

"We walk on the correct side of the road, facing the oncoming traffic. Don't do anything stupid when we're there, like scaring the birds. And no trying to jump over the hole!"

"I promise I won't."

The sign is in both Breton, the local language, and standard French: *Beg an Ifern*, Pointe de l'Enfer, *Kumun Enez-Groe*, district of the island of Groix. The view from the cliff top is extraordinary. The foam from the waves flies up in the wind, the seagulls glide and swoop. But Charlotte is disappointed. There is no devil with a goatee beard, red body, forked tail and sharp hooves to greet us, brandishing his trident. The hole is merely a long crevasse in the cliff, with a pretty little path which leads down to the sea. But it's treacherous; the spot has taken many lives. There have been a lot of accidents recently, mostly fathers, healthy strong young men out walking who ignored the sign forbidding them to use the path. They thought they knew better, but then they slipped and the sea smashed them onto the rocks. I saw their pictures in the paper. I saw the helicopter hovering in front of the cliff, the firemen, the divers, the sea rescue boat.

"It can't be that dangerous, otherwise the footpath wouldn't exist," says Charlotte. That glow in my sister's eye worries me.

"You promised me you wouldn't do anything stupid," I say.

"I swore to leave the birds alone and not to jump," she says, walking towards the crevasse. "I won't get near the waves, I'm not stupid, but there's no harm in going a little way down to admire the scenery."

"The path is slippery, you'll end up smashed against the rocks. Those men I told you about are dead, Charlotte!"

How am I going to stop her if she tries to go down it?

"We'll come back with Daddy," I tell her. "He will tell you how dangerous it is. Do you know why he's in Lorient with Aunt Sarah?"

"Of course. It's for Lou's inheritance."

She has that stuck up, know-it-all look again.

"Dad won't be coming back to Groix again. He's selling his share of the house to Aunt Sarah."

I freeze on the spot. Charlotte points to her new fleece.

"That's why I can't leave this here, as there won't be a next time."

"But Lou is buried here, and there's me and Joe!"

"I heard him talking to Mum. He will arrange for services to be held for Granny. He's angry with Grampy. You're coming with us to the South of France this summer."

My head is spinning. So Daddy wants me to come to the South of France, okay. But I can't just leave Mummy, or the island. With Charlotte, okay, but with Albane, no. How can I leave Joe? Or Mummy? If I say no, Daddy will think I don't love him. If I say yes, Mummy will think I don't love her.

"You're wearing Joe's bracelet," I say, pointing at her wrist. "Would you really betray Groix?"

"I'm just a little girl and I have to do what my parents tell me. My mum made me wear the bracelet today, as it was a present from Joe but once we're back in Le Vésinet, I'll have to take it off."

"Why?"

"Because she's jealous of you, your mum and Grampy. She wants Dad and me all for herself. I won't get another chance to see the path so it's now or never."

She moves towards the hole. I grab her by the arm, but she pulls away sharply. I grab her again but she jostles me, and I wobble before regaining my balance. We're both going to fall down the hole and then Mummy won't have anyone to take care of her anymore.

"It's only a path, Apple, you're overreacting a bit. If every bride and groom from the past had died, there would be no one left on the island. Besides, they jumped, they didn't walk down," she laughs.

I panic. She is out of control.

"Maybe there's a pot of treasure at the bottom, like at both ends of the rainbow," she says. "Then your poor mum could pay for you to have a phone."

She is showing her other face now. It didn't take long.

"I have some other amazing places I want to show you, but you have to come now."

She is standing at the edge of the drop. I'm so afraid, I can't breathe.

"Charlotte, I've got a secret that no one else in the whole world knows."

"Okay, tell me," she says.

"I'll tell you if you swear you won't go down there."

I'm going to betray you, Lou, to save your granddaughter. It's worth it.

"Okay," says Charlotte, walking towards me.

I am so shaken up that my knees are trembling. I sit on the ground. She sits down next to me.

"You could have died," I tell her.

"I'm not scared of dying," she says.

"You mean you don't like life?"

"Not that much, anyway, what's your big fat secret?"

"It's about Lou, and the day we both got burnt," I reply.

"The cat knocked the *grek* over, what's so exciting about that?"

"I lied, it wasn't the cat," I whisper.

My sister thinks she's guessed it.

"What, you did it? You burned Granny? If Joe knew, he would hate you!"

I shake my head. "No, Joe would always love me no matter what. It wasn't me who knocked it over."

"Who was it then?" she asks, intrigued.

"Lou," I say, bowing my head. "She just lost it, she didn't recognize me, and I scared her. She pushed me away really hard and knocked the coffee pot over."

"Is that true?" she asks.

I nod my head in shame. Oh no, now I'm a traitor, I gave your secret away, Lou. I had to because Charlotte is alive and you are dead. I did the right thing. I stand up. My sister is out of harm's way now, Albane will get her back safe and sound.

"Come on, let's go to the Pointe du Grognon," I say, relieved.

Charlotte gets up too and stands on the edge of the drop again. "Thank you for telling me. I'll keep your secret. And I'll only go halfway down."

I'm stunned. "You promised me! I trusted you! I've betrayed Lou now!"

"Yeah, because you're gullible," she says, bursting out laughing. "I'm sick of being a goody-two-shoes who does what her mum says. From now on, I'm going to do what I want."

She places one foot on the path. "Look, it's not collapsing, the ground is firm."

"You'll slip," I say. "And I won't be able to do anything. Like with Lou when she pushed me away."

"In a minute, I'll be waving at you from the bottom. If it was dangerous, they would have blocked it off."

"They can't block off the whole cliff! Isn't the sign enough for you?"

"It's there to scare people," she says cockily.

"What shall I tell Daddy?" I ask.

She stares at me defiantly. "Tell him I may be younger than you, but I'm definitely braver."

She walks off and goes down the path.

I can't bear to watch. I've warned her, she knows what she's risking. Her mum will kill me. Daddy will hate me. A terrible thought then crosses my mind. If I'm all Daddy has left, he'll want to see more of me. He'll come back to the island to see me. We'll play the saxophone together on the cliff and pretend Charlotte never existed. I shake my head and brush these awful thoughts away. I won't let my mind think such bad things; Daddy has two daughters.

"Ahoy, I'm still alive and it's really nice down here!"

Charlotte has disappeared into the hole; her voice is muffled. I turn my back on her and walk off. Well, I can lie too. I'll tell Albane her daughter ran off and left me, and I don't know where she is. The sea won't dump her body for nine days. No one saw us. Daddy won't know anything. I'm not her babysitter. I don't want to die with her. I love life too much.

"Come and join me, it's amazing down here!" she calls out.

"I'm going back," I shout.

"No, don't go without me!" she yells.

Why didn't I think of it sooner? The only way to stop her is to threaten to leave. Without an audience, she has no one to show off to. It will take the wind out of her sails. I smile to myself. I will never be an only child; I'm very fond of my sister. Daddy loves me a tiny bit too. Albane hates me, but we can't expect everyone to like us. I've got Mummy and Joe. I will always have Mummy and Joe. And I've got you, Lou, even if I don't see you anymore.

"I'm coming back up, wait!" she cries, out of breath.

"What do I care, see you, bye."

Charlotte didn't fall, we're going home together, all's well that ends well. I see the top of my sister's head emerging on the path, and her red face. She's out of breath from climbing back up so quickly.

"I'm coming, Ap—"

Her foot slips. She flaps her arms and tries to catch herself. Her head disappears. She utters a long piercing scream that ends in a crash of broken branches. I shout her name and rush to the edge of the hole. I can't see her. I scream out her name again. "CHARLOOOOTTE!"

After what feels like an endless silence, I finally hear her faltering voice.

"Ap . . . ple . . ." she says, faintly.

"You're alive, thank you, thank you, oh thank you!"

I thank Poseidon, Neptune, and all the sea gods who didn't want her.

"I'm . . . not in the water . . ."

"Good! Are you hurt?"

"I'm . . . not far from the edge . . . It's very slippery . . . You were right . . ."

I can't go down and help her. If I slip down there too, no one will ever find us. I lie down on my stomach and lean over the hole, my head sticking out from the edge. I catch sight of her, an orange patch in the middle of a green patch. She has fallen flat on her stomach onto a bush that has caught her. She has great difficulty turning onto her back. I retch; some sick comes up. My sister hadn't zipped up her fleece. A broken branch has pierced her T-shirt and is sticking into her chest.

"There's a piece of . . . wood . . . stuck inside me . . ."

I've never seen a horror film but this is what it must look like. My eyes go blurry and then I pull myself together. This is not the time to crack.

"Don't move! I'm going to get help!"

She slowly moves her hand towards the branch. "Don't leave meeeee ... please! I'm going to take it out ..." she squeals.

"NO!!! DON'T TOUCH IT!!!" I yell, remembering what happened to poor little Tachi in Bhutan. Charlotte must trust me on this. I try to appear calm but my voice is quavering. Sweat trickles into my eyes.

"IT'S EXTREMELY IMPORTANT, CHARLOTTE, DO *NOT* PULL OUT THE BRANCH!!!"

"I don't want it inside me all my life!" she cries, terrified. "I don't want ... a tree ... to grow inside me!"

"Do you know the story of Joe and the little Bhutanese boy?"

"No ..."

"The little boy was hit by an arrow in the chest. It plugged the hole. His mother didn't know that though, and she pulled it out. Joe rushed over and put his hand in the wound and plugged the leak with his fingers. He took Tachi to hospital. The surgeon operated on him and he got better. He still writes to Joe every year to thank him."

"So ... go get ... Grampy ..."

I think she has got the message.

"I'll be back as soon as possible. Joe will save you. Do not touch that branch! You hear me?"

"If I die ... will I see Granny again?"

I mustn't cry.

"If you die, you'll have to eat Granny's cooking every day, so hold on!"

I rush out onto the road trying to remember my grandfather's drawings. The lungs are under the ribs. There is the bone that looks like a tie, I can't remember its name. And there's the heart.

Joe, Groix Island

I'm all alone at the house. Our children have gone to see the solicitor. I've got an ochre coloured "Joseph" on my shoulders today. Maëlle is working and Albane is shopping in the village and probably making sure she avoids the bookshop where Maëlle works. Brakes screech to a halt in the street, and a white Xsara Picasso stops in front of the house. A door slams. I look out of the window. Véronique, the daughter of Lucette, the famous maker of *tchumpôts*, rushes into the garden looking distraught. I may be retired but my doctor's instincts are still intact. Who is ill? Her mother? Her brother?

"Apple . . ." she says, out of breath. "At the Hellhole . . ."

My heart sinks. "Has she fallen?"

"I called the emergency services but I didn't have your number. It's Charlotte who fell and she has a branch stuck in her chest. Apple said to tell you it's 'like Tachi'."

Forgive me, Lou, because for a second, I thanked the heavens it was Charlotte and not Apple. I'm so ashamed of myself. If Apple had died, all the stars would have gone out. Without her, I would have given up on life. I should love my granddaughters equally, but I'm only human. I see one growing up each day, and hardly know the other one. Don't blame me, Lou. I'm going to save Charlotte.

"We need to hurry," I say.

Véronique drives. Despite the bumps, I manage to send a quick text message to Maëlle: "Apple OK, Chrltt fell down hellhole." I'm drenched in sweat despite the cold. Véronique skilfully avoids a pothole.

"The replacement doctor is on call," she says.

My colleagues Alexis and Faustine are on holiday. Shit! Apple said it's a Tachi situation. I only hope that the locum has already worked in A & E and knows what to do and doesn't touch the branch. The surgeon will take care of it in theatre. No one should remove it until Charlotte is on the operating table or she will bleed to death. A child has less than three litres of blood, and loses it at incredible speed. I think back to Pierre Desproges. *I don't have cancer, I'll never get it, it's against my principles.* I have to save Charlotte. I can't let my granddaughter die, it's against my principles.

Albane, Groix Island

There are only a few shops here. It's nothing like the Paris sales ... But as there are fewer customers, I quite enjoy browsing for once. I could replace the Barbour I gave away, which Cyrian has suddenly decided he misses, despite never wearing it! A sweater for Charlotte. A raspberry-coloured sailor jacket for me that I could wear on summer evenings in the South of France. I look at my watch. My husband and his sister must have signed by now, freedom at last. The girls will be back soon. We will cross back over tonight, stay in a plush hotel, visit the Éric Tabarly sailing museum tomorrow morning, then hit the road. This is the last time I'll ever set foot on this island. I would have liked Groix if Maëlle and Apple hadn't been here. I can see the cemetery wall on the other side of the covered market. I head over to say a prayer at my mother-in-law's graveside. We didn't have much in common, but if it wasn't for her, Cyrian and Charlotte wouldn't exist.

At the entrance to the cemetery, the silence is broken by the sound of sirens wailing. It doesn't sound like the ship's horn, it must be the emergency services. My shopping bags suddenly weigh a ton. There are just over a thousand inhabitants during the winter on this piece of rock in the middle of the ocean, that's three hundred and fifty families. But still I sense it. At that very moment I sense it, just as I sensed it with Tanguy.

My blood freezes. I drop my bags. People in the street move in slow motion. They turn to follow the ambulance with their eyes. A woman comes out of the bookshop. She runs towards me, and I recognize her, it's Maëlle. I've only seen her once, at my mother-in-law's funeral. I immediately knew she was a threat. Cyrian married me because I was pregnant. But he loved Maëlle who refused to leave Groix and go to Paris with him. He never stopped loving her. Now he takes comfort in the arms of other women. I know all about his affair with that slut from the hotel where his think tank meets. She's not the first. Before that, there was the bitch from the PTA. He shags them, but always comes home to me at night. My father used to cheat on my mother too. She said it was normal, because men's brains were in their trousers and that we should turn a blind eye or risk losing everything. I could have sworn that Joseph was faithful to Lou, but I was obviously deluding myself. I thought that us four, Cyrian, Charlotte, Oskar and I, were untouchable, until I heard that siren.

Maëlle catches me just before I collapse. I have no words, no tears, I feel nothing but fear. She takes charge and leads me away, and I let myself be taken. A kind teenage girl picks up my bags where I left them on the ground. Apparently her name is Azylis and Maëlle murmurs to her that she should just hold on to them for now. Every step is torture. She makes me climb into her Twingo. She fastens my seatbelt. My head sways, my neck can't hold it up any longer. I don't think of my daughter, I'm thinking about my mother. I see her hateful face, her delirious eyes, and I hear her cruel disgusting words over and over again. *I hope you will have a child and lose it.* I always knew that Charlotte wouldn't make it past Tanguy's age. This is my punishment. I left the ignition key in the moped. I didn't set the lock. By killing my brother, I killed my daughter too.

Maëlle drives, her eyes glued to the road. She is not as beautiful as Sarah, but she is still radiant. I had a beautiful little girl; life is about to take her away from me. Maëlle will see Apple grow up, love, blossom, choose her path. Charlotte will remain a child forever.

Goulven, Groix Island, the Hellhole

This is the first time I've had to replace anyone, and it's gone pretty well. I've mainly been treating patients for what I call "the-morning-after-itis"; problems linked to all of the late-night festivities this week. My colleagues, Alexis and Faustine, will be back tomorrow. There is only one thing I want right now, and that is to be curled up together under the duvet with my girlfriend and sleep for twelve hours. I haven't eaten anything yet; hypoglycaemia is giving me a headache. The paramedics called me just as I was about to bite into my sandwich.

I pull over, grab my bag and run to the scene of the accident. Paramedics who are still roped up have just picked up the patient and cut away her T-shirt. Damn, that's just my luck. The ginger-haired kid, orange fleece on her shoulders, and bare-chested, has a branch stuck in her torso, skewered like a Christmas turkey.

"I'm the doctor, my name is Goulven. What's your name?"

"Char . . . lotte . . ." she whispers.

The piece of wood is protruding from her thorax just below the sternum. My mind races, blowing chest wound, collapsed lung. I think heart wound, internal bleeding, acute tamponade, shock. I request a medical evacuation by helicopter to the hospital in Lorient. I put on sterile gloves and examine the child, take her pulse and blood pressure. Whenever I'm on call at A & E, for some reason it's always quiet, so I never see trauma victims and I don't learn a thing.

My girlfriend seems to attract them, she's lucky; patients flock to her when she's on call, consequently she has more experience.

Assisted by a young, very efficient paramedic, I put the girl on a drip to counteract blood loss from haemorrhaging and to avoid defusing the heart. It's always difficult injecting kids ... Hippocrates has got my back today; I succeed the first time. Phew, I'm doing okay so far.

"Is that your sister?" I say to the brown-haired girl in the blue fleece who doesn't miss a single thing. "Where are your parents?"

"Our grandad is on his way," she says quietly.

The paramedics tell me that the helicopter is about to take off. My patient is conscious. She is breathing normally. Her blood pressure is stable, her pulse is fast but that's because she's panicking. My IV drip is flowing perfectly. Everything is going well. Except that there is dirt and moss on the branch. It's going to infect the wound. I'm thinking septicaemia, pericarditis, pneumopathy. I reach my hand out. The kid in blue starts screaming like a mad thing.

Apple, Groix Island, the Hellhole

Dr Goulven is afraid, I can tell by the look in his eyes. He doesn't know the story of Joe and Tachi. I must save my sister. I scream and stand between him and Charlotte while the paramedics look on in astonishment.

"WAIT FOR MY GRANDAD, DON'T TAKE THE BRANCH OUT!!!"

"Get out of the way, little girl."

"No! It's plugging the hole like sailors plug holes in their boats!"

The doctor asks the paramedics to get me out of his way. Alexandre, the young paramedic, pulls me back and holds me down by pressing his hands on my shoulders. I struggle and scream again.

"PLEASE LISTEN! YOU MUST LEAVE THE BRANCH ..."

Everything happens within a split second. The doctor puts his hand on the branch and gently pulls it out of the wound. He finds himself holding the branch, which is brown at the top, and blood red at the bottom. At first, nothing happens. Dr Goulven places a sterile compress on the wound, then grabs a roll of sticking plaster. Charlotte seems reassured that she can no longer see the branch. I shiver as I think of Tachi. I remember when Joe asked me to help him plug the leak under the sink. Cardiology is like plumbing, it's all about pressure and leaks, flaps and valves. I remember your bookcase, Lou, and the story of *The Silver Skates* about the little Dutch boy from Haarlem who plugs a dike with his finger to stop the water from flooding the town.

Suddenly, the white compress turns bright red. The branch is no longer there to stop the bleeding. Blood gushes out just like it did when Tachi's mother pulled out the arrow. Alexandre lets go of me for a second, so I seize my chance. I slither alongside Charlotte and place my index and middle fingers on the compress to push it into the hole made by the branch, under the horrified gaze of the others. Alexandre starts to yell and Dr Goulven freezes.

A small stream of blood flows from the drenched compress. I grope around as if I'm under the sink, looking for some invisible leak. I have to plug the hole in the dike. The compress prevents my fingers from slipping on the gooey blood. No time to be afraid. I don't want my sister's heart to stop and have to be massaged while we sing "Staying Alive".

Cars screech to a halt. Mummy and Albane jump out of one, and Joe and Véronique out of the other. Joe sees my hand pressing on the wound. When Albane sees us her knees buckle and Mummy stops her from falling. I scream out to Joe without moving my fingers. "The doctor wouldn't listen to me, he pulled out the branch!"

"Bloody fool!" roars Joe.

The paramedic says that Charlotte is no longer bleeding. I found the hole, Lou! Joe and I exchange a look. The helicopter hovers in the sky above us; its rumbling fills the air.

Joe, Groix Island, the Hellhole

Apple has made a compression point at the exact right place. The heart is a muscle, and like any muscle under attack from a foreign body, it tenses up and constricts. The bleeding has stopped. Fantastic! The onlookers watch aghast. I am ecstatic; Apple is ashen faced. I don't believe in miracles, Lou. I don't believe that you are looking down at us, with fluffy white wings, jumping from one cloud to another. I am scientifically minded, hands-on, and pragmatic. We're all going to die one day, it's the human condition. But nobody is going to die *today*.

"I'm a cardiologist," I say. "Don't touch them! Apple has just saved Charlotte's life!"

My young colleague realizes he has made a dreadful mistake and turns white. The paramedics are there with their victim assistance and rescue vehicle as well as their off-road liaison vehicle. They know me well, I've helped them out many times before. I try and comfort Charlotte who is having trouble breathing and Apple who is red-faced with nerves and emotion.

The Lorient air ambulance, *Dragon 56*, lands. A doctor and a nurse get out and run towards us. My young colleague steps aside and lets me take over. I introduce myself and the emergency staff radio a status report to their supervisor. We cannot substitute Apple. If she takes her fingers out of the hole, the blood will start gushing out and Charlotte will bleed to death.

The paramedic attends to my granddaughter. She puts an oxygen mask on her to ensure she has a concentrated supply of oxygen. She regulates the intravenous flow rate and sticks electrodes on her chest to monitor her heart. Heart wounds bleed either throughout the thorax and around the lungs, or in the pericardium, the sack that surrounds the heart. If it's a severe gunshot wound, for example, the patient dies very quickly from haemorrhagic shock. If the wound is small, such as a stab wound or a branch as in Charlotte's case, the patient bleeds less, but may die of cardiac tamponade, as the heart gets compressed by blood trapped between the pericardium and the heart. Apple's fingers are keeping the hole plugged. Charlotte is pale and breathless, and has to be carried in a half-sitting position. If we lie her flat, the blood will put pressure on her heart and she could go into cardiac arrest.

"Don't move a muscle," says my colleague to Apple. "You're coming in the air ambulance with your sister and me. You hang on in there until we reach the hospital, okay?"

Brave little Apple nods. She has never flown before.

"I'm replacing Tachi's arrow," she whispers to me.

"I trusted her, and this is what happens!" moans Albane.

The helicopter takes off with the two girls onboard, siblings in the true sense of the word. I hug Albane for the second time in my life. The first time was when she married my idiot of a son.

"Tell me she's going to be okay," begs Albane.

"Apple averted a disaster," I tell her. "They'll operate on Charlotte in Lorient. We need to tell Cyrian; tell him we'll meet him there."

Albane panics and turns to Maëlle.

"Could you do it?" she asks.

*   *   *

Can you believe it, Lou? Albane just asked Maëlle to call her husband!

My sweater must have fallen off in Véronique's car without me noticing. I'm shivering and suffering from withdrawal symptoms without it. I go and get it and make a few phone calls. Gildas and Isabelle are not answering, but Jean-Pierre offers to take us to the mainland in his inflatable Zodiac dinghy.

Maëlle drops us off at Locmaria port where Jean-Pierre is already turning over the engine of his boat, the *Maï-Taï*. He makes us put on life jackets and sets our course for Lorient. Albane's eyes are sunken and she can't stop trembling. This is like a bad dream. Apple didn't understand the implications, she simply acted on instinct and it paid off. But the battle is far from over. Apple is keeping Charlotte alive. But everything will depend on the doctor who takes over when the helicopter lands. An orthopaedic or gastrointestinal surgeon might be brilliant in his or her field, but utterly incapable of dealing with a heart injury. For Charlotte to stand the best possible chance, she needs a cardiothoracic surgeon with the nimblest fingers possible.

Cyrian, Lorient

"Thank you, sir, that's that all sorted. We won't need to see you again," I say, shaking the solicitor's hand.

"I will though!" says Sarah.

She's actually alluding to the donation of her share of the house to Apple, but he takes it as an invitation to flirt with her and dives right in.

"We can have lunch together next time," he says in a dirty whisper. "The chef at Le Jardin Gourmand is a woman. I love women."

"That's very kind of you, sir. I'll bring my friend Federico along if you don't mind, he loves French cuisine," she replies.

That wipes the smile off his face. We leave soon afterwards.

"Federico?" I ask, a glint in my eye, pointing to her left forearm. "Will Giulietta be there too?"

She shakes her head.

"I meant the real Federico, well a real-life person, he's a film buff."

Just at that moment, my phone rings. I recognize Maëlle's voice, even though we haven't spoken in ten years. The ground feels like it's going to swallow me up.

"What's going on?" I ask.

"Charlotte has had an accident. She's gone to Lorient in the helicopter with Apple. Joe is making the crossing right now with Albane."

I can hear what she's saying but the words don't register. A piece of wood has speared my youngest daughter's chest? And my eldest daughter is keeping her alive? I can't breathe. I must get to the hospital. I would lay down my life for my daughters. If I hadn't wanted to flee Groix, if I hadn't tried to get rid of my share of the house, none of this would have happened. Charlotte wouldn't even be on the island today. This is my punishment.

"Joe has taken charge of everything. Love you," says Maëlle.

Her last words don't come as a surprise to me.

"Love you too," I say in a choked voice, before hanging up.

Our love has not waned over time, but we are like two fish who don't swim in the same waters. She is saltwater and I'm freshwater.

"I'm guessing that was Albane?" says Sarah.

"No, Maëlle. Charlotte has had an accident; she is seriously injured. They've airlifted her to hospital."

They're going to operate on my little girl, fix her, and save her. And I'm going to take time off to be by her side, for as long as it takes, I don't care. She's going to get well again. I can't even begin to contemplate what will happen if she doesn't.

Sandrine, Lorient

It was a mad scramble to get everything ready. It's all good, and I'm on top of things. The air ambulance has landed. The older sister has maintained compression during the airlift. I congratulate her on her courage and composure, and explain to her that I'm the anaesthetist and ask her to be brave for a bit longer. She has to come with us to theatre now without removing her fingers from the wound. We put overshoes on her before going into surgery. We're going straight into surgery and bypassing A & E altogether. We'll do a series of blood tests, including blood type, here in theatre, plus a quick ultrasound scan.

The older sister is trembling with fear and nerves, and her hair is plastered to her face with sweat. I smile to encourage her. Theatre is a scary place for a child. It's a big freezing cold room, full of people wearing face masks and surgical caps, and there are weird cables everywhere and machines making beeping noises. Surgical lights illuminate the table where we position the younger sister. I think about my three daughters safe at home before banishing them from my mind to focus on my patient. Luckily, she's got Claude, a very experienced surgeon who's not easily rattled. He has planned a left thoracotomy, a surgical procedure in which a cut is made between the ribs to reach the lungs or other organs in the thorax. This will allow him to do two things: open the pericardium to release the blood that is compressing the heart, and rapidly stitch up the wound while being careful not to touch the coronary arteries.

*   *   *

Claude, wearing green scrubs, surgical cap and overshoes, scrubs his nails and washes his forearms with soap. He rinses, dries and disinfects himself with a hydroalcoholic solution before entering the block with his hands held up so he doesn't touch anything. A surgical nurse helps him put on his sterile gown. She hands him gloves that he puts on without touching the outside and she ties the straps of his gown. I prepare my little patient by whispering in her ear that everything is going to be fine and not to pay attention to the noise around us. I make her breathe oxygen through the mask while stroking her cheek.

Claude is ready and gives me the go ahead. We ask the older sister to stop the compression and step back without touching anything. She checks that she has understood, that her role is really over, then she takes her fingers gently away from her sister's heart. A nurse takes her out and leads her through to the surgeons' scrub room to clean her bloodied fingers.

Meanwhile, in theatre, the race is on. Upon the surgeon's command, I quickly administer the contents of my two syringes. My little patient falls asleep while I intubate her. Claude paints her skin with an antiseptic solution and positions the operating tables. I haven't yet switched on the ventilator, but he has already made the incision. He puts a retractor between the child's ribs. Blood appears, less than what one might have feared, thanks to the unexpectedly quick thinking of her sister, but still. The suction brings it back with a sucking sound. Claude tells me what he is doing and reports on the state of her injuries.

"Pericardium decompressed."

"Small wound on the tip of the heart, two to three centimetres."

"Bleeding is under control."

"The lung is clear."

"How's she doing?"

I report that her blood pressure is increasing but that I'm going to transfuse her anyway, given how much is in the canisters.

The nurse assisting me took some blood while we were preparing the table. To be on the safe side, I ordered several bags of O negative before obtaining her blood type. The surgical procedure itself lasted less than an hour. But the little girl's body has undergone a severe shock. I monitor her hemodynamics by measuring her invasive blood pressure using a catheter in the radial artery of her wrist. I will keep her sedated to control her coagulation, continue the transfusions, warm her up, let her heart rest, check for complications in the heart, lungs and kidneys, and make sure she doesn't start bleeding again. If all goes well, I'll wake her up within the next twenty-four hours.

Joe, Lorient

Being a doctor is a double-edged sword. You save lives while dicing with death. We protect patients, but we know only too well the prognosis of diseases, including ours and those of our loved ones.

Claude, the surgeon who operated on her, explains that Charlotte had a wound on the tip of her heart with entry at the xiphoid process and transfixation of the diaphragm. I decipher his medical jargon, that special language which separates doctors and those with medical training from the average man on the street. He summarizes his surgical procedures and lists the possible complications. He is not a cardio specialist, just an old-school, experienced surgeon who has also done humanitarian work. Where a younger surgeon would have freaked out and transferred Charlotte to a specialized unit, wasting precious time, Claude didn't hang around. He opened up her chest to suture the tip of the bleeding heart. Just the tip. Charlotte was incredibly lucky; her lung was intact.

"Is my daughter alive?" asks a haggard-looking Albane.

"Yes, madam," answers Claude softly.

He has stitched Charlotte's chest back up. And her heart has been sutured. Now we have to wait. If everything goes well, she will stay in hospital for a week and her stitches will be removed after ten days. Assuming nothing goes wrong of course. If there are no complications, she will have a six-week convalescence period with respiratory physiotherapy.

"My daughter is alive?" repeats Albane.

Apple is trembling and her face is all screwed up. Cyrian holds her tightly against him without letting go of his wife's hand.

"Your sister is still sleeping," says Claude to Apple. "You should take your mummy to get something to eat. I'll update you later."

Apple nods, not bothering to point out that Albane is not her mother.

I order hot chocolates from the local café, but no one drinks them. Thanks to my Dumbo ears, I'm able to listen in on three conversations at the same time. Cyrian calls Maëlle and updates her. Sarah phones a friend, and Albane keeps repeating that her daughter is alive, and blaming Apple for putting her in danger.

"You should congratulate her instead for having stopped the bleeding," I say.

"Congratulate her, Grandpa?" chokes Albane. "After she forced Charlotte down that treacherous footpath? When she tried to kill my daughter?"

Apple tips her chair over as she gets up and runs out. Sarah goes after her.

I've tried to change things, Lou, but I've only succeeded in making them worse. Now Charlotte is lying in intensive care seriously injured and Apple is hurting. I'm hopeless at managing this family. You should have married the guy with the spiky hair and brown eyes.

My phone rings. All conversations come to a halt as Claude announces that we can see Charlotte.

Lou, on the other side

There was nothing I could do to help you. I stood there, petrified and frustrated, watching you struggle. I was so scared for Charlotte and totally in awe of Apple's courage. You make a great patriarch, my *piroche*. Thanks to you, our children were starting to find their way, until Charlotte fell down that hole. She's only nine years old, she's tough, she's in great shape. She will make it, won't she?

Joe, Lorient

Charlotte is under sedation and intubated. Cyrian and Albane wash their hands before putting on scrubs, masks, gloves, and overshoes. Petrified and distraught, they tiptoe into the unit. I'm also in scrubs and stand back to give them space. Sandrine, the anaesthetist, tries to reassure us. While Cyrian and Albane look on in horror, she explains what the tubes are for: intravenous drip, urinary catheter, blood pressure, intubation of the airway. Charlotte's eyes are kept closed to protect them. She has large bandages on her left side from which protrude thoracic catheters, which for her parents are merely large tubes filled with blood. She is artificially sedated to rest her heart. She is not in pain. Though she can't answer, she can potentially hear her parents. Sandrine advises them to talk to her normally, and to touch and caress her.

"Don't hesitate if you have any questions whatsoever," she says softly.

"My daughter is alive?" repeats Albane like a sleepwalker.

Sandrine explains it all again, but Albane isn't listening and Cyrian can't remember anything after five minutes. It's all too frightening for them. The first post-operative tests are okay. Charlotte's coagulation is almost back to normal after the transfusion, her blood gases are normal, and she has no contraction problems following the post-operative echo-cardiogram.

Albane, who has just aged twenty years, takes her sleeping daughter's hand. Cyrian stands on the other side of the bed. I leave them to it and go and find Sarah and Apple. Children under the age of sixteen are not allowed in the recovery ward of the ICU.

Every morning when I wake up on the island, I look out towards the sea. It's visible from just about everywhere, and when it's raging and the wind answers, it can be heard from just about everywhere too. In Paris, however, I would wake up to the sounds of traffic streaming down Boulevard Montparnasse, car rather than boat horns filling the morning air. When I'm in a train station, I'm lulled by the streams of passengers walking past, the sound of boat shrouds rattling replaced by the squeaking of suitcase wheels. And when I'm in a hospital, I'm lulled by the familiar sounds and smells which make me feel at home.

Sarah has sent me a text message from Apple: "Charlotte isn't going to join Lou, is she, Joe?"

I reply: "No, she's going to get better really fast. Thank heavens you were there!"

I find them outside and Apple leans against my shoulder.

"Did everything go okay at the solicitor's?" I ask Sarah, to break the heavy silence.

"We prepared the documents for Apple," she says.

"For me?" says Apple, looking at her aunt in surprise.

"Imagine that the house in the village is a pie," replies Sarah. "The pie belonged to Joe and Lou. Joe still has his share, but Lou's was divided in two, half for your father and half for me. Your father has sold me his half. And I'm giving it to you. Do you follow me?"

"You're giving me Daddy's half that was half of Lou's pie?" asks Apple, stunned.

"Yep."

"You should have given it to Charlotte to make her come back to the island," says Apple.

After a lull, Sarah turns to me. "I saw Patrice again."

I feign astonishment.

"We broke up ten years too late. Now I can see him for what he is and I feel liberated."

"Was that him on the phone just now?"

"No," she replies. "That was my Italian friend. I spent New Year's Eve with him."

"What about your rule? Never seeing a guy more than twice?"

"This is a bit different," she says. "I'm not seeing him properly yet, err . . . in the biblical sense. We're not yet . . . so I can see him again. He isn't my usual type. He's got a film reel for a heart. He makes me feel like I have the star role, not just relegated to the wings. Will Charlotte go back to Le Vésinet when she's strong enough?"

"Her parents will decide depending on the surgeon's advice. The first few days will be decisive. When she gets out, she will go to a rehabilitation centre. She would be better off in Groix, with plenty of fresh air and a personal cardiologist on hand, but they will most likely want to take her home," I say.

"I was supposed to see Federico in Paris tomorrow, but I would prefer to stay here until Charlotte is out of danger. I've invited him to Groix for three days, do you mind?"

Technically, Sarah is as entitled to stay here as I am, she can invite anyone she likes. But Charlotte nearly died. This is not the time to be inviting guests to stay. Just as I'm about to say this, her phone rings. She walks off, standing very straight, without leaning on her stick.

"She's allergic, Joe," says Apple.

"To what?" I ask. "Does she have a rash, red spots that itch?"

"Sarah is allergic to hospitals because of her illness. If she has to go inside one, someone has to go with her. Daddy has Albane, me and Mummy have you, but Sarah has no one."

This kid is years away from going to medical school, but her natural intuition means she's already streets ahead of me.

"Is Sarah's friend a priest? she asks.

"Why would you think that? I ask, surprised.

"Aunt Sarah talked about knowing him *in the biblical sense . . .*"

Charlotte almost bled to death and Apple saved her life. She could have gone into cardiac arrest during the airlift or in theatre. The surgeon and the anaesthetist saved her. Now it's just a matter of being patient. And this is the first time that Sarah has invited a man to the island since Patrice. I feel better for a thousandth of a second, until it hits me. Federico will recognize me; he'll remember that I told him about Sarah's tattoos in Le Vésinet and that I encouraged him to invite her to dinner. Sarah will feel manipulated. She'll dump him and sever all ties with me. And then I will have lost both of our children.

Apple, Lorient

I'm taking the last boat back with Joe, Aunt Sarah and Oskar. Joe told the 7 Gang that Charlotte is in hospital. Some of them have flats in Lorient that they offer to lend him, so Daddy and Albane have got somewhere to stay for the night now. We're going back to the island because I have school tomorrow and dogs are not allowed in the hospital. Joe spoke to the doctors, then he explained to Daddy in simple terms what they had said. Daddy was so exhausted, he just said, "Thank you, Systole". Joe frowned and Sarah grinned. Daddy then admitted he had been calling Joe that for years. In the waiting room, Albane is still looking daggers at me. She thinks I made Charlotte go down the Hellhole. I can't drop Charlotte in it, I'm not a grass, so I go up to her to try and say something comforting.

"Charlotte is very strong, she'll get better quickly," I whisper.

"It's all your fault," she whispers back fiercely.

Daddy doesn't hear her, and puts his big arm around my shoulders as if his body is Joe's sweater. He takes me aside.

"You were exceptionally brave, Apple. Tell me what you'd like, and I'll make sure you have it."

I hesitate, even though I know exactly what I'd like.

"What would make you happy? A trip? A TV? A mobile phone?" he asks.

"I want Charlotte to recover here in Groix with us. Joe will look after her. We'll all be together."

Daddy lets out a big, long sigh.

"No! I meant something I can buy you. Charlotte will go back to Le Vésinet as soon as she's well enough to travel. I'll go into the office every day but will come back early to be with her. You can come and spend the February half term with us if your mum agrees."

"You said I could have whatever I wanted," I insist. "Charlotte won't be going back to school right away. And Joe is a cardiologist, he will look after her really well. Plus, she would be breathing in clean, healthy sea air."

"Albane will never agree to it, Apple, you'll have to choose something else. Besides I have a business to run, I can't stay on the island."

"You could come back every weekend," I suggest.

"I doubt that Systo . . . that your grandfather would agree to it. Things are not good between us right now. He won't want us in his house."

I try absolutely everything to get him to agree. Then I play my trump card.

"I understood what Aunt Sarah said. You sold her your piece of pie from the house and she has given it to me. So I'll be staying in my own house. And I can invite my sister if I want."

Daddy opens his mouth, but nothing comes out.

"If it's Mummy that bothers you, we can go to Locmaria," I add. "You said I could have anything I want, Daddy, and this is what I want!"

I wish he would hug me, but his arms just dangle by his sides, like they did at your funeral, Lou. And I don't dare touch him.

4th January

Joe, Lorient

I enter the airlock leading to the ICU with the others, thinking about the candle I lit for Charlotte this morning in church. My mother used to perform this ritual every time my father went on a fishing trip. She kept it up even after his boat came back without him, as if the flame would keep him warm somehow.

Charlotte had a bad night, which is to be expected because the first three days are the worst. Jean-Pierre drove me and Sarah to Lorient in his Zodiac dinghy. When we arrive, she takes two bottles out of her bag.

"This is a gift for Charlotte from Apple. She bought sterile bottles from the pharmacy and filled them with sand and sea water," she explains.

How thoughtful of Apple, and she even remembered what I told her about the risk of infection. The bottles won't be allowed into the ICU, but Charlotte can have them in two days' time when she is moved to the cardiology ward. Providing all goes well and there are no complications of course.

The anaesthetist joins us in the airlock while we put on our scrubs. She tells us that the tubes assisting Charlotte's breathing were removed this morning. Due to her thoracotomy, she was in a lot of pain when she came round, but she's smart for her age and the pain management consultant was able to accurately assess the degree of pain relief for her. She has a standard drip morphine pump with a booster if needed. She says Charlotte must be hungry because she was asking for an apple, which is a good sign. I clear up the misunderstanding: Charlotte doesn't want fruit, she wants her sister.

No more than two people are allowed in the ICU at one time. I join Cyrian, Albane comes out and Sarah takes her for a coffee. I catch my son's eye. This brush with death means we have temporarily put our differences aside. I check the equipment: the monitor, the IV drip, the drainage catheter. Charlotte is breathing on her own, floating somewhere, high on morphine.

"You're at home here, aren't you," whispers Cyrian. "It's completely thrown me and Albane. It's completely alien to us."

He can't admit in front of his daughter that he is frantic with worry, but I can see it in his face. I reassure him that I saw the anaesthetist, and everything is fine. Then I go up to Charlotte.

"My little apple Charlotte, Apple isn't allowed to visit you, so she is working really hard in school thinking about you. Don't worry about Oskar, he's with us, but he's been looking everywhere for you. Do you know how to work the pump, if it hurts?"

My granddaughter can't open her eyes, but she wiggles her finger. She heard me.

Cyrian comes out and collapses on the bench in the airlock. He tears off his mask and gloves, and wipes his eyes with the sleeve of his green gown. He used to cry at the drop of a hat when he was little, while Sarah just gritted her teeth. I haven't seen him cry in ages, except for the day you left us, Lou.

"This is my punishment isn't it, for selling my share of the house, fate is taking its revenge on my daughter. It's over with Danny, Dad. Why is this happening to us? What has Charlotte ever done? She's only nine years old for God's sake! At her age, you just graze your knees or break a tooth. You don't have heart surgery!"

"She's alive, Cyrian," I say.

"If it wasn't for Apple . . . I have never been there for her. I'm a lousy father and a lousy husband."

I tell him to devote his energy to his daughters and wife instead of wallowing in self-pity.

"If there are no complications, they say Charlotte will be out of the ICU the day after tomorrow," he says. "She'll start her rehabilitation four days after that. Do you remember where Sarah was in Le Vésinet, at the hospital in Avenue de la Princesse?"

"Vaguely," I say.

"Do you think it would be good for Charlotte there?"

"I'm sure it would be," I reply.

"Will she make it? We've already lost Mum . . ." he whimpers.

I put my hand on his shoulder. We haven't touched each other in years. We didn't even hug the day we lost you, Lou.

"She'll be fine. She's got Breton blood in her veins."

He rolls up his jacket sleeve; he's wearing your father's watch, Lou.

"Sarah gave it to me on your behalf," he says.

In our family we're too proud to say thank you. We tend to clash rather than reach out.

Albane, Lorient

"What can I get you?" asks my sister-in-law, counting out her change. "Espresso? Cappuccino? With or without sugar?"

"Tomato soup," I mumble.

Our life has been shattered. Normally we would be back in Le Vésinet by now. Charlotte should be at school. Cyrian should be at work or busy hooking up with his slut. I should be planning dinner, making Charlotte's tea, taking Oskar out . . . Oskar number one, Oskar number two.

Sarah tells me Apple has a present for Charlotte. She shows me two bottles and a letter:

Dear Sis,

Even though Daddy didn't do a paternity test, you are my sister and I think about you all the time. I'm not allowed to see you. I hope you're not in too much pain. Joe says they're giving you something called more-fean, and that there's no telly in the ICU. So I'm sending you a portable beach I made myself. I keep thinking of you in the bush and can't get it out of my mind. I miss you. I'll send Boy and Lola to say hi to you.

Love, Apple

"What a sweet message from one sister to another," says Sarah. "Who are Boy and Lola, are they friends from Lorient? And what's all this about a paternity test?"

I grab the bottles and throw them in the rubbish bin next to the coffee machine.

"May I remind you that Apple nearly killed Charlotte!"

"And may I remind *you* that Apple saved her!" Sarah shouts back.

"You're only defending her because you have no children of your own and you don't understand. Why don't you have children anyway? You don't want to or you can't?"

Normally I wouldn't broach such a delicate subject with my sister-in-law.

"I don't want to risk making a child suffer. Besides, I haven't found anyone to settle down with yet," she replies calmly.

"Well, on the contrary, I took the risk of bringing a child into the world when I knew I had a chance of losing her."

"What do you mean?"

"My little brother, Tanguy, died after being hit by a lorry. He was riding on my moped. I have to live with his death on my conscience. My mother was so grief-stricken that she put a curse on me. She willed me to have a child and to lose it, so I would feel her pain."

Sarah looks at me, shocked. The tomato soup burns the roof of my mouth, and the pain reminds me that I'm still alive.

"I hear my mother's voice in my nightmares. Every night since Charlotte was born, I hear her evil words as I fall asleep. I used to take refuge in Cyrian's arms. Now I'm scared all the time and lie awake. The curse looms over us, because I decided to take on fate."

"Well, it appears that love is stronger than hate, because Apple broke the curse by saving Charlotte."

I refuse to listen to her defend Apple. That girl is poisonous and dangerous.

"She took Charlotte out on her bike during the last school holidays and she forced her to go down that path yesterday. My daughter would never have done such a thing, she's too timid. My mother put a curse on her and Apple's jealousy almost finished things. I will never forgive her, or myself for that matter."

Cyrian, Lorient

Neither of us has an appetite. When Albane and I left the ICU, Charlotte was asleep, knocked out by the morphine. We left her after checking at least ten times that they had our phone numbers. I would love to have held her tightly against me, but all I could do was touch her cheek with my gloved hand and smile at her behind my mask.

"I'll look after her. I know how to deal with little girls, I have three at home," says Sandrine, the anaesthetist.

*   *   *

I collapse onto the bed. One of Joe's friends lent us this place. We stayed here last night too and got back so exhausted that we didn't even speak before we both crashed out. Albane is perched on the sofa, looking bizarre and awkward like a distant relative at a family gathering. I wish I could just fall asleep, curled against her, touching her skin, and wake up to discover that this was all just a bad dream.

"We need to talk," she says in a small voice. "It's long over-due. We should have had this discussion after that first tart."

I look at her bewildered.

"I know all about the slut from the PTA who had a voice like Minnie Mouse. And I know about the slag from the hotel."

Can it get any worse? I'm worried sick for my daughter who is hooked up to all sorts of machines and wires, and is being cared for by strangers. I'm totally exhausted, I don't need this. I don't want to get Danny involved, today of all days.

"This is really not the time or the place for . . ."

"It's been over for a long time now," she says wearily. "Let's put all our energy into Charlotte. And we'll deal with the rest afterwards."

"What does that mean?" I ask in dismay.

"I mean it's time to bring down the curtain. Show's over. I'm done with play-acting and pretending."

Yesterday, I had a family, a loving wife, a beautiful little girl. In the space of one day, I have lost it all. My daughter is bleeding from the heart. My wife is leaving me. You said in your will that Systole betrayed you, Mum. Why didn't you leave him?

"You and Charlotte are my most precious possessions," I plead.

Apple too of course, though this is hardly the right moment to mention her. And Oskar, whom I miss more than I thought I would.

"You're sleeping on the sofa and I'm in the bed. This conversation is over. We'll continue it when Charlotte is out of hospital. *If* she comes out."

I shudder. Albane looks anguished.

"I killed my brother, Cyrian."

"That's not true," I protest.

"And our daughter almost died because of yours. So just shut up!" She's shouting now. "We will continue to live together and raise Charlotte if God doesn't take her from us. But you're dead to me."

"It's over with that other woman. I swear."

"I don't give a damn."

She goes into the bedroom. I stand there in a daze, staring at the empty sofa like an idiot. I grab a bottle of gin from the kitchen and pour myself a glass. I knock it back neat, with no ice, just to numb the pain. Then I put it back in the cupboard. I need to be able to drive should the hospital call.

If I had Baz with me, I'd play until dawn. I have to convince Albane to forgive me. Forgive me for giving up the saxophone, forgive me for becoming a bad person, forgive me for falling out of love with her. When Charlotte is better, I'll go back and see the solicitor and I'll make sure that my daughters and their mothers are provided for. Then I'll get out of here, as far away as possible.

5th January

Joe, Lorient

I arrive in the airlock as Cyrian comes out of the ICU. He throws his overshoes in the bin. His face is furrowed, and he has gone an odd grey colour.

"Charlotte is in pain, they've increased the morphine."

"It's the thoracotomy," I tell him. "The pain will lessen."

He feels her suffering, his nostrils are twitching.

"I had it out with Albane last night," he says.

"Does she know about Danny?"

He nods.

"Does she want a divorce?"

"She wants to blot me out, pretend I don't exist."

The only advantage of being a widower is that you no longer have to partake in domestic squabbles like this.

"I wanted to thank Apple for her bravery," Cyrian goes on. "I asked her what she would like me to get her. I was expecting her to say a TV or a phone, or something like that . . ."

"Did she ask you to come to the island more often or to get back with her mother?" I ask.

"I still love Maëlle, Dad, but we are *not* compatible, like the water and oil after the sinking of that tanker, *Erika*. I always hoped Maëlle would change her mind, and that she would join me in Paris. I mean you dared leave your precious island to go and study in Rennes, didn't you?"

"I had no choice, old chap, as far as I know there are no medical schools in Groix."

"You could have gone back there afterwards, instead of parading around in that Parisian hospital."

"I wanted to impress your mother. So, what did Apple choose as a gift?"

"She doesn't want a TV or a trip. She wants Charlotte to come back to Groix for her rehabilitation and to be looked after by you. I've been thinking about it. I'm going to stay in Lorient while she's in hospital. Then she'll go to your house, where she'll be safe. I'll miss her but I will come back every weekend."

I can't believe my big Dumbo ears.

"I would be more than happy to look after her! What does Albane think?"

"She's not talking to me anymore, I'm the invisible man. She'll agree if the surgeon thinks it's a good idea. I'll come down every Friday night on the train."

"I'll be able to pick you up. I'm going to buy a small boat; I've seen some for sale at the port," I tell him.

"I can contribute to the cost if you like."

"Stop flaunting your salary, it's very aggravating! I'll come and get you, no arguments. It's a shame your mother isn't here anymore, she would have been able to make Charlotte some decent meals."

I think I went a bit far, Lou, but Cyrian is hugging me. We stand there like two idiots, clinging to each other. We are full of tears and laughter, and memories of your culinary disasters mingled with sorrow and love for you.

Apple, Groix Island

Last night I dreamt that I squeezed my sister's heart so hard that it burst like a balloon. I've been practising my saxophone every day since the beginning of November, except the day Charlotte fell down the Hellhole. Today I am rehearsing with the Tuna-Cats band, which is composed of about thirty musicians. They're mostly women. The children play the trumpet and trombone. Fred, Joe's artist friend who does the dinners for the 7 Gang, is playing the cornet. Yves switches from saxophone to piano. They rehearse a piece called "Bésame mucho" that I don't know, then "Ain't She Sweet" which "swings real good" as Charlotte would say. I play "Saint James Infirmary Blues" with them, which is an American folk song. Some tunes are happy like "Tequila", "Mirza" or "Titine". Others give me goose bumps, like "Le Temps des fleurs" and especially "Amazing Grace", which I taught myself to play. I think of Lou and feel all sad. I also think of Isabelle who lived in Groix. Her husband shot her with his rifle. She wrote a funny, beautiful book called *The Big Feet Tribe and Other Stories*. Children from school did drawings to go with her text. I think of the teens from the mainland who came to spend the night on Red Sands Beach and whose campfire set off a wartime bomb. It killed one of them and wounded another. Music makes me feel strong. When I play I'm not scared of that evil look Albane gives me because she thinks I nearly killed Charlotte. When my left hand plays the top notes on the saxophone, I'm helping Charlotte's heart keep on beating. When my right hand plays the lower notes, I'm helping her lungs work. When I blow into the mouthpiece, she runs after Oskar. The night Daddy said I could have anything I wanted, I nearly said "a saxophone".

I go home. Mummy thinks I was at choir practice. I've had a tummy ache since Albane started blaming me for nearly killing Charlotte. Hey, if it's an appendicitis, they might airlift me to hospital and put me in the same room as my sister!

Joe and Sarah are back from Lorient. I tell Joe I need an operation. He asks me to lie down and rubs his hands to warm

them up before pressing them down hard on my tummy. He
asks me to bring my thigh up against my stomach, then he
asks me to walk. He diagnoses a serious attack of the blues. He
prescribes me a Nutella crêpe. I make sure Oskar gets a piece.
On the day of the accident, the poor thing stayed locked up in
Daddy's car the whole day, with no food or water. He peed on
the leather seats, but no one told him off.

Maëlle, Groix Island

Yves asked me right away whether I minded him giving
Apple saxophone lessons to surprise her father. I respect my
daughter's privacy, and don't ask her any questions when she
pretends she's been to choir practice. I hope Cyrian won't let
her down again. I loved him for what he was and can already
see certain traits of his—courage, loyalty, and impulsive-
ness—in Apple. Our love story lasted two years. I thought he
would stay, but he wanted to be one better than Joe. I was
afraid he would do something stupid after failing his entrance
exams, but Albane turned up just at the right time. She may
well be married to him, but she is as alone as I am in raising
her daughter. He is never there.

"Federico is arriving tonight and he'll stay for three
nights," Sarah says.

"I assume the pair of you will be sharing a room?"

"We spent Christmas Eve and New Year's Eve together,
but nothing happened on either occasion. I'll make up the
blue room for him."

Sarah then sighs heavily. "I told Albane that Apple saved
Charlotte but Albane won't listen."

"Apple can't defend herself because it would mean grass-
ing up her sister," I tell her.

"When me and Cyrian were kids, we were so close we
would take punishment for each other. I experienced that

bond again when we both played music with that idiot, Patrice. Cyrian was a gifted musician."

I nod, remembering how he played saxophone for me on the clifftop before asking me to marry him and follow him to Paris. He didn't imagine for a second that I'd refuse.

Federico, Groix Island

I wasn't seasick, but I sway when I finally set foot on land. What am I doing here? What has Sarah got over the others? The face of a Madonna and the body of a goddess . . . She is overwhelmingly fragile, fascinating, intense, and mad about cinema. In Rome, it was as if I'd known her all my life. We were supposed to have dinner in Paris tonight, yet here I am on this minute island. It took four hours by train and a fifty-minute boat crossing to get here. *Sono pazzo.* I must be crazy. *Pazzo di lei.* Crazy about her.

The ferry I took is big compared to the sailing boats and moored fishing boats here, but it's ridiculously small compared to the giant cruise ships that pass under my windows along the Giudecca Canal in Venice. At the last minute I stuffed some clothes in a bag decorated with the colours of AS Roma football club that a friend had left at my place. They'll think I'm a football fan.

"Ahoy! 1 2 3!"

"Sarah!" I cry, and hug her, before reluctantly letting her go.

"Welcome to Groix!" she says, spreading out her arms like the tour guides leading Asian tourists around St Mark's Square.

I look around me and pretend to introduce myself to the north, the south, the east and the west. "Federico, delighted to meet you, *piacere.*"

*   *   *

"Hi everyone!" calls out Sarah to anyone listening.

A curly haired brunette comes out of the kitchen and puts out her hand. A young girl, a mini version of her mother, points at my football bag.

"Gryffindor?" she asks.

"There are two teams in Rome," I explain. "Lazio whose colours are light blue and Roma whose colours are orange and red. It's not my bag by the way."

"Apple is a Harry Potter fan," says Sarah to clear up the misunderstanding. "At Hogwarts, Harry is in Gryffindor, which has the same colours as your bag."

"Oh! Grifondoro! We call it Hogwarts, like in England," I say.

Apple's eyes go all big. "Is Harry called Harry? What about Ron? And Hermione?"

"Yes."

"And Albus Dumbledore, the headmaster?"

"Albus Silente."

"And Minerva McGonagall, Harry's main teacher?"

"Minerva McGranitt," I answer.

"I'm going to see if my father is in his study," says Sarah.

She goes up the stairs slowly. I want her so much. As she reaches the landing, the front door opens behind me. I swivel round.

I recognize him immediately. It's the man I saw on Christmas Eve in Le Vésinet when I went to visit my neighbour, Eric. I'm on the verge of reminding him, but he is shaking his head fiercely. Sarah comes back downstairs. The man is still shaking his head, so I guess I'm not supposed to know him.

"Daddy, this is Federico, like the *maestro* himself."

Ah, it's coming back to me now; I thought Sarah was a patient but he soon set me straight and told me about her tattoos. It's thanks to him that I invited her to dinner. I wonder why he is lying to his daughter. We shake hands as we size each other up.

"You're both wearing a 'Joseph'," says Sarah.

She turns to me. "That's our name for the sweater that my father has permanently draped over his shoulders."

"Where did you meet?" asks Sarah's father, who knows full well.

To my surprise, Sarah looks at me and says, "In an Italian restaurant in Chatou."

Lying appears to run in the family . . .

6th January

Charlotte, Lorient

I had another echocardiogram this morning. They seem happy with it. I'm leaving the ICU and they're putting me in a room on the cardiology ward. Mum and Dad say it's good news. I have no say in anything. I sleep, I'm in pain, and I'm scared. I remember that Apple tried to stop me from going near the Hellhole. I was so frightened in the helicopter. The oxygen made my throat really dry. I was freezing cold, and felt like I was floating. They're going to take my morphine pump away. What if the pain comes back? They're also going to take out my tubes, and I know that it's really going to hurt.

"How are you feeling, my poor darling?" asks Mum, who looks even worse than I do. She looks like she hasn't slept since my accident.

"Why can't Apple come and visit?" I ask.

"It's her fault that you're stuck in this bed!" she says angrily.

I squirm and screw my face up in pain. It burns every time I move.

"But she saved my life!" I insist, on the verge of tears.

"She almost killed you, you mean."

Mum is sitting on the edge of my bed. I squeeze her hand. The effort takes every bit of strength I have. She doesn't understand that Apple replaced Tachi's arrow.

"She stopped me from bleeding to death!"

"She forced you to go down that dangerous path. You would never have done such a foolish thing by yourself."

"She tried to stop me, but I pushed her away. It's all my fault."

Mum goes pale.

"When I accused her she didn't deny it!" she snaps.

"That's because she didn't want to tell on me."

"She could have denied it at least!"

"And get me into trouble? She's my sister, she was protecting me."

It hurts my ribs to get angry and pulls on my scar.

"Grampy saved me too. He stopped the doctor from pushing Apple out of the way while she was plugging the hole with her fingers."

Mum twists her hands nervously. "I blamed Apple just like my mother blamed me. Sarah's right, Apple broke the curse. She is ten years old, the same age as Tanguy . . ."

I don't know who she's talking about. My eyes go all heavy.

"I'm falling asleep, Mum. I'm lucky to have a sister. You don't understand because you haven't got one."

Mum's eyes glisten strangely. She says she has something urgent to do and rushes outside.

I wake up when the nurse comes in carrying a tray of medical equipment.

"I'm going to take your tubes out and then you're going up to cardio," she announces cheerfully.

"I don't want you to take them out, it's going to hurt a lot, isn't it?" I say.

"Yes, I'm not going to pretend otherwise, but we don't have a choice. I'm going to give you a dose of morphine, which will make you feel a bit floaty. I'll be back in six minutes. You'll have a TV in your new room and your sister can come and visit you."

Six minutes is a long time when you're freaking out. I'm glad Mum isn't here; she would just make it worse. The nurse comes back. She puts on gloves. She has already prepared the bandages.

"Here we go, Charlotte. You take a deep breath and hold it. Okay? Are you ready? Right, breathe in."

I breathe in and hold my breath. She rips them out really fast. It hurts so much it takes my breath away. I want to scream at her to stop but I can't speak. It hurts so much, I'm going to fall down the Hellhole again, it hurts very, very . . .

"It's over! You were very brave, well done!" the nurse says, smiling.

"It's over," I whisper, drenched in sweat.

Next thing I know, I'm out like a light.

Cyrian, Lorient

Charlotte has been moved from the ICU into a white room. I'm sat there in a plastic chair that squeaks every time I move. She opens one eye, then the other, and looks around in amazement.

"Did they move me while I was asleep?"

"Yes, they did," I say.

She looks down at her IV drip, the morphine pump is nowhere to be seen.

"What if the pain comes back, Dad?"

"They've put painkillers in the drip. If that's not enough, we'll ask them to give you more. My train to Paris leaves in forty minutes. I'll stop by the office and come straight back. Mum is staying. We're not leaving you."

She nods. She looks like a little bird that has just fallen out of the nest.

"Did it hurt a lot when they took the tubes out?" I ask.

The nurse had told me that she was very brave.

"A bit. You will come back, Dad, won't you? You won't abandon me?"

"I promise I'll come back, my darling."

"What if you change your mind? And decide your work is more important?"

"Nothing is more important than my little girl."

"But you abandoned Apple, so you could do the same to me."

I reel with shock. Kids know exactly where to hit you where it hurts.

"I didn't abandon Apple," I protest. "I don't happen to live in the same place as her. And, yes, I miss her. But I'm lucky to live with you."

Her eyes are hollow. Hardly surprising, given that her chest has been cut open, her ribs sawn and her heart stitched up.

"I was mean to Apple," she confesses eventually. "She tried to stop me from going down that path, but I liked provoking her."

"Why?" I ask, baffled.

"Because you prefer Maëlle to Mum, even if you don't talk to her anymore. Apple looks like Maëlle. I was afraid you'd love her more than me."

I am astonished, and saddened by her jealousy.

"I swore to Apple that if she told me Granny's secret, I wouldn't go down the path," she adds.

"What secret?" I ask, rubbing my face. My train for Paris leaves in thirty minutes.

"She told me everything, but I did it anyway. I betrayed her, and she saved my life," sighs Charlotte, pale and listless.

Panic comes over me. I ask her to tell me Granny's secret. Secrets are toxic. Like acid that eats away at you until there's nothing left.

"Have you seen the scar near Apple's eye?"

"Yes, the cat knocked the *grek* over."

"No, Dad. They lied to you. The coffee pot was knocked over, but it wasn't the cat. Granny lost it, she didn't recognize Apple and panicked and tried to push her away. And the *grek* got knocked over and burnt them."

My train leaves in twenty-two minutes. You lost your mind, Diastole, and nearly disfigured my daughter, who kept your secret out of loyalty. You were a danger to others and you knew it, and yet you hid it from us.

I'm appalled and so sorry for you, my poor Diastole. You must have suffered terribly! I'm also very hurt and furious too that you didn't trust us. I could have helped you! I grind my teeth wondering whether Systole knew about this? I'm gripped with jealousy and my stomach is in knots. You chose to confide in him but not me. I cringe. You knew what was coming next. You couldn't risk it happening again. So it was true then? It was your idea to move into the nursing home? Systole didn't force you? For the last six dreadful months, I thought I was defending you against him. But, no, you were my mother right up to the end, until your memory went. Systole didn't force you to do anything. And you made Apple swear not to tell anyone. You kept your dignity, right up to the end.

My train leaves in nineteen minutes.

"I have to run to the station, darling. I'll be there when you wake up tomorrow, I promise."

"Dad, it was me who cancelled the hotel room in Lorient. I'm sorry."

Now that Charlotte is no longer in the ICU, I don't have to wear gloves anymore. I can touch her. I feel her cheek, her skin is all warm to the touch. Her ribs are too sore for me to hug her, but I stroke her face tenderly.

Cyrian, on the train from Lorient to Paris

I barely make it onto the train in time. A woman wearing green glasses asks if we can swap seats so she can face forwards. I nod, I couldn't care less where I sit.

I check my text messages. Danny is hounding me. Her tone has changed now. Though we are two consenting adults, I am now the nasty married creep who has dumped his mistress. I have completely gone off her; I don't know what I ever saw in her. I used my family as an excuse to finish things, assuming the role of the bad guy so that she'd be put off. She's hurting and isn't giving up so far.

She sent me a long message just this morning: "I know your wife is putting pressure on you, threatening to stop you from seeing your daughter, but no one can make you happier than me. Kids grow up and leave. Forget about your daughters before they forget about you. They don't love you. I should know, I'm a girl. My father may as well be dead for all I care."

If she knew about Charlotte's accident, she would be delighted. I reply: "My daughters will always come first."

I delete her contact details from my phone and resign from the think tank.

Diastole you knew, didn't you? You knew what the disease would do to you, but you didn't let it destroy you. You departed before it could ravage your brain. I need to know the truth. There's only one person who'll tell me. I send her a text: "Charlotte is a little better. How did Apple burn her face?"

I wait, eyes glued to the network bars.

"The cat knocked over the *grek*," she replies.

"That's the official version. Do you believe it?" I ask.

"No. Lou and Apple made a pact."

My fingers tremble as I type the next question: "Who decided on the nursing home?"

The train rushes into a tunnel. I'm frantic until the network returns. Maëlle replies: "Lou. The day after the burn incident. Joe didn't want her to go."

The train rushes on and on through the enchanting Breton countryside.

"Is something wrong, sir?" asks the woman in the green glasses who took my seat.

There are tears rolling down my cheeks.

Joe, Groix Island

Charlotte's drainage tubes have been removed. There is always a risk of pneumothorax, but it turned out alright. I'm able to breathe easier now too. The Groix islander who sold me my new boat used to sail with my father. He hands me the ignition keys.

"May she give you as much pleasure as she gave me. I don't fancy feeding the fish. They've munched their way through enough of my friends. I prefer to die in my own bed. Shall we have a tipple to celebrate?"

"Some other time," I say. "I have to go to Lorient to see my granddaughter in hospital."

I'll deal with the name change tonight. *Lou of the High Seas* sounds grand. With your name on the hull, I'll never feel alone when I'm onboard.

Federico, Groix Island

"Does this cinema remind you of anything?" asks Sarah.

There at the crossroads, between a restaurant, a workshop and a bicycle hire shop, stands a big grey building with light blue letters on the front: *Cinema des Familles*. There's a poster stuck to the double glass door.

"Is it meant to be Cinema Paradiso?" I ask.

"You guessed it!" she says.

The island's only cinema is a replica of the one in Tornatore's film. It's open during the school holidays and used by the film club all year round. The poster is advertising tonight's Soup Festival at the old factory in Port-Lay.

"The idea is that you bring your own soup and taste everyone else's," Sarah explains. "Shall we go along?"

We've been behaving more and more like a couple since I arrived, but we're sleeping in separate bedrooms. Apple liked my Grifondoro bag so much that I let her have it. She offered to carry it up to my room when I arrived and asked Sarah where I was sleeping.

Sarah's father overheard Sarah say that I was in the blue room.

That night I got into my little bed, daring to imagine her in her New Year's Eve red underwear and then without . . .

"I waited for you in the blue room last night, Sarah," I say.

"I waited for you in the peach room," she replies with a smile.

"How am I supposed to guess where your room is?"

"My room is at the end of the landing. My door has an 'S' on it; it's my old childhood bedroom."

I can't stop myself from grabbing her and kissing her in front of the legendary cinema. Not a fake film kiss, but a larger than life kiss that Philippe Noiret would most probably have censored in his films. If we hadn't been at her father's house, we could have spent the day in bed. If we hadn't been on an island where people gossip, we could have booked into a hotel.

We'll have to be patient. In ancient Rome, time was counted from six o'clock in the morning to noon and from noon to six o'clock in the evening. Night-time hours didn't count, but for us they'll count double.

I love cooking and had the best teachers: my mother and four sisters.

"Shall we make my Aunt Mirella's winter soup for the festival?" I ask.

"What's in it?

I send a quick text to my cousin, Carla, to find out. Carla used to work in cinema too, dubbing films with her distinctive voice. Now she helps her mother at the restaurant. She answers *subito*: "Shelling beans, porcini mushrooms, peeled chestnuts, onion, celery, carrots, garlic, chilli, cured ham and olive oil."

There are twenty soups on the list, plus ours, and one hundred and fifty participants. The locals have hearty appetites and empty their bowls with gusto. Our tureen steams deliciously. Apple and her grandfather are in charge of serving. First, we taste a red cabbage soup; then one with chicken, pumpkin and sweet potatoes. The men all turn to look at Sarah.

"Hey, that's Joe's daughter, isn't it?" they say. Their singsong accent sounds like an Italian lullaby. My neighbour tells me that in the Middle Ages soup was a slice of stale bread that served as a plate, on which meat or vegetables were placed. After the meal, the nobles gave the leftovers to the poor or to their animals. When the first terracotta plates appeared, the bread was placed at the bottom and the broth was poured on top, but the name, "soup", remained the same. It was very different from nowadays. We try a soup made of chayote and cream cheese, one made from local mussels, and, to finish, one made from watercress, pears, and croutons, topped with blue cheese and a local spice.

We take over from Joe and Apple; our tureen is three-quarters empty. Joe joins his friends, and Apple films the festival on her iPad.

"I love your soup, mate!" says one of the locals to me.

My aunt Mirella is a fantastic cook. She was a dressmaker before opening Al Cantuccio. She handles food carefully like she once handled valuable silks.

Then several islanders get up and start singing an old mariners' song.

"*I'm a pirate, I don't care for glory, the laws of this world or death so bold. For I have staked my victory on the high seas and I drink my wine from a cup of gold.*"

More and more people join in and the rest of us applaud.

"Now a song by Michel Tonnerre. A song by Michto!" someone calls out.

Sarah stands up, leans against the table and sings in a husky voice.

"*On the coast at nightfall, we still sing to the sound of the violins. At Beudeff's on the accordion, it's not the beer that'll make you weep. And old Joe's accordion sings an old sea shanty. Drink in the sea spray with your eyes, and it'll come back to haunt you each time it rains ...*"

She continues, staring into my eyes and emphasizing the first line.

"*Come on, Joe, do the Irishman for us, tell us what you learned when you were sailing. While over in Galway, when you navigated the seas.*"

I hold her gaze. Other voices join in, but I only hear hers.

"It's your turn, mate!" a guy in a faded jacket calls out to me, as he fills my glass with wine.

My mother used to send all eight of us to the Irish choir to give herself a break. I get up, clear my throat and sing the classic "When Irish Eyes Are Smiling".

"*There's a tear in your eye, and I'm wondering why, for it never should be there at all ...*"

I sing the whole song and then sit back down, out of breath and out of practice.

"Keep going, mate," says the islander who had taken a liking to Mirella's soup earlier.

"Do you know 'Danny Boy'?" asks the guy in the faded jacket.

I nod slowly. All Irish people know it, we sing it on St Patrick's Day and at funerals.

"Well, what are you waiting for?" he says. "The tide to come in?"

"My brother used to play it on the saxophone," whispers Sarah.

The last time I heard that tune was when me and my three brothers carried our mother's coffin.

"Oh yes! Please sing it!" begs Apple. I give in to please them.

"*Oh Danny Boy, the pipes, the pipes are calling, from glen to glen and down the mountain side, the summer's gone and all the roses dying . . .*"

All conversations around us come to a halt. Apple and Sarah can't take their eyes off me.

I sit down, exhausted. The guy in the faded jacket thinks Sarah is my wife. I don't tell him that this is only the third time we've met. Cyrian phones from Paris. He's coming back to Lorient on the first train tomorrow. Albane calls to say Charlotte is a little better. The islanders sing another song by Michel Tonnerre.

"*Fifteen men on a dead man's chest, Yo ho ho and a bottle of rum! A drink and the devil be done for the rest, Yo ho ho and a bottle of rum!*"

I feel like I've been on this island forever.

Later that night, we walk back to the house with the empty cooking pot. Sarah, Apple, Joe and Maëlle are all singing.

"*We were three sailors from Groix, tra la la la. Enlisted on the* Saint-François, *tra la la la. The north wind blew in a storm. The wind from the sea torments us. The wind from the sea torments us."*

Everyone goes to bed. I slip down the corridor to the peach room.

"I have an unbreakable rule," murmurs Sarah. "I never see anyone more than twi—"

She is interrupted by my mouth on hers. The long wait has fuelled our passion. We are already a couple; the Christmas kiss and the New Year's Day kiss had already sealed our fate. We roll and sway in unison, we are captivated, our bodies joined in a passionate frenzy. Then we cling to one another, amused, fulfilled, finally back to port. The wind from the sea no longer torments us. I fall asleep on my side, facing Sarah, my arms around her waist, holding her fast like a mooring rope.

7th January

Apple, Groix Island

The brass band will be giving a concert soon. Yves wants me to play in it.

"But I'm not ready yet," I say.

"Yes you are," he replies. "You play well."

"Do you know the song 'Danny Boy', that my Aunt Sarah's friend sang? Is it too hard for a beginner?"

Yves laughs into his beard. He rummages around in his bookcase, takes out a booklet and leafs through it.

"It used to be called 'The Londonderry Air'. I have the music for alto saxophone and piano."

He plays it on the piano, then on the saxophone. It's so moving, powerful and tender, that it takes my breath away.

"We could play it together at the concert if you like?" suggests Yves.

"But I don't know how to play it," I protest.

"Well learn it then, what are you waiting for? The tide to come in?"

Albane, Lorient

Charlotte is asleep. Her results were good. The door opens. Sarah creeps in on tiptoe. Joseph is with the cardiologist. It's such a relief to have a doctor in the family, it makes things easier; he understands exactly what it all means.

"Are you alone?" I ask Sarah. "Charlotte admitted that Apple tried to stop her from going down that treacherous path. You were right; love really does conquer all. My mother's dreadful curse has been broken. Tell Apple she can come and visit tomorrow."

Sarah reaches into her bag and pulls out two bottles that I recognize.

"But I threw them in the bin!" I say.

"I took them out again, hoping you would see sense and change your mind. Here's her letter too, will you give them to Charlotte tomorrow?"

I nod.

Sarah, Groix Island

Dad is eating at Fred's house tonight with the 7 Gang. Federico and I were invited but we prefer to spend the evening by ourselves. The Ocre Marine crêpe restaurant in Locmaria has closed down permanently. It's such a shame; their camembert and salted butter caramel crêpes were to die for. We try another crêpe place instead, there are lots to choose from here on the island.

"What do you fancy?" I ask him.

"Grilled fish," he replies.

"But this is a crêpe restaurant."

"Okay, I'll have pasta then," he says.

"You can only eat crêpes in a *crêperie*, you know."

"Why? You don't only get pizza in a pizzeria . . ."

"Can you stay on for a few days longer?" I ask.

"I wish I could. It's so annoying, I only have a two-hour lesson the day after tomorrow in Paris, then a whole week off."

"There is a solution, you know," I say. "When I was a child, I stole a sheet from my father's prescription pad so I could bunk off school. I copied it all out to the letter: *I, the undersigned, hereby certify that I have examined Sarah today and her condition requires that she stay at home*."

"Did it work?"

"It was perfect, except for the fact that instead of forging Dad's signature, I stupidly signed my own name. What an idiot! Dad had a double helping of your soup. If you ask him nicely, he'll give you a doctor's note. Besides, you don't look too well. You're sleep deprived and you need strict bed rest . . ."

9th January

Apple, Lorient

I did the crossing on Joe's new boat, *Lou of the High Seas*. He keeps telling me Albane wants me to come, but I'm really anxious. Luckily, she isn't there when we arrive. My sister looks much thinner and she talks in a faint little voice like we do in class so the teacher won't hear us.

"Thanks for the beach," she mumbles, pointing to the bottles on her bedside table. "But Boy and Lola didn't come."

"They must have got the wrong floor," I say.

I sit on the squeaky plastic chair. Joe leaves us to it. He goes off to talk to the doctor. I tell Charlotte about the Soup Festival and show her the little video I made on my iPad. She looks at the decorations and listens to Federico singing.

"Daddy asked Joe if you can come and stay on Groix when you get out of hospital," I tell her.

"Really?!"

"He said I could choose anything I wanted to thank me for helping you, so that's what I chose. You'll have your own personal doctor at home. Isn't that cool?"

"So I won't be going back to Le Vésinet? Wow, you're amazing!"

"Daddy will come every weekend and you'll have my room downstairs, so you won't have to go upstairs. It's a bit messy but I'll tidy it up first."

"Downstairs I'll be far away from my mum!" says Charlotte excitedly.

"Did I hear my name?" asks Albane, opening the door.

Did she hear? Charlotte goes red. I get up, squeaking the plastic chair and move it back against the wall. Albane no longer gives me that killer look, but I still don't trust her.

"I owe you an apology, Apple," she says straight away.

I wish Joe would come back.

"I'm sorry," she says. "Charlotte told me what really happened. It was unfair of me; I accused you wrongly. I was so afraid . . ."

"I've brought you something," I say to Charlotte, to change the subject.

I hand her the little jar that I bought at a local delicatessen.

"Charlotte has to eat the hospital food," Albane intervenes.

"It's not edible," I say quickly.

Charlotte looks at the label: *Iodized air, origin: Groix Island.*

"Is it filled with air? That's amazing!" she grins.

"Thank you so much, Apple," adds Albane.

She's gushing and it's making me uncomfortable, so I tell her I love my gift, and don't need anything else.

"What gift?" she asks, looking perplexed.

"Charlotte is coming to Groix to recover."

"Grampy will take care of me. I'll have my own personal doctor like the Hollywood stars," adds Charlotte gleefully.

Albane stares at us blankly and then leaves the room.

"She didn't know," murmurs Charlotte.

I wonder why Daddy didn't tell her?

Albane, Lorient

He is sat at a table in the café, typing away. I notice the empty cups in front of him, the stain on his sleeve, his furrowed brow, his bitten thumb nails, his pallor, his charm, the new creases on his forehead. Despite it all, I still love the man.

"Cyrian?"

He looks up, then he remembers I've left him and his smile fades. He looks at his watch, in astonishment.

"Is it already time for me to take over?" he asks.

I tell him Apple is with Charlotte. He closes his computer and nudges his files out of the way, then stands up like a gentleman. I sit down. I can't keep quiet any longer.

"Charlotte seems to think she'll be convalescing on Groix!"

"I wanted to talk to you about it. The surgeon thinks it's a good idea. Systo . . . my father does too," he says timidly.

"But I thought you had arranged everything with the hospital in Le Vésinet?" I reply, my mind reeling. "So, were you just going to tell me at the last minute? When everything had already been decided?"

"You'll be rid of me in the week. The air is much cleaner on Groix. It's reassuring to have Dad around. Besides, Apple being there will stimulate Charlotte. She would have been alone at night in Le Vésinet. Here, she'll be with you," argues Cyrian.

Not seeing him anymore will be a relief, that's true. And he's right, Joseph is an esteemed cardiologist. And when I went into the hospital room earlier, Charlotte seemed happier now that Apple is allowed to see her.

"I'll think about it," I say eventually. "I've been unfair on Apple. I hope she'll forgive me."

"I miss you."

I get up and leave without saying a word.

10th January

Apple, Groix Island

I'm rehearsing a lot with the band and I'm getting more confident. It's easy, because if I make a mistake no one can hear it, and I've even figured out how to catch up with the others. I'm doing well with the "Danny Boy" piece. When I play with Yves accompanying me on the piano, it feels like I'm surfing the waves. I love this melody, it just *does* something to me, a bit like when I eat cake baked by Martine. When I play it, my heart beats to the rhythm of the saxophone. It puts everything in the world to rights, as if nothing can ever go wrong again on Groix. As if Daddy lived with us and Lou wasn't dead.

Federico stays a few more days. Aunt Sarah has been walking better since he got here. Charlotte and Albane are arriving tomorrow. Mummy will go back to Locmaria, but I'll still see her every day. Daddy will come here on Friday night and sleep in his own room. Albane has moved into the blue room because Daddy snores and stops her sleeping. It's like musical chairs in our house. I gave my room to Charlotte. Federico left the blue room to sleep with Aunt Sarah in the peach room. Joe is the only one who hasn't changed rooms.

12th January

Charlotte, Groix Island

They brought me here in the Cayenne; I sat in the front in Mum's usual seat. Dad said I should be as snug as a bug in a rug. I can't imagine a bug being in a rug, it would just get crushed. Grampy doesn't like Dad's car usually, he calls it a tank. He didn't say anything this time though. On the boat, I used the lift instead of the stairs, and I didn't even go out on deck. Now I'm in Apple's bedroom. There is a tiny picture of Dad on the bookshelf, which you can only see from the bed. I didn't tell him though.

I was so excited about coming back here, but nothing is like I thought it would be. I feel so old, like thirty or something. I can't run or walk around; I can't even carry a plate. I have to have help with washing myself; I panic when Oskar comes near me wanting to play. I can hardly breathe, and when I cough it's a nightmare. I was looking forward to seeing Apple again, but she must be fed up with me because I can't do anything. I'm weaker than Grampy. He's going to remove my outside stitches in two days' time. The inside stitches will disappear by themselves. Grampy has a steady hand. I'll still freak out, but I'll be *stoic*. Apple taught me that word, "stoic". I like it, it's cool. I'm better off here with Apple than alone in Le Vésinet.

Grampy gave me some delicious Groix caramels coated with Peruvian chocolate and pistachios. He gives me pain killers too. The physiotherapist is nice, I am his youngest patient on the island. He teaches me how to spit to clear the mucus so I don't get an infection. He says that I'll be able to breathe normally within six weeks. I've been breathing since I was born without even noticing, now it's an effort. I'm learning a lot of stuff from him, like the fact that not everyone breathes the same way, it depends how old they are. Babies breathe quicker than children who breathe quicker than adults. I won't be going back to school for ages. I'm tired all the time. I'm so scared that I'll never run, shout or dance again. I wonder if Aunt Sarah feels like this when she sees everyone else dashing around normally. If Granny was here, I would talk to her about it. She understood everything. I nearly joined her in heaven.

I help Apple revise her poetry for school: *The grasshopper, so blithe and gay, Sang the summer time away. Pinched and poor the spendthrift grew, When the sour north-easter blew.* I have a good memory; I learn it by heart and I can recite it all in one go. Apple moves her hands and arms around and mimes the story to an invisible audience. In her poem, everything is moving, the ant, the grasshopper, the sun, the wind. Not like me, stuck in this room like a butterfly pinned to a board.

22nd January

Cyrian, Groix Island

My stomach churns as I catch sight of the name of Systole's boat: *Lou of the High Seas*. I haven't been a better father than him, but he was definitely a better husband than me. He protected Mum to the end. I'm even beginning to wonder if he really did cheat on her.

Charlotte is down in the dumps. Apple is doing her best to distract her. Oskar brings her toys but doesn't understand why she won't throw them to him like she used to.

"Do you want to take over?" Systole asks me.

"I can't," I say.

"You've got a boating license, haven't you? There's no roll-on roll-off at this hour. What's the problem, don't tell me you're scared?"

Here we go again, just like when I was younger, when I would dive from the highest board or abseil down from the mast to prove to him that I wasn't some stupid wimp. Speed is restricted to three knots in the harbour. I accelerate in the channel, then go full tilt through the waters of the Courreaux once we're far enough away from the coast. The boat vibrates beneath my feet. I'm surfing a wave, I accelerate again. *Lou of the High Seas* rears her head, but I'm calling the shots.

"It's great, isn't it?" yells my father. I nod and concentrate on looking out for the cardinal buoys. The north cardinal mark has both arrows pointing upwards, the south cardinal mark has both arrows pointing downwards, that's easy. The east cardinal mark has arrows pointing up and down. The west cardinal mark has them pointing towards the centre. I know Systole, he won't help me, he'd rather let me crash the boat and then hurl insults at me afterwards.

"You were right about the nursing home," I shout over the noise of the engine. "It was Mum's decision."

He's standing behind me, so I can't see the look on his face. Here I am, steering his boat at night, heading for his island. My arms are stiff from grasping the rudder. I turn around as I approach Groix. I recite under my breath: *when entering the harbour you put on a green sweater and bright red stockings.* The green sweater refers to the green cone beacon on the starboard side. The bright red stockings are the red cylinder beacon on the port side.

"I'll let you dock, Dad," I call out.

"No, you can do it," he insists.

"It's been ten years since I last manoeuvred in a port, don't you think it would be wiser if you did it?"

"Not scared are you, son?"

Same old story. Grinding my teeth, I drop speed and aim for the dock at a forty-five-degree angle. I put the motor into neutral so that I'm parallel and straighten up a tad. Then I reverse slightly so that we come to a stop.

"That's how it's done," he says, before jumping off and mooring the boat with surprising agility for a man of sixty. "You haven't forgotten anything."

"How are things going with Albane?" I ask.

"She's cheerful, helpful, nice, I hardly recognize her. Lou and Thierry are good judges of character."

"What has your friend Thierry Serfaty got to do with anything? He hardly knows her!" I say, wondering whether my father is losing his mind too.

"He has a fine knowledge of the human mind, Cyrian. Lou said that Albane was a kind-hearted person. I'm sure Thierry would agree with her."

"You and Mum have so many friends. I've lost touch with all of mine. My wife and daughter don't have any either. Why is that do you think?"

"You used to have friends," he replies. "Charlotte is becoming friends with Apple now, that will help her recovery no end."

We fall in step and walk home, passing in front of the Ty Beudeff. If I wasn't in such a hurry to see Charlotte, I would treat my father to a beer at the legendary bistro for the first time. My daughters are in the kitchen with Sarah and Federico when we arrive. They are playing *burraco*, an Italian card game similar to *canasta*. Charlotte smiles when she sees me walk in. She makes an attempt to get up and stops suddenly, her body contracting in pain. I kiss her forehead. She has lost even more weight. Apple waits her turn. I kiss her forehead too.

"Where's Albane?" I ask.

They tell me she has gone to sing with the local choir.

I must be dreaming. My daughters are now best friends. My father and my wife are getting along. And my wife is singing in a choir with people she hardly knows; she hasn't socialized with anyone in Le Vésinet in the ten years we've lived there.

"Do you mind if we finish the round?" asks Sarah.

I'm delighted to see them all getting on so well, but I feel a little in the way. I ran like an idiot to get here. I spent the journey imagining our reunion. And now I'm here I feel really out of place. Apple, who has always been hyper-sensitive and intuitive, says sorry with her eyes. Pale-faced Charlotte is called to order by Sarah.

"We're winning, concentrate please, Charlotte, otherwise they'll be hell to pay!"

"We're winning, Dad. Aunt Sarah says we're jammy buggers!" cries my little girl.

If she uses language like that in front of her mother, there will indeed be hell to pay . . .

We'll be eating in three quarters of an hour when Albane gets back. I go outside and stroll towards the rugged coastline, passing in front of the glassblower's workshop. It was eleven years ago that the owner, Damien, designed the first gift I ever gave Maëlle, a beautiful string of glass beads which matched her eyes. He also made the bracelet I gave Albane on her first visit to Groix. This guy has a big family and is always smiling. I only have two daughters and I'm grumpy all the time. What went wrong I wonder? All of a sudden, a car draws up beside me.

"Cyrian?"

I see an honest face surrounded by red hair sticking out from under a turban. She's a shrimp of a lady but massively generous: it's Martine, the famous baker of chocolate cakes. She lives in Lomener with Olivier, her guitarist husband.

"Can I drop you somewhere?" she asks.

I wonder if Lou sent her to me?

"I'm off to Locmaria," I say.

She tells me to hop in.

Rabbits run along the windy roadside. The road itself curves round in front of Locqueltas, skirts Kermarec and continues on to Locmaria.

"Joe gave us a fright, but he's better now," she says.

I go cold.

"I work in Paris, and couldn't take care of him," I say, instantly on the defensive.

"Of course not, I only wanted to reassure you! We all stick together here. We miss Lou. One year, I wrote on my jams 'pear, banana & kisses'. In return she gave me jars of 'burnt apples, cinnamon, calva & friendship".

"Did you pretend they were delicious and throw them away?" I ask.

"That's exactly what I did," she laughs."

She drops me off in Locmaria. I can see a light on downstairs in Maëlle's cottage. Smoke is bellowing out of the chimney. I have plenty of fond memories here. I recall Maëlle's grandmother with the two lace wings in her hair. On Sundays, she wore the full headdress. She used to tell us about her childhood, the boys who dropped the water jugs when they came back from the fountain, cakes which were made communally using the baker's huge oven, and the wind swept villages where large families lived in tiny houses. Despite her modest background, she carried herself like a queen. I remember throwing pebbles up at Maëlle's windows at night so that she would come and meet me. I remember her parents, who died in an avalanche when Apple was only a few months old. It was the first time they had been to the mountains after winning a competition. Her father had survived countless storms at sea only to succumb to the snow. I was already with Albane by that time but didn't know Maëlle was expecting Charlotte. I had hoped that she would finally come and join me in Paris since her parents were no longer around to keep her on Groix. I obviously underestimated the power of the dead. If her parents were alive, she might have left them one day; but once they died, she could never bring herself to abandon them.

I knock at the door.

Maëlle, Groix Island

What the hell is *he* doing here?

"Is Apple okay?" I ask anxiously.

"She's fine. Can I come in?"

I kept the furniture from my parents' living room but redecorated the bedrooms and renovated the bathrooms in the guest rooms. I point to my father's armchair.

"Take a seat. He's not going to come back and kick your arse."

My dad once chased Cyrian down to the beach intending to give him a good hiding because I stayed out all night. Cyrian outran him and they eventually made up. They had a mutual respect for one another, at a time when Cyrian couldn't see eye to eye with Joe.

"The girls are playing cards and Albane is at choir practice."

"What do you want?"

"I want us to call a truce," he says.

"I wasn't aware that we were fighting . . ."

He looks at the framed photos of my parents, my grandmother in her headdress, and Apple as a baby.

"You leave town as soon as I arrive. You won't let me pay towards my daughter's upkeep. You do everything you can to avoid me."

"If you had come to find me, I would have gone back to the village. Apple isn't just *your* daughter, she's *our* daughter. If you had presented things differently, I would have accepted your help. I'm not running away from you, I'm just avoiding your wife," I explain.

"You made me out to be the bad guy. The scumbag who abandoned his child."

"You didn't abandon anyone, I refused to go with you. Apple is an incredibly special little girl, you would see that if you bothered to get to know her," I throw back at him.

"She looks just like you," he says. "I lost you and I knew from the outset that I would lose her too."

"What do you expect, locking yourself away in Paris with Albane and Charlotte?"

I offer him a cigarette. He tilts his head back, makes himself at home in front of the fireplace, and smokes it eagerly.

"I also came to thank you. For helping Lou and taking care of my father which should have been my responsibility."

"They are Apple's grandparents, and they took me in after my parents died. I will always be grateful to them."

"On the day of the accident, when I said I love you, I meant it," he whispers.

"So did I. But we're incompatible," I say.

"I know. Are you seeing anyone at the moment?"

"No, not right now. I was, but I didn't tell Apple."

"I'm going to lose Albane."

"Do you truly care about her?"

"Yes, though I didn't realize it at the time."

"Then fight for her."

"I cheated on her. She knew and accepted it. I've stopped cheating on her now, but she resents me. She really seems to hate me. I always thought she would love me forever."

"You men are unbelievable! Put your energy into winning her back instead of whining about it. Seduce her like you did the first time you met. You've got a head start, my friend, you're her daughter's father."

"I'm not your friend," laughs Cyrian.

"It's time you became one then," I say, feeling a renewed affection for him. "Because as your daughter's mother, I've got a head start too."

Charlotte, Groix Island

Federico and Apple beat us at *burraco*. Aunt Sarah is furious.

"Where's your father?" Mum asks when she gets back, surprised not to see him.

Since my accident, she doesn't call him by his first name anymore.

At that moment Dad walks in. "I went outside to get some fresh air while my daughters were learning how to gamble," he says smiling.

Since my accident, he says "my daughters". Plural. I scrunch up my nose.

"Have you been smoking, Dad?"

"I only had one."

"It's very bad for Charlotte!" says Mum angrily.

Dad goes over to kiss her, but she turns her head away and opens the cupboard to get the plates out. Apple picks up the cards and sets the table. I feel useless.

"I'm going to go and get a jumper," I say.

"I'll go," offers Apple.

"Which one do you want?" asks Mum.

"She's recovering, she's not made of bone china," says Grampy. "Her bedroom is on the ground floor, it's not far."

I get up slowly, walk to my room and sit on the bed for a while to get my breath back. I can only wear cardigans now, because of my ribs. I wouldn't be able to put on a polo neck or round-necked sweater. Apple has given me a shelf in her wardrobe for my stuff. I can see the orange fleece I was wearing when I fell. It was covered in dirt, grass and blood, someone must have washed it. It's waiting for me, all clean, and nicely folded, looking all fluffy and cosy. I hurt myself trying to put it on. Someone knocks at my door. Dad comes in and sits down next to me.

"It's hard isn't it, sweetheart," he says.

"I feel so weak, Dad. The physiotherapist says I will get stronger, but I don't believe him. Apple must be fed up with me, I can't even go out. Do you think I'll ever breathe again like before?"

"You're going to take care of yourself, eat, sleep, get your confidence back and then you'll get your life back too. Do you have your iPad? I'll show you what helps me hold on when I'm feeling down."

He taps on the tablet and hands it to me. I see docks lit up by two flashing lights, one green and one red, sailing boats lined up along the quay and various moorings.

"It's the webcam at Cap-Lorient in Port-Tudy," he explains. "It's a live view of Groix harbour. Beautiful isn't it?"

"Do you look at it when you feel sad?"

"Yes, and also every morning and every evening. I see the roll-on roll-off ferries docking, passengers and cars getting off, dock workers unloading cargo, sailing boats and fishing boats going in and out. I see the rain pouring down and the sun reflecting on the water. I see life by day and the sea at night. Once I even saw Apple and Granny pull over to buy a ferry ticket!"

"Dad, I'm so sorry I went down that hole. I felt like I was in prison with Mum but at least I could breathe."

"In prison?" he says, stunned.

We live in the same house, did he not notice anything?

"I'm not allowed to have any friends, I'm not allowed to eat lunch in the canteen. I can't invite anyone round or go to anyone else's house. I'm Mum's plaything," I mutter.

"Aren't you exaggerating a little?"

"Now it's going to be even worse!" I say. "She's going to lock me up until I'm eighteen."

"And after that, what will you do?"

"I'll go so far away that she'll never find me. Apple's the only one who'll have my address."

"What about me?"

"You would probably just give it to Mum."

Dad's smile fades.

"That means I've got nine years left to stop you from disappearing off the face of the earth," he says seriously.

Lou, on the other side

At the beginning you used to talk to me. Now I'm just a relic of the past. You no longer say "you would have liked that, Lou", instead it's "Mum or Lou, would have liked that". I'm redundant now, my *piroche*. It's normal, that's life, or should I say that's *death*.

Seeing the family together in the house warms my heart. You fight, you clash, you grapple with each other, it's a highly emotional time for you all. You're trapped in the same warped world as before, except this time you're all in it together. At least you're not alone.

Albane, Groix Island

The door of the blue room squeaks open, I wake up with a start.

"Who's there?"

"Cyrian."

I turn on the light, feeling fuzzy from the sleeping pill.

"Is Charlotte in pain?" I ask.

"She's asleep. Get dressed. I need to talk to you."

My husband has a sailor's cap on his head and hasn't shaved for three days. He looks like an ad for a fashionable *eau de toilette*.

"Why? Won't you talk to someone in pyjamas?"

"I'm taking you outside."

"In the middle of the night? Have you been drinking?"

"No. I'm leaving on Sunday; you'll be able to sleep in peace afterwards. Come on, let's go."

He is stubborn as a mule and won't take no for an answer. I throw on some clothes, grumbling, still numb from the sleeping pill.

He hands me my scarf and jacket. We go outside. The wind is raging, and happy to have two new bodies to blow over. Cyrian puts his arm around my shoulders and drags me towards the street and down to the harbour.

I shiver in the icy wind, staggering along the path, propped up by the man I love, who is also the man I'm leaving. The port is deserted yet noisy; the shrouds beat against the masts, and the hulls creak. There's not a soul in sight, no sailors, no seagulls, just us two idiots sitting on the quay, our legs dangling over the edge. The green light on the left is flashing brightly.

"Charlotte's not doing great," he says.

"I could have heard that from the warmth of my bed," I retort.

"She said she felt like she was in prison before the accident. And she's afraid it's going to get worse now," he continues.

"She's wrong," I say sarcastically. "She's really proved to us that we can trust her. I'm going to enrol her for bungee jumping and hang-gliding. She needs to spread her wings!"

"Her heart is strong, Albane. Her ribs will knit together. She's a fighter, she survived. She's not Tanguy."

I try to stand up, but he stops me, so I sit back down. He pulls me close to him. I sit there furious, out of breath, saddened, my eyes misted with tears.

"I wish I had known your brother; I wish I could have made you happy, I wish I could have made my daughters carefree. I went to see Maëlle last night in Locmaria before dinner," he says.

I ask if they are getting back together, trying my hardest to sound indifferent.

"I'm not getting back together with anyone, you're my wife. And I love you. Maëlle and I have just agreed to be friends."

He puts his handsome face next to mine. If I wanted, I could push him into the icy water and he would sink to the bottom. The perfect crime. The port is deserted. I would go back up to my room, go to bed, and act all surprised with the others tomorrow morning when he doesn't appear at breakfast. That other bitch would be waiting for him a long time.

"Give me a second chance, Albane. Let's start again. I'll change. I promise. I don't want to lose you."

"What about that woman?"

"I told you, it's over."

"Why did you want to talk to me here?" I ask.

He turns around and shows me a camera behind us. "That's the port webcam. I was angry at Groix for snatching my mother from me. I was angry at Maëlle for having Apple. But whatever happens, I can't keep away from this piece of rock. I grew up here, these are my roots. I look at the harbour every morning and evening, and imagine myself arriving by boat. This is my haven, my refuge. The webcam is filming the exact part of the quay where we are now, up to the roll-on roll-off on the right. In Groix nothing matters but the truth, no cheating, just the truth."

"So if I'd pushed you into the sea just now, there would have been hundreds of witnesses?"

Suddenly, he kisses me, like he used to. I let myself go. After all Charlotte is safe and sound at home with her personal doctor, it's freezing cold and there's just the two of us.

We walk back up the street to the town reminiscing. Is this really me? This woman clutching her man in the darkness on a small island? Is this tender, passionate man really my husband?

What follows is incredible. Unexpected, unbridled sparks and passion, as though it were our first time, complete with delightful, awkward fumbling and surprises. My mother's curse has been broken. Charlotte has her life ahead of her. I am finally free. Love really does conquer all.

Charlotte, Groix Island

I used to sleep on my side. Now I have to sleep on my back, which means I don't sleep very deeply. I hear the front door open and close. I recognize my parents' voices, even though they're whispering. Where on earth are they off to in the middle of the night?

I wait but they don't come back. Has Mum asked Dad to jump over the Hellhole? Are they going to kill each other on the cliffs? If they both die, what will happen to me? Granny's gone; Grampy can't look after me. Sarah thinks I'm a spoilt brat. Maëlle wouldn't want me. Mum's mum hates children. What about Oskar? Will they put him in a dog's home and stick me in an orphanage? What if they put him to sleep? Apple won't know where to find me, we'll lose touch with each other. Maybe my prison life wasn't so bad after all. Mum treats me like a baby, but at least she loves me. Dad is never around, but he does love us really.

My heart pounds at the thought. If my stitches break, will I bleed to death? I need to calm down. I'll do what Dad does when he's sad. I fetch my iPad and click on the Groix harbour webcam. I can see the back of a man and a woman. They are sat together, watching the harbour. The image freezes, it often does that. Dad told me the views last sixty seconds and are updated every two minutes. The woman wants to get up, but the man stops her. She looks like ... hey wait, is that Mum? Is that Dad? The image freezes. They both turn around. It freezes again. He is showing her the webcam. I wave madly but they don't see me. The image freezes. Yuck! They're kissing now! How disgusting. The image freezes. They walk off, looking like they're glued to each other.

Did I really see them, or am I going crazy? I hear the door of the house open and close slowly. It's them, whispering and laughing. They go upstairs. Dad didn't jump over the Hellhole then. And they didn't kill each other. So I won't go to an orphanage, and Oskar won't be put to sleep. We'll stay together. Dad was right, his webcam really does cheer you up!

30th January

Apple, Groix Island

I'm so nervous. We rehearsed all morning. The concert was supposed to be held outside, but it's raining cats and dogs, so we'll have to perform in the village hall instead. The musicians and backup singers are all wearing black. Charlotte lent me a lovely soft polo neck. None of my family knows I'm in the brass band, they all think I'm in the choir.

We take out our instruments and get ready. The grown-ups are as nervous as the children. Me and Yves are up fifth with "Danny Boy". I'll then play with the brass band for the sixth song, and after that I'll leave the stage and I'll listen to the choir in the audience with my family. I have reserved seats for them by taping their names on the plastic chairs. Charlotte is arriving with Dad in the car and will come in just before the concert starts so that no one knocks into her. I take a few deep breaths that make me yawn. I know both scores off by heart. The other children have already played in front of their parents at parties or competitions, but Daddy has never seen me play before. The hall is filling up. The only seats left are the ones I reserved. The back door opens, and Charlotte and Daddy walk in. Charlotte looks really pale compared to everyone else. They sit down and the lights go out.

The brass band starts the concert with a happy catchy tune, and the trombones, trumpets, piston horn, saxophones, and drums all play together. I wait at the back of the stage watching the others play. Armelle suddenly appears and whispers in Jacote's ear who then whispers to Yves. He stops playing and steps back into the shadows. He whispers to me that I need to set up my saxophone quickly, and then grabs the microphone.

"Friends, we have a bit of a problem. One of our musicians has punctured a tyre in the rain in Port-Mélite, so we need to go and fetch him. We hadn't planned on playing "Singin' in the Rain" tonight but there you go! This means there's a slight change of programme. We'll go straight to the piece that was going to be performed a bit later on, a piano and alto saxophone duet."

I scramble to set up my instrument.

"Apple, are you ready?" My hands are sweaty and my mouth is dry. Yves is sat at the piano waiting for me. The whole room is waiting for us.

Yves plays the first bars of "Danny Boy" alone, as normal. The saxophone feels really heavy on my neck, the strap is digging into my skin and my fingers are hot, but I'll feel better once I start playing. I don't look at my family, I just think of one thing: the butterflies I get in my stomach every time I play this magical song. Yves's fingers fly over the keys, I put my lips over the mouthpiece and the familiar notes pour out. Well at least they're meant to . . .

My heart is racing. My fingers are on the right keys and I can hear the music in my head. My mouth is in the right position too. I'm not clenching my teeth too much. I blow but nothing comes out. Nothing at all! All you can hear is the piano. My saxophone makes a sshhhhhh noise, like the sea, as if it's broken. I panic. Has someone played a joke on me? My saxophone won't play for Daddy? Have I made it angry? Yves can't help me, he's playing the piano. All this practising for nothing! I'm a laughing stock. I blow again: shhhhhhh. I feel sick to my stomach and turn to look at Daddy at the back of the room. He's talking to Charlotte and hasn't even noticed. It was for him, it was his piece. I may not be Sidney Bechet or Stan Getz, but this morning I was playing "Danny Boy" really well.

Yves's fingers dance all over the piano. No one understands why I'm not playing, and some people even think it's a joke. I grit my teeth, take the strap from around my neck, place the saxophone on the floor, and creep off stage. I'm so embarrassed I could go through the floor. I slink towards the door in the dark, and just as I close it, the piano stops playing, and everyone claps for Yves. I run across the road in the pouring rain without looking and almost get hit by a car that brakes suddenly on seeing my dripping body dart out in front of it. I run to Lou.

I sit on top of her gravestone. I tried to show off and made a total fool of myself. I'm going to hide until Daddy leaves tonight. I lie on my back and look up at the sky to Lou. I'm soaking wet and freezing. A hand touches my shoulder; I scream.

"Don't be afraid, it's me!"

It's Daddy holding a big umbrella over us.

"You'll catch your death. Take off your sweater."

"It's Charlotte's. I've got nothing on underneath."

"No one's looking. Here, put my sweater on instead."

I take off the polo neck which is sopping wet and put on Daddy's big sweater with long sleeves that hang over the end of my arms. He only has a thin polo shirt on. We both shiver in the cold.

"We'll go back in the warm, but first, you must finish what you started. Remember what Lou used to say? When you fall off a horse . . .?"

"You get right back on," I reply. "But the saxophone isn't a horse and I'm rubbish at it, Yves lied to me."

"The saxophone is a reed instrument, darling. You forgot to put this on."

"What?" I ask, alarmed.

He carefully places the saxophone case on the grave next to us and asks me to hold the umbrella over all three of us, me, Daddy, and the saxophone. Daddy puts it together really quickly without putting the reed in. Then he blows into it. It goes shhhhhhh, like the sea. Exactly like me on stage.

"You see? Without the reed, there's no vibration, no sound."

I get it now. I thought I had all the time in the world, but when they hurried me onto the stage I forgot to put it in. Dad hands me the reed box.

"Can I have my umbrella back? You're on in two minutes."

"I can't go back there."

"No, you're going to perform right here, for me and Lou."

I'm speechless.

"Don't tell me you're scared?" he says.

I may be dripping wet but I'm not some scared little wimp. I grab a reed from the box, moisten it with my tongue, put it on the mouthpiece, and tighten the ligature. My dripping hair is stuck to my face, Daddy sweeps it back behind my ears and stands there, holding his huge umbrella over us. His sweater is so big, he has to push the sleeves higher up my arms.

"We're waiting," he says.

This time I don't need the score. I put the instrument to my lips and play "Danny Boy" in the rain while Daddy holds the umbrella over me.

The earth starts spinning again. The saxophone doesn't care if I'm drenched, it has come alive again, playing a beautiful song about love, friendship and a Celtic land similar to Brittany. The sailors buried here recognize the old tune which has been bellowed by many a mariner in the bars across the ocean. Dad listens too, holding onto Lou.

2nd February

Charlotte, Groix Island

Dad has gone back to Paris for work. Before my accident, I was cocky and grumpy. Now I feel weak and helpless.

"You have dark circles under your eyes," says Mum.

"Joe could drive us to the beach in his car, so you can get some sea air," suggests Apple. "Why do you stay locked up inside all day?"

"If you're fed up with me, then go and play with your friends who can run around and laugh, you don't *have* to stay here," I reply bitterly.

"You haven't seen the sea since you arrived!" cries Apple.

She doesn't know that I go on the harbour webcam every day. My heart doesn't hurt, but it's really painful when I breathe, as they had to saw my ribs to get to my heart to sew it back up. Grampy explained to me that it's like moving the T-shirts in my wardrobe to the side in order to get to the sweaters at the back.

"Did your enthusiasm for life fall out of your pocket in the Hellhole?" asks Apple to provoke me.

Aunt Sarah says that sounds like the first line of a novel.

She's sad because Federico goes back today. Grampy examines me every day, and we talk together. Since my accident, I've been asking him all sorts of questions, like what goes on in peoples' heads, why you can be so happy one day and end up skewered in a bush the next, and how you fall in love.

"Your heart is beating like a Swiss watch, and soon all this will be nothing more than a very bad memory," says Grampy.

"I feel so alone," I tell him. "When Granny was here, everyone was alone, except the two of you. Even though she's gone, you're still together. Sarah has Federico. Apple has her Mum. Mum and Dad are back in the same room now; after that kiss at the harbour she doesn't mind his snoring anymore. But I don't have anyone, except Oskar."

"What were your parents doing at the harbour?"

I tell him what I saw on the webcam. Grampy seems keen to know if I think Dad and Aunt Sarah are happy.

I nod and he looks glad. I tell him that it's like everyone else is enjoying the spring sunshine and I'm stuck in winter.

"You mean they've got great lives and you haven't, is that it?" he asks.

"I can't breathe," I say.

"Oh yes you can. But you're afraid to because it hurts. One morning, you'll wake up without even noticing that you're breathing, like before."

He gently places his hand on my scar; the scar frightens Mum and fascinates Apple. "You'll be back in the sun long before spring arrives."

Sarah, Groix Island

Federico bought a new travel bag to replace the one he gave Apple. He doesn't like goodbyes.

"Go away, Sarah, or I won't board this boat and I'll lose my job."

Before he gets carried away, I tell him if he's dreaming

about a perfect Italian family with a *mamma* who makes pasta and a *bambini*, he's in the wrong place.

I don't have any particular dream; I was just looking for the right man. In Rome, people in the streets are naturally Fellini-esque; they have a certain Italian sophistication while retaining their earthiness. Here, Groix islanders are just islanders, without even trying. Being surrounded by sea shifts your perception. Being surrounded by Federico has shifted my perception.

"Don't put your head on the line for me!" I yell.

"1 2 3," replies Federico. "In Venice, when security guards do their rounds, they stick bits of paper on houses and shop doors to prove they've been there. I want to stick bits of paper with your name on them all over my life. I'll be back in Paris in a month's time."

A month is ages. I don't know if I can wait that long.

"What colour is your room?" I ask.

"Pompeiian red," he says cheekily.

Apple, Groix Island

At the time, I didn't really take in what Aunt Sarah said. Suddenly, her words come back to me. I storm into Charlotte's room.

"Hey, I've got an idea!" I yell, my hair all ruffled from my hat.

My sister, wearing two golden hair slides in her perfectly styled hair, is curled up in bed.

"I was asleep," she grunts.

"You're nine years old, you're too old to be napping," I say.

"I'm recovering," she snaps at me.

Joe told me all about "hospitalism", and what it does to young children who have been in hospital for a long time and separated from their mothers. They stop developing and let themselves die. Charlotte was used to being treated like a baby by her mother. She felt secure in the ICU and on the cardiology ward, but now she's back in the real world again, and she's aware of how fragile she is.

"You'll like my idea!" I insist.

"You shouldn't have woken me up. When I sleep, I forget that I'm stuck in this room."

"You need to stretch your legs."

"It hurts every time I take just three steps. You'll have to go on your own."

I tell her that the journey I've got in mind won't tire her out at all. "Remember I asked you if your enthusiasm for life fell out of your pocket in the Hellhole? Well, Aunt Sarah said it sounded like something from a book. Right now, you can't move around on your legs, but you can travel on words. We could write a short story together, a bit like Lou's Clara Prize. Don't look at me with those cow eyes, otherwise I'll wonder if they transplanted a cow's heart in you by mistake."

"What will your book be about?" she asks.

"It's not mine, it's ours," I say. "Anything we like."

"How about my accident?"

I stop and think about it. "Yeah, we could tell the story through your eyes and then through mine."

"Maybe my heart could tell the story, it could be the narrator," says Charlotte.

I know what she means. When I was small, Lou gave me a book where a drop of water told the story of its journey into the taps, the bathtub, and eventually the sea.

"That's a great idea," I tell her.

"Cool!" says my sister. "Grampy told me that a heart is like a house with four rooms, you go in through the atria and out through the ventricles. What shall we call our book?"

"*Yolo! You Only Live Once!*" I shout.

Charlotte's eyes sparkle, her colour is coming back. She tries to give me a high five to clinch our deal, and stops short, wincing.

Albane opens the door and asks us if we need anything.

"No thank you," says my sister, smiling for the first time in ages.

Albane, Groix Island

I get lost in the endless maze of streets; I'm going round in circles and end up back at the church of Notre-Dame-de-Plasmanec every time. Locmaria was the most populated village on the island before Port-Tudy rapidly expanded at the end of the nineteenth century. My father-in-law told me to turn off after the threshing yard. What does a threshing yard look like? I find the house eventually.

Maëlle invites me to sit in front of the hearth and gives me a cup of tea. I must look like a tea drinker as everyone offers me tea, even though I don't actually like it.

"We should have had this conversation ten years ago," I say, diving straight in at the deep end.

"You knew where to find me," she answers mildly.

"My husband still loved you."

"It was a holiday romance, not the love story of a lifetime, Albane. If we'd really cared about each other, wild horses wouldn't have kept us apart. Lou gave up her castle for Joe. He left his island for her. Neither Cyrian nor I would budge."

"He married me because I was pregnant," I say.

"He would have married me for the same reason. Forget the past, Albane. He loves you. He panicked at the thought of losing you. Do you still love him?"

I nod. "Your little Apple is a real hero. She saved my daughter's life. I can never thank her enough."

"She acted on instinct," says Maëlle.

"There's something I want to suggest to Cyrian, but I'd like to have your opinion first."

"Of course," says Maëlle. "I'm all ears."

5th February

Joe, Groix Island

I've no idea what my granddaughters are up to, but Charlotte's got some colour in her cheeks now. She's eating and breathing without even noticing. She and Apple are forever giggling away together. Even Oskar seems happier.

Cyrian arrives by train, and Apple and I go to Lorient to pick him up in *Lou of the High Seas*. He gets into the boat carrying two rectangular cases, one black and one grey. He hands the grey one to Apple, who blushes with excitement.

"It's a second-hand Yamaha. It's been around a bit and has a warm mellow sound. Perfect for you. I put a Selmer mouthpiece on it for you."

She gives her father a big hug. As I watch them, I silently rejoice. We did it, Lou; I think our children and grandchildren are finally happy. I don't know if it will last, but it's wonderful to see.

Once I get home, I deactivate my Google Alerts, gather the family around the kitchen table and make a speech.

"Last November, the solicitor read out part of your mother's will, then he asked you all to leave the room. The rest was for my ears only. He showed me a small bottle in which your mother had slipped a message for us. I'm picking it up tomorrow."

"Couldn't you have taken it with you at the time?" asks Cyrian.

"No, but I can now."

"Do you want us to come with you?" asks Sarah.

I tell them I need to do this alone.

What fun we had this evening. Apple christened her new saxophone and played a duet with her father. Though they've never rehearsed together, they instinctively played in sync. They followed the score glancing at each other while their instruments vibrated in unison. I'm impressed. I hope you can hear them up there, Lou.

Cyrian asks Apple what she is going to call her saxophone. Apple looks at Charlotte, who shouts out, "Clara!"

I go outside to look at the night sky. You can't see anything in Paris because of the pollution. In Groix we sleep under a star-studded sky. Unfortunately, your herb garden is no more, Lou. I forgot to tend to it, I'm afraid. Your basil, mint, chives, parsley, sage, marjoram, verbena, lemon balm, lemon thyme, and your favourite herb, *marensa maritima*, or "oyster leaves", which really do taste of oysters, have all withered and died.

I think back to that dreadful night I found you in my office. If I hadn't woken up in time and if you had gone through with it, we wouldn't be sat here tonight . . .

Eight months earlier

Joe, Groix Island

I take a walk along the coast with Bertrand, Jean-Luc and Marie-Christine, and return to find that you and Apple have managed to burn yourselves. Thank God Apple had the sense to run cold water on your burns, but she didn't think to put on any ointment. I coat you in it, relieved it's not worse. I examine Apple's eye with my ophthalmoscope and bandage up your hands. I give you both painkillers, and then I bawl at Tribord, the guilty party. He turns his back on me, humiliated.

The next night, a noise awakens me. I automatically reach out to your side of the bed. You're not there and the sheets are cold. I search the house for you. Eventually I find you sat in my armchair, in my office, shivering in your nightdress, your bandaged hands gripping my rifle. The box of cartridges is open on the desk and the barrel of the Verney-Carron is aimed at your throat.

"Lou, what the hell are you doing?"

"Who are you?" she says, looking at me blankly.

An icy chill runs through me.

"Put down the gun, Lou!"

"Get away from me!" she screams.

"Lou, it's me, Joe, your husband!"

"It's loaded, I'm warning you!"

I don't recognize your voice anymore.

"Please my darling . . ." I'm begging now.

I move forward and the unthinkable happens: you turn the rifle on me, you point it at me. I freeze.

A tear runs down your cheek as you tighten your grip. Your bandages are in the way, but your index finger is just two millimetres from the trigger. If you shoot me at that height, the bullet will go straight through my chest and shatter my heart. If you shoot lower down, it will pierce my abdomen. I'll have to be airlifted to Lorient, operated on and would probably die in theatre. Or it'll get lodged in my spinal cord and I'll end up in a wheelchair for the rest of my life. I could always customize it and have wheelchair races with Sarah.

I smile at you amidst my panic. And then something happens. Suddenly you reconnect. Your neurons start functioning once more. Your brain does its job. Your memory sorts, filters, and puts you back on the right track. I utter your name.

There's a look of absolute horror in your eyes. You stare blankly at the rifle in your bandaged hands, the rounds of ammunition, and suddenly notice me at the other end of the barrel. You immediately point the gun at the ceiling. I grab it from you, take it apart and remove the bullet.

"Have I lost it, Joe?"

I struggle to keep smiling.

"I lost it the first time I set eyes on you, and never got it back again," I reply.

"Joe, it wasn't Tribord that knocked over the boiling coffee, it was me."

My face drops.

"Yes, you heard right. I nearly blinded little Apple, my *piroche*. I didn't recognize my own granddaughter. I tried to push her away."

"What happened? Were you asleep? Did she startle you?"

"No, she didn't even startle me. I just have moments when my mind goes completely blank. I don't know who I am or where I am anymore. That's why I took the gun, to stop me from hurting any of you."

I sit down and you snuggle up against my shoulder.

"We're going to get you checked out, treated and fixed," I say cheerfully.

"You're a terrible liar, my love. I'm a doctor's wife so you can't pull the wool over my eyes. I've heard you say a thousand times that it's over for so and so, or that you wouldn't want to be in their family's position. I'm not afraid for myself, I'm afraid for all of you."

I reassure her that I'm there and that I'm going to protect her. But she insists that it could happen any time, while driving, in the street, on the boat, or in the kitchen with the gas on.

"I'll never leave you alone again," I say.

"You're not my baby-sitter, Joe! I wanted to end it all with your rifle but I can't remember anything after that. Did I aim it at you? Did I nearly kill you, Joe?"

You looked like a frightened little rabbit when you put your bandaged hands on your head. You don't cry, you're past that stage. You're in a very dark place, and nothing can get you out, not even our love.

"What if one night, while you're lying next to me, I forget who you are?" she asks.

"I'll hide the gun."

"It's not only guns that are dangerous. There's boiling water, gas, knives, scissors, fire!" she says.

"Calm down, my love."

"A sleeping sumo wrestler is as vulnerable as an ant. And it's not just you, there's Apple. And Maëlle. And Charlotte, Cyrian and Albane when they come to visit. There's Sarah. I don't want to wake up one day discovering I hurt or killed one of you!"

"That won't happen," I say.

"If you want to prove to me that you love me, give me the gun back."

"No way!"

"Well, there is another solution, my *piroche*."

"Yes, I know, treatment!"

"Cut the crap, my *piroche*. It's too late for that. I want to make the most of the time I've got left; but on one condition."

"What's that?"

You stare into my eyes and utter the words that no one should have to say at only fifty-six years of age.

"A nursing home."

6th February

Joe, Lorient

I killed you by not letting you take your own life eight months ago. It was the lesser of two evils. Your mind packed up and left, and you moved into a nursing home. It's ironic really that I helped create the Society for Aiding the Wives of Inadequate Husbands to help my friends' wives, yet I wasn't able to help my own when it really mattered . . .

Today, your solicitor is wearing a pink polo shirt without a crocodile motif. It's the same shade of pink as the "Joseph" on my shoulders. I get straight to the point.

"My children are happy," I say.

He opens his drawer and hands me the bottle, which I stuff into my jacket pocket.

The taxi drops me off in front of the ferry terminal. Jean-Louis Aubert's song, "Alter Ego", has been on my mind since this morning. I hum it as I walk towards the warehouse next to the carpark where the vehicles board: *My life is missing some time, Missing time down the line, I miss you, my alter ego.* I greet the lorry drivers and sailors who work there and ask if anyone has a pair of pliers they could lend me.

I sit on a rock out of the way and pull out the cork. The wax breaks into tiny blood red pieces. I uncork the bottle and put it to my ear. The memory of your voice tickles my cheek, the echo of your words dissolves in the wind. I could swear you just said you love me.

There are two folded up pieces of paper inside: the agreement we made and your message. I struggle to get at them, my fingers won't fit inside the bottle neck. I could smash it on a rock but risk wounding myself on the broken glass, not to mention any passing children or dogs.

I put my hand in my pocket to look for my glasses. Damn! I left them on Groix. You had perfect vision, but I'm lost without my spectacles. I shall grow old while you'll never have another wrinkle. I shall become a crotchety old widower and you'll remain young in our memories forever. If I make it another twenty years, I'll be old enough to be your father. It's tantalizing; your words are so near yet so far, I just can't get to them. I close my eyes and travel back in time ten years, to that summer solstice evening . . .

Ten years earlier

Joe, Groix Island

"To love!" I yelled, that summer solstice evening on the beach.

"Look at me as we toast, Joe," you said, "otherwise seven years of no sex!"

I obeyed instantly.

"Can you think of a song that would fit this moment, my *piroche*?" you asked.

"*An island between the sky and Lou! An island with no men or ships.*"

You were sad, because your grandfather had just died. He was a brilliant and warm-hearted man, who had become senile and aggressive. You were angry with his doctors and accused them of prolonging his life with strong medication. Then out of the blue, our conversation took a different turn.

"Can I count on you, Joe?"

"Yes," I said, "I'd lay down my life for you."

"But would you *take* my life? You fight for your patients. I need you to swear that one day, if need be, if I get like my grandfather, you'll save me."

"Save you from what?" I asked. "From that sand flea that's about to suck on your leg?"

You let out a squeal and moved.

"You know how to treat people, Joe, you know how to alleviate suffering. You injected that man who had no head."

*   *   *

I was a young intern with the paramedics at the time. I had just attended my first home birth and was on cloud nine. Just afterwards, I found myself at the scene of a road traffic accident in which the driver, an old man who hadn't fastened his seat belt, had practically no head left. He was literally a mouth with nothing above it, no nose, no eyes, no hair. His skull had shattered, and his brain was splattered on the windscreen. His heart was still beating uncontrollably, his abdomen was crushed. His legs had been broken by the metal side panels. His hands were still gripping the steering wheel. He was a heavy smoker and drinker, so his diseased organs wouldn't be of use to anyone. His wife, who looked like my grandmother, had been pulled out of the car in a daze. She slowly came to, asking how her husband was. He was still drunk, he had fallen asleep at the wheel. "How is my husband?" she asked again. I didn't want her last image of him to be of an old man with no face and no legs, a mangled body hooked up to a beeping machine, keeping him alive in a vegetative state. The scene was utterly horrifying. So, I injected him with a substance that stopped his heart in a matter of seconds. Technically, I killed him. I killed a dead man walking, a fibrillating thorax. That night, I told you about it. Then I got drunk in the warmth and safety of your arms, not behind the wheel. I've never told anyone else about it.

"I'm not proud of that, but I don't regret it."

"We're happy together, my *piroche*. But who knows what the future holds? If I get an incurable disease, or if I'm dying and in intolerable pain, or if I go insane and start slurring my words, I want you to promise to release me."

"You're crazy!" I shouted.

"Yes, crazy about you. And I swear I'll do the same for you if you ask me. Otherwise, I'll be your devoted nurse, in sexy underwear, until your dying hour. I couldn't bear to leave this world not remembering that I love you."

"I'm a doctor, I save lives, I don't take them. That man you mentioned was practically dead already. If one day you're as bad as him, I promise I'll stop your heart . . . Is that okay for you?"

You shook your head angrily, that wasn't what you wanted to hear. You didn't think your grandfather, the only person in your family who told you about your mother, had deserved to go that way. I tried in vain to bring you to your senses.

"Why are you worrying about this at forty-six years old?" I asked.

We stayed on the beach, huddled together, until late that night. A seagull finished our sandwiches. You wouldn't drop it. You kept on and on, eventually bursting into tears. I gave in, thinking that it was just an idle conversation that didn't commit me to anything. You gave me a delicious French kiss. *This is a 21st of June kiss, darling, never to be forgotten!* You took a piece of paper from your pocket and wrote on it:

Joe and Lou, of sound mind and body, hereby promise, as of this day, with immediate effect, to release each other from suffering should the need arise.

You dated and signed it. I signed it too, to stop you crying. You wrapped the bit of paper around your finger and slipped it into the empty bottle. Then you put your mouth around the bottle neck and whispered words that I couldn't hear into the bottle. You pushed the cork in and scratched the label until the last two letters of Mercier disappeared, leaving only "Merci": "thank you".

6th February

Joe, Groix Island

The sun is streaming down from the bright blue sky onto the roll-on roll-off, and shines on the sailing boats, fishermen, walkers, cars, dogs and seagulls. Sarah lent me her iPod, and I listened to Didier Squiban play "Molène" on the piano during the crossing, it helped me relax. I take off my earphones and jump off the boat, the bottle bulging in my pocket.

"Hey, Systole! Dad!" calls out Cyrian.

I turn around. Our children have come to meet me. We find a table at the Escale café and order three glasses of Muscadet. I take the bottle out of my jacket pocket, you're lying at the bottom of it, like the genie in the lamp. Your words are waiting for me, Lou.

"I couldn't get your mother's message out."

"Soaz must have something we can use," suggests Cyrian.

He comes back with a piece of string and folds it in half. He lowers the loop down to the bottom of the bottle and tilts the neck, so that the loop goes under the papers. He gently pulls the string and the messages come up with it. First, I open the famous agreement, which I failed to honour. Then I hand your message to Cyrian. He passes it to Sarah, and she reads it out.

11th August

I am writing to all three of you from my room in the nursing home. I know you won't release me, Joe, even though you signed my agreement, promising you would. And I thought I'd been clever in marrying a doctor! Cyrian, Sarah, I played a bad trick on you, yes, sorry. I deliberately misled you into thinking that your father had cheated on me. He betrayed me, yes, but he didn't cheat on me. He didn't go with any other woman (as far as I know!), though it's true that he did like ogling them. Ten years ago, on Les Grands Sables beach, I made him promise to help me if I ever had an incurable disease, was in intolerable pain or lost my mind. Men can't resist tears so he promised, which reassured me. I knew he wouldn't keep his word, but I still felt relieved in a funny way.

You were born into a privileged family. The flip side of the coin is that you didn't get to see much of your father. You both have your own sorrows and hardships to deal with and you faced them with courage. The reason I lied was to force you all to confront each other, to make you discover who you really are. If it has brought you all together, then I have succeeded. Your father didn't want me to move into the nursing home, I forced his hand, because I almost disfigured Apple when I knocked over the grek. I had a memory lapse and didn't recognize her.

You made me so madly happy, all three of you. Joe taught me the incredible joys of life. I hope you both get to experience the same adventure. And please know that every disgusting meal I gave you was made with love.

I hope that Apple and Charlotte will grow up to be fulfilled and free women. It's not children or grandchildren that make us happy, it's the love they bring us, the love we give them, the love which envelopes us all.

We don't know how we'll die, but we can decide how we'll live. Joe, I forced you to become better acquainted with our children and I stopped you throwing in the towel and going under. You stopped me from ending things that night, so I did the same for you. I got here before you, Joe, so I'm going to book us the best table in a five star restaurant in the sky. Loving you was intoxicating.

Thank you for Groix, really. I've got the best view from this piece of sky. I can see the waves caressing the jagged coastline, the earth and the rocks, the evergreen broom and the low walls, the tuna on the bell tower, the harbours, the creeks and the islanders; it's at once simple and extraordinary, powerful and unique. Groix was the icing on the cake, not my burnt cakes or Martine's magical culinary creations, but the icing on the tchumpôt.

I love you all,
Lou

6th February

Joe, Groix Island

We walk home at Sarah's pace. I've finally become a father. Better late than never, one could say. Albane and the girls are playing Monopoly in the kitchen. Albane places a red hotel on Rue de la Paix and looks at Cyrian. He nods back.

"Albane and I have something to tell you."

I shudder. Are they getting divorced? Are they having a baby?

"We have decided to buy a house on Groix, so we can come for the holidays and be closer to you and Apple without crowding you, Dad."

Apple has a massive grin on her face, she reminds me of a Pac-Man.

"Are you kidding me?" I exclaim.

"We thought you'd be pleased, Dad!"

"So my house isn't good enough for you?"

You should have seen his face, Lou.

"I'm only kidding, son," I chuckle. "Your mother's not the only one allowed to joke. No, it's amazing news. Just one thing though, please get a normal car to drive around on the island, not that tank, okay?"

He nods. There's a knock at the door. We're all sat here, so who can it be?

"We have a guest for dinner," announces Albane, adding a plate.

Maëlle walks in and takes her place at the table as if it were the most natural thing in the world. Cyrian looks on, speechless.

"You'd better put some weight on, Charlotte," says Albane. "I'm warning you, when you go back to school, you'll be eating at the canteen!"

Charlotte and Apple grin at each other slyly. It reminds me of that last piece we listened to together at the nursing home, "After a Dream" by Gabriel Fauré, with Yo-Yo Ma on the cello. I imagine even the grub at the school canteen is preferable to your culinary delights, my love.

Lou, on the other side

I would have given anything to capture this moment of pure joy in our kitchen tonight. It was as unforgettable as a saxophone note held to the count of five, and as powerful as an equinox tide. The pressure is off now, phew! You're reunited at last, my darlings; the future is yours. And the past is mine to dream about, as I soar above the clouds to an incredibly beautiful melody. Silence has given way to music.

I find myself on a cliff edge under the Milky Way, with the sea below. I hear "After A Dream" by Gabriel Fauré in the distance. I get closer to the musicians. I can't believe it: Wolfgang Amadeus is at the harpsichord, and Johann Sebastian is at the organ! But Bach died six years before Mozart was born, who in turn died fifty-four years before Fauré was even alive. Barbara, the tall brunette, and Italian singer Reggiani are sitting with the English artist, David Bowie. My parents have reserved a seat for me between them. A fisherman in a sailor's sweater that looks like you is smiling at me, Joe. A little boy who looks like Albane is listening, spellbound. Fellini is waltzing with Giulietta. I'm not alone.

We must go our separate ways now, my love. I'm not sad. Though I'm setting sail without you, I'm taking delicious memories with me. I'm terrible at maths, but I've had some free time on my hands since All Saints Day so I've come up with some figures. One double-digit for the number of years we spent together and the other a hundred digits long for the number of times we laughed. Fauré's piece ends. Wolfgang and Johann take a bow. The audience stands up to dance, each swaying to their own music. You're not here to stand on my feet, my *piroche*. I don't hear bells ringing like Capra's angel, Clarence, just a fantastically funky disco beat: *Ah ha ha ha, stayin' aliiiiiiiiiive!*

Paris, Groix Island, Rome, 2015
Kenavo d'an distro, goodbye and see you soon

Music

"Audite Silete", Michael Praetorius

Various film scores for Federico Fellini, Nino Rota
"And Then" (*Et puis*) & "Paul's Song" (*La Chanson de Paul*), Serge Reggiani/Jean-Loup Dabadie
"Pie Jesu", Gabriel Fauré
"An Island" (*Une île*), Serge Lama
"Sing, Life Sings" (*Chante, la vie chante*), Michel Fugain
"Staying Alive", Bee Gees
Adagio for Strings, conducted by Leonard Bernstein, Samuel Barber
"Caballitos", Laurent Morisson, adaptation of a poem by Antonio Machado
The Italian Concerto, Johann Sebastian Bach
The Magic Flute, Wolfgang Amadeus Mozart
"Message in a Bottle", The Police
"Danny Boy", Frederic Weatherly
"Amazing Grace", John Newton
"Manu", Renaud
"Go West", Swing Cajun/Pat Sacaze
La Forza del destino (ouverture), Verdi
"When Those Who Go" (*Quand ceux qui vont*), Barbara
"Cinema Paradiso", Ennio Morricone
St Matthew Passion, Choirs 1 & 2, Johann Sebastian Bach
"It's a Wonderful Life" (film soundtrack), Dimitri Tiomkin
"Bianco Natale", Mina

"I'll be Home for Christmas", Barbra Streisand

"It's a Wonderful Life", Frank Capra

"Saint James Infirmary", performed by Louis Armstrong

"Le Forban", French sea shanty

"My Little Boy" (*Mon p'tit garçon*), Michel Tonnerre

"When Irish Eyes Are Smiling", Olcott, Graff & Ball

"Fifteen Sailors" (*Quinze marins*), Michel Tonnerre

"We Were Three Sailors from Groix" (*Nous étions trois marins de Groix*), French sea shanty

"Alter Ego", Jean-Louis Aubert

"Molène", Didier Squiban

"After a Dream" (*Après un rêve*), Gabriel Fauré, with Yo-Yo Ma on cello

Recipes

Lucette's *tchumpôt*

Ingredients: 1 kg flour, 2 eggs, 1 large pot & 1 small pot of fresh cream, 2 plain yogurts, 1 packet of brown sugar (this is known as *sucre vergeoise*, granulated sugar must not be used), yeast, raisins (or prunes), 100 g salted butter.

Put the flour and yeast in a mixing bowl with a little salt, and make a well. Add the fresh cream, plain yoghurts and eggs, and mix everything together. Spread out a clean tea towel and sprinkle it generously with flour. Turn the contents of the mixing bowl upside down onto the tea towel and knead the dough using one corner of the tea towel without touching the dough with your hands (it's sticky). Form the dough into a loaf shape, and then divide it into 3 pieces. Flatten each piece of dough like a pancake until they measure 15 to 20 cm in diameter. Add the brown sugar in the middle of the pancake until the sugar forms a layer 2 to 3 cm thick. Leave a margin of 1.5 cm without sugar all the way round. Add strips of salted butter, raisins (or prunes), and wet the edge of the dough. Fold it in half like a turnover, sealing the edges without piercing the dough. Wrap up each turnover either in greaseproof paper, a cabbage leaf, or a tea towel, and tie it up like a parcel. Do not make it too tight, otherwise the cake won't rise.

Bring a saucepan of salted water to the boil and plunge the *tchumpôt* into it. Leave it to cook for 20 minutes, then remove

without piercing the wrapping. *Tchumpôt* cake should be
made once guests have already arrived, as it hardens quickly.
Cut into slices before serving. Any leftovers can be eaten the
next day, cut into slices, sautéed in hot salted butter and left
to caramelize.

Mirella's *Al Cantuccio* soup

Ingredients: beans (shelled or white), porcini mushrooms,
peeled chestnuts, onion, celery, carrots, garlic, pepper, cured
ham, olive oil, salt, wholemeal bread.

The night before, rinse the beans well and put them to soak
in water with the finely chopped carrots, onion, celery and
garlic.

The next day, cook the beans, carrots, onion, celery and
garlic in the vegetable water. Keep a saucepan of boiling
water nearby to add as you go along, so that the water level
doesn't drop. When the beans and vegetables are cooked, add
the porcini mushrooms, previously sauteed with olive oil and
chilli pepper. Chop up the chestnuts and cured ham or
bacon, add them to the vegetables, mix everything together,
and sprinkle with olive oil. Toast small pieces of wholemeal
bread; serve the soup and add the toast on the top.

Afterword

Where do *you* normally go for your holidays?

As a child, I used to spend the holidays at my grandmother's house in Antibes on the French Riviera and with friends in Sainte-Marine in the Finistère area of Brittany. As a teenager I went to Antibes, and Belz in the Morbihan area of Brittany. Then my grandmother died, and I couldn't get the beguiling view of the Garoupe lighthouse out of my mind. Then one winter's day, fifteen years ago, I took the ferry from Lorient to Groix. The sun glistening on the cliffs gave me the urge to dance and write. The rain mingled with the sea spray was intoxicating and made me want to throw caution to the wind. I gazed up at the star-studded blackness of the night sky, while the beams of the island's two lighthouses, Pen-Men and Les Chats, embraced the ocean.

I told Nicole, a friend from Lorient, that I dreamed of writing from a lighthouse or an island. When her friend sold a little whitewashed house with blue shutters on the island, she thought of me. I was a stranger to Groix. I took the ferry with my long-eared basset hound, Guinness, the spitting image of Inspector Columbo's basset hound. At the port, I asked the taxi driver if he minded dogs. To my astonishment, he took out a small step which he placed before Guinness so that he could climb in. I knew instantly that this island was unique. Six months later, poor Guinness passed away and I set off for the island on my own. I couldn't stop looking for

him, until Uriel came into my life, a black and white cocker
spaniel I fell in love with. He had a passion for befriending
rabbits. He forced me to walk miles, throwing his saliva-
coated ball just so he could fetch it. With him I shed my extra
weight from hours sat writing, sipping coffee and nibbling
chocolate.

That piece of rock in the middle of the ocean, five miles
long and two and a half miles wide, inspired this novel, which
seeks to demonstrate that it is never too late for people to find
happiness. I'm delighted to be able to share the island's
storms, sensitivity and seagulls with my dear readers today.
Though imaginary, my characters are based on real island
folk. These locals are essential, if not key to the plot, each one
an important link in the island chain.

Don't get me wrong, Groix is not some fairy tale paradise.
In days gone by, life was harsh, and it's still pretty much the
same today. But there is something authentic about the
island. When Groix islanders smile, it's genuine, like their
sentiments, and there is true solidarity between them. The
island is magnificent. Each time I leave, I'm grateful to have
spent time there and fret at the idea of never returning.

I really believe that there is a book out there for each
one of us, that will change the course of our lives; whether
that be a novel, love story, comic, detective story, collec-
tion of poems, technical, scientific, historical or sci-fi book.
This book is waiting for you somewhere. Maybe in a bookshop. Maybe in the local library. Wherever it is, I hope you
find it. Maybe Lou has inspired you to go and live on an
island or reconcile with your family? Many stories have
profoundly affected my life, but Groix turned my whole
world upside down and inside out, leaving me with
emotional whiplash!

This island holds a special place in my heart. I wasn't
born here, and I'll never be one of them, as I haven't got

four generations of family buried in the local cemetery. Groix, with its tuna fish on the belfry weathervane instead of the traditional cockerel, is steeped in fortitude and bravery, be it the fishermen who set off on their *dundee* tuna boats or their proud valiant women, who stayed on the island, tilling the land and raising the children while their men were at sea.

My father died of a heart attack when I was seventeen years old, just a month after I passed my baccalaureate exams. He was as strong as an ox but collapsed like a house of cards. It was time enough to love each other, but not long enough to talk to each other. He loved Brittany and had just purchased a plot of land in the forest to build a house on and write his third book. I would love to have shared this island with him in the way I'm sharing it with you. I would have introduced him to all my friends here, including the 7 Gang. I would have taken him to the covered market, where I really did see the silent ball mentioned at the beginning of the novel (though not during a funeral). He would have bought his newspaper at the local newsagents. He would have loved Loïc's "Gangster pâté" and Gwenola's prune cake (a traditional Breton recipe known as "Far"). He would have taken me to The 50 for dinner and I would have taken him to the crêpe restaurant. Lucette would have made her famous *tchumpôt* cake for him. We would have watched a film together at the Cinéma des Familles.

We would have gone for brisk walks along the gusty coastal paths with Uriel, and sat around a roaring fire in thick sweaters, trying to set the world to rights, happy to be together like any father and daughter (like Joe and Sarah in the book). I was too young to lose my father, so I make up for it through my writing. He left us one summer. I was about to start law school. He phoned me from the hospital and said being a medical doctor was the most noble profession in the world.

He died the next day. I became a doctor so that I could resuscitate other people's fathers.

Lou appears regularly throughout the book. Originally I had intended to delete these short paragraphs. Their purpose was to guide me, and help me personify her character. She got the better of me, however, and I decided to leave her in.

By the way, I'm a really bad cook, just like Lou. There are only two things in life I'm good at: writing and cheese soufflés.

Nowadays when I arrive on Groix, I imagine I can see Joe and Lou on the hillside. If you come here one day, maybe you'll see them too? No need for a visa, there's no time difference, no air strikes, or booked out flights. The sky belongs to the birds, the land belongs to the islanders, the ocean belongs to the valiant, and the night belongs to lovers. Friendship cannot be bought here; it can only be given. There are no traffic lights, directions are painted on the tarmac or on a boulder by the roadside. You'll meet some delightful people, mysterious cats, laughing dogs, mischievous rabbits, proud pheasants, greedy gulls, silent owls, dignified lobsters and graceful spider crabs. The multicoloured hortensias will throw up a kaleidoscope of colours, and the broom will burst with flecks of gold. You'll idly stroll through the village doing your shopping, with all the time in the world. If you lose your way, you'll soon find it again. One toughens up living on an island, its physical, magnetic energy is contagious. They didn't teach me that at medical school. I felt it when I was there. You'll buy your newspaper opposite the post office; you'll hear the wind playing the harp on the shrouds of sailing boats, and then you'll finally understand the local proverb for yourself: *Groix ahoy, feel the joy.*

*   *   *

And if you can't come, then listen to the songs, "My Little Boy", "Danny Boy" and "Molène". Or make Lucette's *tchumpôt* cake, like Apple and Charlotte. Most importantly, make sure you savour it with someone you love.

Enjoy!

Have a safe crossing!

Kenavo d'an distro!

Acknowledgements

I wish to express my sincere thanks to Héloïse d'Ormesson and Gilles Cohen-Solal, Sarah Hirsch, Roxane Defer, Anne-Marie Bourgeois, and the whole EHO team. It's been an absolute pleasure to work with you all.

Huge thanks go to Nicole de Pol and Christine Soler for the island house, to Jean-Pierre and Monique Poupée for introducing us to their friends, to all members of the 7 Gang at Fred's, to Mylane Corvest for the bracelet, Lucette Corvec for the *tchumpôt*, Brigitte Adam, Joe *nav*, Joe Le Port, Soaz who is now Françoise again, and to Groix islander, Anita, for her blog.

Special thanks to Anne Goscinny for the reunion with our fathers, to Éric Frachon for the "Frachon" on his shoulders, to my mother for the Keryargon roses, to Doctor Catherine Ferracci, Doctor Claude Fuilla, and Doctor Sandrine Paquin for their medical expertise, to Ywes Ballan, Amandine Jendoubi, Renata Parisi, and Antoine-Basile Mercier for their beautiful saxophony.

Thanks to Thierry Serfaty for his books in which he does away with me, Grégoire Delacourt for making me laugh, Évelyne Bloch-Dano for Illa, Valérie Lejeune for teaching me the local dialect, Caroline Vié for the tattoos, Sylvie Overnoy for the talking stick, Jean Failler for Mary Lester, and François Boulet for the great Charles.

Thanks to Yveline Kuhlmey for all those bottles of cider, Christel Pernet for *piroche*, Nausicaa Meyer for the lively conversation, Didier Piquot for everything, Martine Pilon for the chocolate cake, Mathilde Pouliot for the *burraco*, Philippe Chambon for New York, Isabelle Preuvot for her sensitivity, Silvia and Alessandro for my goddaughter, Livia.

Thanks to the butterfly tattooed on my shoulder and to my cocker spaniel, Uriel, who doesn't care if I say number one or number two.

Thanks to Christian Fouchet, Hughes Ternon, Alberte Bartoli, Isabelle Redier, I miss you all; to my aunt Talel who fed the homeless of Saint-Germain-en-Laye, who used to seek refuge at our gate at night.

No animals were harmed while writing this book; wine flowed, music was played and enjoyed. I bought a one-way ticket to Groix each morning as soon as I switched on my computer. This island has got under my skin.